Thicker Than Mud

Thicker Than Mud

Jason Z. Morris

RESOURCE *Publications* · Eugene, Oregon

THICKER THAN MUD

Resource Publications
An Imprint of Wipf and Stock Publishers
199 W. 8th Ave., Suite 3
Eugene, OR 97401

www.wipfandstock.com

PAPERBACK ISBN: 978-1-5326-8724-2
HARDCOVER ISBN: 978-1-5326-8725-9
EBOOK ISBN: 978-1-5326-8726-6

Manufactured in the U.S.A.   JUNE 12, 2019

To my Marilyn, my wife, with all my heart,
and, with immense gratitude, to my parents, Eric and Willa Morris.

Adam digged

—SHAKESPEARE, HAMLET, ACT V, SCENE 1

Contents

Acknowledgments

I am truly grateful to my terrific friends, family, and colleagues who offered their support and their insights, who shared their expertise with me, and who read drafts of this book: Frank Boyle, Lenny Cassuto, Christy Coch, Bill Cummings, Joyce Cummings, Anne Hoffman, Karina Martin Hogan, Ben Hollister, Eve Keller, Anna Kruyer, Jillian Leitman, Max Leitman, Karen Lightfoot, Matthew Maguire, Zese Merion, Eric Morris, Marilyn Morris, Nate Morris, Sonia Morris, Willa Morris, Simon Rosenbach, Allison Koweek Schnipper, Michael Scharf, Eden Stevenson, Jon Swartz, Carl Tramontana, and Nancy Tramontana. I am indebted to all of you. I am grateful also to this book's copy editor, Julie Fifelski, and to all the people at Wipf and Stock who helped bring this book to fruition. I want particularly to thank those doughty souls who read multiple, early drafts: Marilyn, mom, and Karina. Finally, I would be remiss if I didn't acknowledge the students and faculty at Fordham who continue to inspire me with their dedication to learning, teaching, and scholarship, and their work in the service of others.

Chapter 1

The dun-colored sediment of Tel Arad was so dry it was almost powder, and even though Adam dug with slow precision, he was covered in dust. It clung to his work boots and his legs. It coated the roof of his mouth.

The heat pressed on him from below as well as above: as the sun's rays poured down through the cloudless sky, those that missed Adam's back caught his face and neck after reflecting off the clay. Adam put down his spade and pulled three water bottles out of his pack. His student Maggie was digging on her knees, her back toward him, so that he could see the map of the Belmont College campus under the Jesuit coat of arms on the back of her t-shirt. Adam had seen the shirt many times over the summer, but he still smiled at the caption: "Because God so loved the Bronx…"

He called out to her, "Maggie, it's a furnace out here. Take a water break!" He tossed her one of the bottles when she turned to face him. "You should go back to the tent," he said. "You still have time to grab some lunch and get to the afternoon lecture."

Maggie glanced at Adam over the wire frame of her sunglasses with a look of perfect resolve. "I'm not afraid of the heat, Professor Drascher," she said. "We have heat in Puerto Plata, too. And my skin won't burn. Not as easily as some." All summer, she had been mocking his twice-a-day slathering on of suntan lotion. "Besides," she said, "I just know the second I leave, you and Dr. Renaud are going to find something and then I'll be kicking myself."

Claudia Renaud sat cross-legged, her notebook and pen on her lap, as she pulled the loose strands of her sun-bleached hair off her tan, graceful neck and back into a ponytail. She looked up at the mention of her name and she caught Adam's gaze. Her eyes were a brilliant, piercing blue. "You were the same way on your first dig, Adam," she said. "You still are. Evidently, we all are." She wiped at her forehead with her red plaid neckerchief. "Toss me one of those bottles and let her work."

1

Adam walked over and handed Claudia a bottle. He had known her for over a decade, ever since he was one of her star-struck students back in the first year of his Ph.D. in archaeology at Fletcher University. Claudia had been fairly new then, but she already outshone everyone else in a department full of luminaries. Adam had been spellbound, he remembered, as she told her class about the lost world she was bringing to light in the Judean desert.

There were still moments like this one—too many, Adam chided himself—when he would catch himself seeing Claudia as he had seen her that first day. He turned away and drained his bottle. "All right, Maggie," he said. "You can stay through the lecture if you can listen while you work. Dr. Renaud and I can probably teach you something while we all roast."

"Maybe we should start with a quiz," Claudia said. "I'd like to see how well Dr. Drascher has taught you."

Adam smiled at the mischief in her tone, but he wasn't sure if Maggie could hear it. Claudia had always had a gift for provocation and for courting controversy, which went a long way toward explaining how she had become an academic celebrity. The high-end journalists knew Claudia was always good for a quote, and the few people Claudia failed to charm, she could incite.

Adam gave Maggie an encouraging nod. Maggie was the best student Adam had taught at Belmont. She would be applying to graduate school in the fall and Claudia's letter could get Maggie in anywhere if Maggie impressed her enough.

Maggie finished her water and picked up her spade. "Ask away," she said. "I'm not scared."

"That's a good beginning, then," Claudia said. "We'll start with an easy one. What do you expect to find here? Coins with Alexander's face on them? A Roman dagger?"

Maggie raised an eyebrow as she dug. She shook her head and brushed her straight, black hair out of her eyes. "Much too recent," she said. "Alexander died in what? Three hundred BC? Three-fifty? The Romans were long after that. The upper layers of dirt must have been carted away before we got here, right?" She waited for Adam to nod confirmation before she said, "You and Dr. Drascher focus on the monarchy, between about 1000 and 600 BC. We're digging down around... was it seven-fifty, Professor?"

Claudia gave her an approving glance. Adam smiled his encouragement.

Maggie scratched lightly at the dirt as she framed her answer. "Amos was prophesying then," she said. "We were reading about it just before the midterm. Assyria would crush the Northern Kingdom before too long, but here in Judah things were okay, right?"

"Good!" Adam said.

"All right," Claudia said. "You have the context. Go on. Say you got really lucky. What might you expect to find here?"

Maggie looked up at her. "A cup? A piece of jewelry?" She caught Adam's eye and she laughed. "Those are pretty safe answers, aren't they? I wouldn't even give myself credit for that."

Claudia looked at her intently. "What if you found an Egyptian scarab? Or Greek pottery?"

"I wouldn't be shocked," Maggie said. "Egypt is close by and it had been interacting with Judah for a long time, since the beginning. A Greek artifact, though . . . I wouldn't assume that came directly from trade with the Greeks. It probably would have come from Phoenician traders, maybe from Tyre."

Claudia looked pleased. Adam wanted to roll his eyes. It was typical of Claudia to be impressed by an answer based so closely on her own lecture, he thought. She had spoken about cultural exchanges in the ancient Middle East the first week they were at the site, and Maggie had listened, enraptured. If Maggie won Claudia over by parroting Claudia's ideas, then that was all right with him, but he knew Maggie was capable of much more.

"What about you, Dr. Drascher?" Maggie asked. "If you could find anything here, what would it be?"

Adam wasn't sure what to answer, but Claudia interrupted. "Something religious, no doubt, right Adam?" She said. "A Baal statue, or some hymn dedicated to Asherah?" Adam thought he could detect a suppressed smirk, and it set him on edge.

"Most people in Judah probably prayed to the Canaanite gods," he said, "even if they worshipped the God of the Bible. Just finding a statue wouldn't really teach us anything new, but it might get us on television, right Claudia?" He paused for a reaction, but if she noticed his jab, it didn't register on her face. He turned toward Maggie. "But if we found something more revealing, something that gave us an insight into Canaanite religion, that would be something, wouldn't it? When a Canaanite prayed to his god, what did he feel? The prophets were constantly hectoring the people to leave off their worship of other gods, but we have nothing in the words of the people who worshipped them. What was it that drew them? What was so attractive? Was it beauty? A sense of security? Of comfort? Of belonging?"

"This is an old disagreement Dr. Drascher is drawing you into, Maggie," Claudia said. "He thinks he can get into the minds of these people. He thinks if he's clever enough, he can interpret fragments of inscriptions or snippets of poetry and think like a Canaanite, or like someone from Judah." She fixed Adam with her gaze. "It can't be done. We have artifacts. We can get their age and where and how they were made. We can discuss the political or economic structure of a settlement. We can talk about what they ate and how large their families were and what kind of house they lived in. But that's all. It should be enough."

Adam didn't offer any response. He just wiped the sweat off his forehead with his callused hand. He didn't want to discourage Maggie, but more and more, this spadework that he had once loved so much felt futile. There's only so much time a grown man can play in the dirt, he thought, looking for buried treasure and coming up with nothing. And here he was out in the August heat; another summer had almost gone. His tenure deadline was coming closer and closer and he had little to show for all his work.

They dug in silence for almost half an hour. Claudia looked like she might have something, but she kept her head down and Adam didn't ask. He turned to see how Maggie was faring and he saw her take up her brush to clear away a bit of loose dirt without risking damage to whatever lay underneath. He heard her mutter, "¡Ay, Dios mio!" and then she looked up and called to him, "Professor! Would you take a look at this?"

Adam nodded and moved alongside her to see what she was pointing at. He didn't get his hopes up. A couple of times before on the dig, Maggie had found blank, uninformative pieces of pottery. Once, she had uncovered a piece of a very plain knife. Claudia had kept copious records on them, but even she hadn't been very excited. Now Claudia wasn't even looking up from her work.

"What have you got?" Adam asked. Maggie showed him the squared-off corner of red clay pottery that she had exposed. It lay nearly horizontal in its bed of dirt. "Good eyes." Adam told her. "Be delicate with that, now. Take your time with it."

"Do you want to take over?" She asked. "If I ruin this, I don't think my stipend would cover it."

Adam shook his head. "If it turns out to be something your stipend wouldn't cover, neither would my salary. Shift over. I'll get the finer tools and we can both work on it."

"What have you found?" Claudia asked.

"No way to know yet," Adam said. "There's a fragment of something buried here, maybe an ostracon. It'll be a while before we've got it out." Adam photographed the piece where it lay, and then he and Maggie worked together with brushes and picks of varying caliber. She spoke to him in whispers as if she were afraid her voice would disturb the ceramic. The labor was slow and painstaking, but Adam felt himself caught up in Maggie's enthusiasm and the time passed quickly.

They finally unearthed a flat piece of ceramic, straight and approximately ten inches long, almost undamaged. Adam and Maggie noted the precise placement of the tablet: its location and depth, the angle at which it had lain in the ground, and the features of the dirt surrounding it. Adam then took the artifact in his hands and examined it. The tablet was covered in writing in the ancient Hebrew script that was in common use before the Babylonian Exile. The writing would have been done while the clay was still damp. Adam could almost picture the thin stylus held in the hand of a professional scribe or a priest, its tip cutting each line of the deeply engraved letters. The tablet could only have been preserved if it had been baked, and the color suggested it wasn't made in Tel Arad. The clay was too dark. That suggested the tablet was fired in a kiln and then brought here.

Adam scanned the text. Most of the inscription was still clear. He felt his grip tighten involuntarily when his eyes struck on a cluster of letters about a third of the way down the tablet that spelled "*Refaim*." Healers! His heart began pounding so hard that Adam thought the others might be able to hear it, too.

Adam looked over at Claudia, but she hadn't looked up from her spade-work. Adam had been fascinated by the Healers since he first encountered them in grad school. They were figures of the Canaanite underworld, but they also appeared in several places in the Bible. For a short while, Adam had considered writing his thesis on them, but he had realized even without Claudia's admonitions that the topic was a career killer. It was clear that there would never be enough evidence to draw solid conclusions from just the few texts that have survived on the *Refaim*. Still, for someone like Adam, the call to understand how the Canaanites saw the afterlife was strong. He looked at the tablet again. "*Qirvu elai Refaim*," it said. "Come to me, Healers." If only it were that simple—as if you could just ask for the dead to appear and you would feel their presence and know that you remained connected to them. Even as a child, Adam had lost belief in anything that could make loss less permanent.

"Professor?" Maggie was pulling on Adam's sleeve. She must have been trying to get his attention for a while. Adam hadn't heard her say anything. He wondered how long he had been lost in his thoughts.

Adam didn't want to tell Maggie what he had seen just yet. It would take too long to explain, and he didn't want her to get too excited until he could confirm what the rest of the text said. Besides, he admitted to himself, he had caught a glimpse of something that had been buried for thousands of years and he wasn't quite ready to share it. Adam took a deep breath. "The writing looks very old," he said. "It's consistent with our time period. Nice find! Do you know the old alphabet?" He was pretty sure she wouldn't. They teach only the modern, Aramaic style of writing in Hebrew classes. "Well, you'll want to learn it. I'll show you when we're back in New York."

Claudia looked over. "There's writing? Can you make out what it says?"

"I'm not sure yet," Adam said. "Probably just a snippet of religious poetry. I doubt you'd be interested."

Claudia scurried over to look, ignoring his sarcasm. She gave Maggie a high five. "Let's see how you recorded the find." She nodded approvingly as Maggie displayed her documentation of the tablet. "We'll have to celebrate!" she said. "The legal drinking age in Israel is eighteen, isn't it?"

Maggie smiled broadly. "It is."

"I have a bottle of champagne back at the hotel," Claudia said. "Let's work until dinner and then we'll have a toast."

Adam took out his phone; Claudia stepped beside Maggie and put her arm around her shoulder to pose for a picture. The three of them were still grinning when Adam's phone rang. He jumped at the sound. The phone was only for emergencies; everyone he knew in Israel was at the dig. Adam's first thought was that it could be his grandfather, but he almost always waited for Adam to call, especially when Adam was away. With a stab of guilt, Adam realized he had let almost two weeks pass since they last spoke.

Adam shielded the screen from the sun's glare as best he could with his hand. The call was from Danny. Adam had a bad feeling. Almost two decades before, for reasons that had always escaped Adam, Danny had ceased to be just a kid from the neighborhood in his grandfather's eyes. Adam had never been consulted, but somehow Danny became virtually a part of their household, loud, needy, and omnipresent. "Maybe he just wants something," Adam thought. But he knew Danny's call would mean trouble.

"Excuse me," Adam said to Claudia and Maggie as he tapped the screen, "I should take this." He spoke into the phone as he climbed out of the trench where they had been working. "Hi Danny," he said. "What's going on?" Despite the poor connection, Adam could hear the strain in Danny's voice. "Hold on a minute, Danny, I'm in a dead zone. I'm going to try for a better spot."

He walked toward the tent. It was probably the best he could do out here.

"It's Hank, Adam," Danny said. "There was a slight pause. "I think you should come home."

Adam felt the muscles in his neck and shoulders stiffen. He had been holding his breath, he realized, and he let it out. "What happened? Can you put him on?" His grandfather had seemed fine when they last spoke. He hadn't complained about anything on the phone. Of course, he wouldn't have, Adam thought.

"No, Adam; he's in the hospital. He's not awake. They said to call you. Can you come?"

He had planned on flying back two days later. "Yeah. Yes. Of course I can come. I'll find a flight and I'll call you back." Everything around Adam seemed to be moving in slow motion. At his feet, a tiny beetle was scurrying into a hole, underground, home. Back in the trench, Maggie and Claudia were kneeling beside each other, their heads close together. Inside the tent, Adam could see the afternoon lecturer, gesturing at his presentation screen.

Adam checked the time. It was almost two-thirty. He called El Al to see if he could fly out that evening. It was a Friday night and he wasn't sure what running up against the Sabbath would do to the schedule of flights out of Israel. He was on hold for a while before he got to an operator, but when he explained his situation, the woman on the line was sympathetic. She put Adam on hold again while she checked the flights.

Adam looked back at the dig site from where he stood, and he remembered standing there a few summers before, watching Claudia's husband Theodore. That was less than a year before he died. Theodore had been painting a gorgeous landscape of the ancient city of Tel Arad, restored, fully alive, superimposed over the modern, unimpressive skyline of the neighboring Israeli town. Adam had understood without being told that the sky in the painting, a luminous blue, was the exact shade of Claudia's eyes. Theodore had loved Claudia with a passion and single-mindedness that she reserved for herself, Adam knew. Adam understood that, too

The woman came back on the line. There was nothing leaving that night, she told him. El Al's flights the next day were booked as well. She said it was possible he might find a flight tonight if he went standby, perhaps on another airline. But the best he could do would be to get to the airport and figure things out from there. Adam walked back to the dig. Maggie and Claudia looked up from the tablet when he approached.

"Sorry I had to take that," Adam said. "That was . . ." was there even a word for what Danny was? He wondered if there was any language that had a word for someone you grew up with and could never shake loose?

Maggie sounded concerned. "Are you okay, Professor?"

"Just a family thing," Adam said with a curt wave. He didn't want to explain. They didn't need to know. "I have to fly back tonight. I should probably pack up my stuff now; there's a bus to Tel Aviv at four." He glanced over at Claudia. "I'm sorry I can't stick around, but you and Maggie can celebrate without me." Claudia acknowledged his comment with a nod, but she was still lost in the tablet. Adam wondered what part of it had captured her attention, but there was no time to ask. It would have to wait until they were all back in New York.

Adam retrieved his daypack and handed Maggie the remaining water bottles he had brought. "I'll see you both in a few days." He looked over at the tablet. "Send me your pictures when you get a chance, okay, Claudia? Please say goodbye to the others for me."

Adam rode his rented bike the six miles back to his room in Arad. It would take him only a few minutes to pack; he had been living out of his suitcase since June. He took a quick shower, changed into the only clean clothes he had left, and arrived at the bus stop with a few minutes to spare after checking out of the hotel and returning his bike.

Arad was near the beginning of the line, so the bus was nearly empty when Adam boarded, but the ride would last almost two hours as the bus traveled its route, first due west, then almost due north. It would pick up passengers all along the route: black-hatted *haredim* rushing to be home before the Sabbath, soldiers on leave, grandmothers.

The more Adam thought about Danny's phone call the more concerned he felt. The bus seemed so slow that it was all Adam could do not to get out and push. He was in no mood to speak to strangers trying to be sociable or looking to practice their English. He set the music on his phone to shuffle and he stared blindly out the window as he slipped the headphones into his ears.

Adam skipped over several songs that didn't suit him, until he came to "Meditations for Moses." It was Charles Mingus solo at the piano, and Adam felt each jab of Mingus's fingers on the keys as if he had been struck. The next song was Bill Evans's mournful, disquieting "My Man's Gone Now," and it sucked Adam in whole. For the rest of the trip, Adam's consciousness drifted unfocused and disconnected. He had only the faintest awareness of the bustle all around him as people boarded at each stop.

Adam's mind drifted back over his last few conversations with his grandfather. There wasn't much to them, Adam thought. His grandfather was usually reticent on the phone, especially on international calls. Adam wondered if his grandfather knew he was sick. He was in his eighties, but he never talked about his health. "It is what it is," he would say. "Tell me how you're doing."

The final stop was in Tel Aviv. It was only about an hour until sunset, but Adam managed to catch a cab to the airport. By a quarter to seven, he was speaking to a ticket agent, but as he had feared, there were no seats available that night with any airline. It took him until nine to straighten out his itinerary. The best he could get was an outrageously expensive seat to New York via Kiev, leaving at eight-fifteen the next morning. He resolved to hunker down in the airport instead of finding a hotel room.

Adam tried to call Danny several times during the evening to let him know when to expect him, but without success. He tried his grandfather, praying he would be at home, the crisis over, but he only got the machine: "We can't pick up the phone right now. Please leave a message after the beep." "We," Adam thought. His grandfather had lived alone since Adam had moved out many years before, but he had never changed the message.

"Hi, it's me," Adam said. "I hope you get this in the next few hours. Danny said you weren't feeling well, but I'm on my way home. I'll see you soon." Adam bought a sandwich in the food court and then slumped into a chair for the night, his legs resting on his suitcase and his daypack on his lap, a prop for his elbow so he could rest his head on one of his hands. He dozed fitfully, starting at every sound out of fear that he would sleep through his departure time. He needn't have worried. He was fully awake by five the next morning, and when the gate opened, Adam was first in line to check in.

When he landed in Kiev, Adam had to wait nearly two hours for his connecting flight to JFK. It was four-thirty a.m. in New York. Adam checked his messages. Nothing. After an internal struggle, he decided couldn't call for at least another hour and a half. The wait was excruciating. He drank a decaf coffee as slowly as he could and then decided to try killing time in a bookstore. Most of the titles on the shelves were written in Cyrillic and were useless even as a distraction, but he did see a guidebook written in English. As far as Adam could make out from the maps he found in the book, the places his family had lived for centuries—almost all within a hundred miles of Kiev—didn't even exist anymore. Whole villages had succumbed to butchery, had been erased.

He paced as he watched planes take off, feeling more and more on edge. "There was no way that coffee was decaf," he thought. The frequent announcements in Ukrainian or Russian, he wasn't sure which, weren't helping his nerves, either. The music of the language was close enough to Yiddish to call out for his attention, but the words meant nothing he could understand. He tried to read his biography of Duke Ellington, but he couldn't focus. He wondered if the Ukrainians around him would recognize the Hebrew lettering on the bookmark he had picked up at his hotel; he put the book back in his bag. He checked his watch and decided it was late enough to call Danny, at least. If his grandfather had gotten home from the hospital already, Adam didn't want to wake him this early.

The phone rang only twice before Danny picked up. "Adam, where are you?"

"I'm in Kiev. I'll be boarding for New York in a few minutes. How is he?"

Danny didn't answer.

"He's steeling himself," Adam thought. But he still couldn't bring himself to articulate what that meant.

"He's gone, Adam." Danny said then. "Hank died last night. I'm sorry. I tried calling but you must have been out of range or in the air. I didn't want to leave a message."

"He died?" It didn't feel possible.

"It was peaceful." For a second, Adam thought Danny might sob, but he pulled himself together. "He was peaceful at the end. The room was all full of lights and beeping machines. That was horrible. I was with him, though." Now Adam did hear a sob. "I was with him until the very end. It was a heart attack. They couldn't get him stable." Danny paused. "I'm so sorry, Adam. I can't believe Hank's gone."

Dead. Gone. Adam couldn't even process what that meant. His grandfather had been his one enduring constant. Everything else could collapse; everything else did collapse, but not him. He was like the Western Wall. "I should have been there," he said.

There was a long pause before Danny answered. "What do you want to do about the funeral, Adam? I could start calling people. We could do it on Monday. I'll handle everything."

"No. No. Don't call anyone." Adam was surprised by the vehemence of his tone, and he lowered his voice. "We should do it ourselves, okay, Danny? He wasn't close to anyone else the way he was with us. We don't need to get other people involved. It will be more meaningful this way."

"What?" For a second, Adam thought he had lost the connection, but finally, Danny said, "Look, we're both in shock. We can talk after you land. Just call me from New York and we can work out all the details then, okay?"

"OK." Adam said. "They've already started boarding my flight. I'll call you from my apartment." He hung up the phone, felt in his pocket for his boarding pass, and walked over to the gate.

Chapter 2

Adam didn't sleep from Kiev to Queens, though he did his best to ignore the passengers' chatter and the constant rattling of the flight attendants' carts. He folded himself into his middle seat and did his best to disappear, emerging from his mental cocoon only to accept some pretzels or some water when they were offered. He wondered if his grandfather had been aware of his absence and if he died angry, or afraid, or disappointed. Or maybe Danny's presence had been enough, Adam thought. But he took no comfort from that possibility. Picturing Danny in the cardiac unit, sitting by the bedside, holding Adam's grandfather's hand and leaning in to listen to his last words only left Adam feeling more bereft.

When they landed, Adam moved through the airport automatically. He must have waited to retrieve his suitcase and then to catch a cab back to Larchmont, but he had no memory of that. He got out at a restaurant a few blocks from his apartment to order a burrito and he finished it on the walk home, dragging his suitcase with one hand and eating with the other. It was just after seven in the evening when he opened his apartment door and dumped his bags on the floor. He showered, pulled on some boxers, took a deep breath, and called Danny.

"Adam, are you back?" Danny asked.

"Yeah. I'm back." Adam closed his eyes. "Are you all right?"

"I've been better. I made some arrangements, but I needed to talk to you before I could schedule the service and burial."

Adam shook his head. It was all going to spiral out of control if he didn't stop it. It would be just like when his grandmother died, just like what had happened when his parents died, probably, though Adam had been too young to remember much about that. He had just a hazy picture in his mind of an apartment full of strangers looking sad and standing in a herd around his grandparents, a collection of legs in suit pants and stockings packed so close together that he couldn't break through.

"Tomorrow?" Adam asked. His throat was tight, so his voice was inaudible at first and he had to repeat the question. "Can we do it tomorrow, Danny? First thing? Just us?"

"You weren't serious about that, Adam? There's no way. It's a huge job. There's no way we could do it ourselves." Danny was part owner of the cemetery and his family had worked in the funeral business for generations. "We should take a day and let people know and arrange a service." He paused for a second; before Adam could reply, Danny added, his voice gentle, "You sound awful, Adam. You must be exhausted. Just leave it to me. I'll take care of it."

Adam shook his head. "No. Please, Danny. No strangers. I'm so beat, I can't argue with you now."

Silence. An aleph. A glottal stop. Then, "It's not respectful . . . Adam, come on . . . no rabbi, no people . . . What kind of a ceremony could we have? There are people who'd want to come."

"We don't need any of that, Danny. It's better with just us, okay? You loved him. I loved him. This is the last thing we can do for him, this private thing, this most personal, private thing." Adam caught himself biting the knuckle where his index finger met the back of his palm. He hadn't done that in years. He hated begging. "Don't take this from me, Danny, please . . ."

"I don't feel good about this, Adam."

Adam bit his lip. He breathed out slowly. "I need it to be this way, Danny, all right? Just us."

Danny paused for what felt to Adam like a long time. He said, "I could tell my guys to have the grave dug by the time we start. But if it gets late, I'll have to call them in to finish. It would be easier with more people . . . We have to be done with the burial before nightfall, so we'll need to get an early start."

Adam sighed. "Can we do it with three? I'm sure I can get Steven. We could do it with just the three of us, right?" Steven was Adam's friend from college, and they were still very close. They were both on faculty at Belmont now.

"It's back-breaking work."

Adam nodded into the phone. "He'll be up for it. I'll call him. We'll be there by eight."

Danny sighed. "OK. I'll make sure Hank's coffin will be there when you arrive. We can be there to help lower it into the grave. I'll have someone standing vigil over Hank at the funeral home all night. The body won't be left alone until we arrive."

"I know, Danny." Adam said. "Jewish law. I know the drill."

"I know you do. I know. Look, we're both a little raw right now. Just call Steven, okay? I'll see you tomorrow."

"I will," Adam said. He reminded himself, as his grandfather would have reminded him, that he could try to be gracious. "Thanks Danny. I know this is tough on you too."

"Don't thank me," Danny said. "I mean it. Don't. We both want to do right by Hank. Try to get some sleep, Adam. Tomorrow's going to be a long, hard day." He hung up.

Adam called Steven next. They were on for less than three minutes. "I'm so sorry," Steven said. "What can I do? I'll be there. Just tell me when and where." That was it. Adam let out a breath when he hung up the phone. No one was better in a crisis than Steven. Steven would help him get through this and he would he help him deal with Danny and there would be no drama. It was going to be all right.

Adam brushed his teeth and got into bed, but, worn out as he was, he couldn't sleep. When he closed his eyes, he felt hyperaware, like every nerve was firing. He could almost feel his hair growing out of his scalp.

He got up and pulled up Miles Davis's *On The Corner* on his computer. It was one of the first albums that got him into jazz, back in high school. It wasn't the kind of music that would help most people relax, but at the familiar skittering rhythms of the opening bars Adam knew he had found his medicine. He lay back on his bed and let his head sink into his pillow. The music was electric, distorted, complex. Bursts of trumpet and guitar wove in and out of the underlying bass and percussion, complementing and canceling out the insistent, chaotic chatter in Adam's brain.

Adam closed his eyes and he could almost see a woman coalescing from the music, pulling him toward her, inviting him to dance alongside her. In his mind's eye, he could see the curves of her hips and her breasts as she moved. She undid her ponytail, and her hair fell over her face, covering her eyes. All of his focus was on her, on his desire to bury himself in her embrace. He could almost feel his fingers against her smooth, cool skin as he swayed with her, taken by the music. His breathing slowed and steadied. He slept.

The next morning, Adam showered and dressed, but he didn't shave. He wouldn't be shaving for a while. He packed a day-bag with water bottles and suntan lotion before heading to a diner to eat a quick breakfast and pick up some sandwiches for lunch.

His grandfather's coffin was already there when Adam arrived at the cemetery. A bearded, middle-aged man in a black hat and black suit stood sentry, reading psalms. He looked up disapprovingly and left without a word when he saw Adam approaching in his shorts and work boots.

Next to the coffin, the grave lay open like a wound. A mound of loose dirt lay alongside. Danny's crew had prepared the site before Adam had arrived and Adam could see the scars left by the teeth of their mechanical digger along the side of the grave closest to the headstones.

Adam took a breath as he looked back at the coffin. It was a simple pine box with three rope handles on each side. As prescribed by Jewish law, nothing was to interfere with the decomposition of the body.

Adam saw that Danny had left three shovels out for them, much larger and cruder than the tools Adam had used at Tel Arad, but when Adam hefted the one closest to him, it sat comfortably in his hands. He probed the soft, moist soil with the toe of his boot. He was anxious to get started, to be digging. He badly needed this to be over.

Adam looked up and saw Danny striding toward him on his short, powerful legs. The four men he had brought with him were in work clothes, but Danny wore a dark sports coat and dark jeans. When Danny caught Adam's eye, he put his arms out wide as if he could pull Adam to his barrel chest from thirty steps away. "Adam! Adam!" he called.

Adam winced. Danny always spoke too loudly for Adam's taste and with too much physical contact: an arm around the neck, a pat on the shoulder, a two-handed handshake. Danny cried in public. He got into loud arguments over nothing. In hundreds of small ways, despite his grandfather's hopes that he and Danny would become close, being associated with Danny had always embarrassed Adam.

As Adam walked over to take Danny's hand, Danny shook his head. "I can't believe he's gone, Adam," he said. He squeezed Adam's arm. He glanced over his shoulder, gesturing toward his crew. "We should get started," he said. "I'm sorry I'm a little late. I had to drive Henry to daycare. Rose was a real treat this morning. A total bitch."

Adam never had much to do with Rose when he could avoid it. She had always been cold toward him, and prickly. But then he imagined it was no picnic being married to Danny. "How is Henry doing?" Adam asked. "How old is he now? Eight months?"

Danny nodded. "Eight months last week." He glowed with pride. "One of his teeth just came in. He's such a trooper. It must have hurt, but he barely fussed at all. Hank was telling me just the other day what a special kid he is." Adam recognized the flash of pain on Danny's face as a mirror of his own, and for just a second, he felt their shared bond as something more than a burden.

Danny looked at his watch. "We should get started," he said. "These guys need to get going." Adam nodded, and at Danny's signal, one of the men distributed short ropes. Danny walked to the front right side of the coffin and he gestured for Adam stand across from him on the other side. The other men lined up behind them. When Danny gave the word, they all looped their ropes through the rope handles on the coffin.

"You're going to want to stand straight, Adam," Danny said. "We'll go slow. Lower the coffin hand under hand."

Adam kept his eyes on his hands. It was one more loss alongside all the others, he thought. He focused on his breathing and on Danny's whispered count before each incremental descent of the coffin. When the box finally came to rest at the bottom of the grave, the men pulled up their ropes and handed them back to the leader of Danny's crew.

Steven drove past then in the beat-up Chevy he had bought back in grad school. He parked and walked over to Adam and embraced him. "How are you doing, Adam? Are you okay? You look like crap. Have you slept?" As usual, Steven looked every inch the prep school graduate. He was wearing jeans, but he had a summer sports coat draped over one arm.

"I've been better," Adam said. "I'll feel better after today. I'm really glad you could come. It means a lot." He gestured at the jacket. "I hope you don't mind getting those clothes dirty."

Steve shrugged. "I wasn't sure what to wear," he said. "I wanted to be prepared." He shrugged apologetically. "I've never been to something like this before."

"No one has been to something like this before," Danny said. He must have dismissed his men when Steven arrived. They were already about a hundred yards away, walking back the way they had come.

Adam gestured toward Danny. "Steven, Danny, you remember each other, right?"

Steven nodded and extended his hand. Danny took it in both of his and pumped it up and down. They hadn't seen each other for years, but Adam had kept Steven up to date about Danny's more irksome habits, as well as the favors he had asked.

"Adam doesn't want to have a ceremony," Danny told Steven. "'Just a burial,' he says. "It isn't right. Will you tell him it isn't right? Maybe he'll listen to you. I'm only third generation in the funeral business, so what do I know?"

Adam started to protest, but Danny interrupted. "I'm not asking for me, Adam. This is for Hank and your grandmother and your parents." Danny gestured at the headstones marking the graves of Adam's family. "Don't you think they would want some kind of service? This isn't how you do a Jewish funeral."

"Don't," Adam said. "Don't. I don't need a guilt trip." He had been so young when his parents died. His memories of them were no more than faint impressions, and they were so enmeshed with stories his grandparents had told him that he didn't know whether they even belonged to him. He remembered his grandparents telling him the driver who killed them had been drunk. He was sure of that. The memory of the crack in his grandfather's voice, of his grandmother turning to the wall, trying to stifle her sob as Adam absorbed the words: that memory was his.

"They're dead," Adam said to Danny. He took a breath and tried to push the bitterness back down. "You can't please them. Believe me. I've tried. The dead are implacable. Or maybe they just don't want anything. It comes to the same thing."

Danny set his jaw. It was an expression Adam knew well. He was digging in. "We're not going to just bury him without any prayers," Danny said. "It's not right. I won't go along with it. This is a kosher cemetery, Adam. There are some things that you just do. I shouldn't have let you get your way about not having anyone else, but I'm not giving in on this. We're having a service."

Adam knew there was no way Danny could understand. Even Steven probably didn't understand how personal this was, how private his grief felt. His grandfather had raised him, and Adam hadn't been there when he was dying. If Adam could have, he would have placed the coffin in the ground himself. He would even have done it with Steven's and Danny's help—just the three of them, instead of Danny's workers—but Danny had convinced him that it was clumsy and difficult work, and they would be likely to drop the coffin. They could bury him, though, Adam thought. He didn't need strangers intruding on that: people for whom this meant nothing, or almost nothing, just some pious duty, some ritual they could participate in before getting on with the rest of their day. Adam didn't need some rabbi reading stock phrases from a book. And he didn't need anyone telling him to pray. Not today. If he had anything to address on high, it wouldn't be pleasant. It wouldn't be respectful or submissive. It definitely wouldn't be any prayer he had ever heard of.

Steven interceded in a soft tone. "Look, Adam. A service couldn't hurt, could it? Maybe later you'll wish you did something more traditional. You certainly won't regret it, right?"

Adam wanted to scream. Sure he could regret it, he wanted to say. He seemed to have a great capacity for regret. But he knew Danny and Steven meant well. "Be amiable," his grandfather had often told him. "Don't make things harder than they need to be."

Adam looked in Danny's eyes. Soon, this would be just one more horrible memory. "This is important to you, Danny?"

"Not just to me, Adam. It's important."

Adam nodded. "OK, Danny. Do it. Let's go. But no long sermons, okay? No big productions."

Danny took yarmulkes out of his pocket. He put one on and passed the others to Adam and Steven. Adam gave his back. He was wearing an old, worn Mets cap that he had bought to watch the Mets on television with his grandfather the last time they were in the World Series. He wasn't taking it off.

"Adam," Danny asked, "are you going to tear some part of your clothes?"

Adam was surprised that the custom felt right to him. He would want to carry a part of this day with him for a while. But he didn't want to have to wear his t-shirt or jeans for the rest of the week. "My cap," he said. "Do you have a scissors?"

Danny shook his head. "I forgot them." He took the Mets cap and pulled hard with both beefy hands, slowly ripping the fabric about three inches up the side. He handed the cap back to Adam.

"*Baruch Dayan Emet,*" Danny intoned. "Blessed is the Righteous Judge." He waited for Adam's response. Steven looked at his feet.

"Amen," Adam said. The whole cemetery seemed still except for a few birdcalls in the distance. Blessed is the Reaper, Adam thought. He looked again at the headstones. Blessed is the Destroyer. There was no one left. Adam was the last of the Draschers, now.

Danny said the prayer supplicating God's mercy for the dead in his expressionless Sunday School Hebrew. Adam translated the phrases in his head as Danny read the words: "the Master of mercy will protect him forever . . . will tie his soul with the rope of life. The Everlasting is his heritage . . ."

Automatically, Adam responded "Amen" at the prayer's close.

"I don't think we should say *Kaddish*, Adam," Danny said. We don't have a *minyan* and the burial isn't over, so you aren't a mourner yet."

"No. Not technically," Adam said, keeping his voice even. Steven caught his eye and Adam made an effort to unclench his jaw. They were trying to help him, he reminded himself. But he imagined himself reciting the traditional mourner's prayer, the Aramaic formula tumbling from his mouth like a nursery rhyme when his mouth tasted like ashes. There are limits to amiability, he thought. Out loud, louder than he meant to speak, he said, "let's skip it."

Danny fumbled with his prayer book. "Does anyone want to say something now?" He asked.

Adam shook his head. Steven didn't respond.

Danny bowed his head as if he were addressing the coffin along with Adam and Steven. He said, "Hank was . . ." Adam looked up as Danny's voice broke. He waited in awkward silence as Danny wiped his forehead and collected himself.

"Hank meant a lot to me," Danny began again. "I was getting in trouble in school, and my parents were ashamed of me. They always told me I was lazy and ungrateful. They made it pretty clear they didn't have much use for me. The school sent a letter home one day after I got into a fight, but I got to it before they did. I ran away the next morning." Adam and Steven were silent, but Danny shrugged as if in answer to a question. "I had maybe thirty dollars on me," he said. "I don't know how far I would have gotten if Hank hadn't found me when he was on his way back home from the newsstand. I knew him a little from the neighborhood and I knew that he knew my mom. I figured Hank would bring me home and I would catch hell, but he didn't bring me home." Danny choked back a sob. "He looked me in the eye like I mattered," he said. "He put his hand on my shoulder and said he would walk me to school. He told me if I ever needed to get away for a while, I could visit. I could just hang out and watch TV, he said, until I felt ready to go home." Danny turned to look at Adam. "I don't know what he saw in me, but no one else ever saw it. I know you wondered what the hell I was doing there all the time, Adam, but I couldn't stay away. Hank was my lifeline. He made me feel like I had a place where I was wanted."

Danny paused for a moment. He cleared his throat and looked first at the coffin and then down at his feet. "I think of you all the time, Hank, when I try to raise my son. I want him to feel what you made me and Adam feel—that he's worth something, that he always has a place. I will miss you terribly, Hank." Danny stepped back from the grave.

Adam felt like he should say something, anything. But the words wouldn't come.

When Danny looked at him, Adam just bit his lip. Steven hunched his shoulders and offered Adam a wan smile. No one spoke for a while. Finally, Adam picked up his shovel and managed to croak out, "Let's get to work."

Danny took off his jacket, folded it and put it on the ground several steps from the grave. He laid his prayer book on top of his jacket while Steven went to put his jacket and dress shirt in his car. By the time Steven returned, Adam and Danny had already picked up their shovels and had begun moving the dirt from the pile to the grave. The dull thud as the dirt struck the coffin was much louder than Adam had expected.

Danny worked like an animal, his muscles straining in the hot sun. He used his shoulders, his knees, his back. Within a few minutes, the sweat was dripping from his forehead and staining the armpits of his shirt. It wasn't long before his undershirt was drenched. You could see its outline through the shirt above. Adam was determined to match Danny's labor, but Danny was relentless and Adam couldn't keep pace. He looked over at Steven, but Steven went at his own speed, pausing every once in a while to make a comment or a small joke.

The three men worked steadily for a couple of hours, stopping only for a few short water breaks until the hole was filled at last. Danny had overestimated the time it would take them, but not the effort. Adam was exhausted.

He wiped the sweat from his face and the back of his neck and planted his shovel deeply into the small pile of dirt that remained next to the grave.

The others stopped as well. Danny wiped his forehead. Steven bent forward, hands on his knees to catch his breath. Adam surveyed the gravesite. He hadn't been to the cemetery in a long time. The three older graves holding his parents and grandmother lay flat under their headstones, the grass growing over all of them so that you couldn't tell where one grave ended and the next began. Adam realized for the first time that there wasn't any space for him there in what his grandmother used to call "the family estate."

Soon, Adam thought, Danny's crew would flatten the loose mound on top of his grandfather's grave and before long, they would plant grass there. In a year, they would put up a headstone and the Drascher family plot would be complete; a tidy little story with a beginning, middle, and end. He wondered if it ever occurred to his grandparents that they had left him floating, rootless.

"We should eat," Adam said. "Are you hungry?" I've got sandwiches in the car. Egg salad with pickles."

Danny smiled. Adam's grandfather had served that to them countless times. Adam went to his car and brought back a small cooler filled with the sandwiches and more water. Steven had a blanket in his car, and they spread it out on the grass next to the graves of Adam's parents and sat down to eat.

"I'm glad you're here," Adam said. "Both of you." He looked at the ground between his legs and then up at Danny. "I should have been there when he died, Danny. I had no idea how sick he was . . ."

Danny shook his head. "You couldn't know, Adam. He hid it from everybody. Even when I called you, I thought he'd pull through. And he was really proud of you, being on that dig. He told everybody he met. 'My grandson is in Israel,' he would say. 'He's an archaeologist. He studies ancient history.' He joked about it, but he was really proud. 'I have no idea what he's doing,' he'd say, 'but it's very impressive.'"

"Did you find anything on the dig?" Steven asked. "How was it over there?"

Adam looked out over the cemetery. He shrugged. "Maybe. I think so. We found some writing that could turn out to be something."

"Ancient prophecies?" Steven asked. "Magic incantations? An ancient genetics textbook?"

"I haven't had a chance to read it yet," Adam said. He tried to force a smile. "If it turns out to be genetics, I'll let you know. We can collaborate."

Adam glanced over at Danny and gestured toward the rows and rows of headstones dotting the ground—all different sizes, colors, and textures as far as he could see, in blocks about a hundred yards square separated by narrow, tree-lined roads. Many of the newer stones were granite or polished marble, tall and engraved in deep letters in Hebrew and English. Some of the older stones were in Yiddish." So many graves." Adam said. "Do you ever wonder what's going to happen to all of them?"

"They'll be here." Danny said. "That's kind of the point, right? Cemeteries are forever. That's part of why I bought in. It's permanent."

"Yeah, but I mean in a really long time: a thousand years, two thousand years. I've been on digs where the site was a lot younger than that. A lot changes in that amount of time." Adam stood up and picked up three small stones from the ground. He placed them in front of the headstones of his mother, father, and grandmother in the traditional mode of marking a visit in a Jewish cemetery.

"In a couple of thousand years I don't even think much of the DNA would be left in these bodies," Steven said, his voice low. "Not in this climate. I doubt if there would be enough to identify them." He looked down at the ground, as if he could see the chemical decomposition taking place at his feet. "Just about all the original molecules would have been degraded. A lot of them would have been built up again into new molecules in worms, or plants, or insects, or bacteria. That would have all happened many thousands of times in two thousand years. Everything that had made up the people while they were alive would be growing in some other body in some other place."

Adam sat back down and ran his hand along the lush grass in front of him. "Chemical recycling. It's hard to get any comfort from that."

Steven shrugged. "I don't find it disturbing. We're all a part of something bigger, something oblivious to our concerns. It's been going on for billions of years and it will continue for billions of years if we don't screw it up too badly. That's something. And also, it's true. I see that as a big advantage over a lot of beliefs people have."

Danny shot Steven an angry look. "Hank wasn't just his body," Danny said. "Science doesn't know everything."

Adam caught Steven's patronizing smile and he intervened before Steven could respond. "We see bones at the digs, sometimes," he said, "along with jewelry and tools, and a lot of trash." He tore off a few blades of grass as he spoke. "Everything gets buried one way or another, and some of it gets dug up later, sometimes with some sense of reverence, but not usually. There's nothing magical about any of it, you know. The bones won't live again any more than the rest of it will, I don't think. The people aren't in their bones, and they aren't in their stuff. We can sometimes learn about the people or how they lived, but they're gone."

He gestured toward the grave they had just filled. "My whole family is here, but nothing that's really them." He looked at Steven. "Maybe in a couple of thousand years they could be part of someone's PhD project."

Steven smiled. "That's a kind of immortality I could believe in," he said. "And if I could help someone get a degree, so much the better."

Adam looked at his feet. "Sometimes I hope for a little more," he said. "Not anything physical; not the bones or the chemicals. But I'd like to be able to hear them again, to see them again." He tried to smile. "Wouldn't it be great if I could just download my grandfather from the Cloud when I wanted to talk to him?"

Danny looked reprovingly at Adam. "You think Hank was just data? Come on, Adam, don't even joke about that. Heaven isn't just some big hard drive."

Adam shrugged. "I have CDs and MP3s of concerts I've been to that sound just like the real thing," he said. "Somehow, the whole experience is there, stored on my computer. Maybe data really is all we are, or all we are that matters, anyway. Zeroes and ones."

"You can reduce everything to zeros and ones in principle," Steven said. "Even the way each neuron functions and the patterns of their connections. With a hundred billion neurons in your brain, each connected in thousands of ways, that's a lot of zeroes and ones, but it's still just zeroes and ones."

Adam took pity on Danny. He didn't want to gang up on him. Not today. He gestured toward the gravestones in their neat rows. "This is a beautiful place, Danny," he said. "You should be really proud."

Danny was quick as usual to accept a peace offering. He looked around with obvious satisfaction. "I do love it here," he said. "Rose thought it made sense financially, but it doesn't really. I'm managing it better than it was, but it's never going to be a real moneymaker. I like that it gives me a chance to work outside part of the time. And it's not from my parents. It's something I did on my own."

Neither Adam nor Steven seemed about to reply, so Danny continued. "What are you doing for the rest of the week, Adam?" Danny asked. "Are you sitting *shiva*? It's not the full seven days, you know. Rosh Hashana starts on the fourth, on Wednesday night."

"I don't know what I'm going to do. I have classes on Tuesday and Wednesday, and they aren't prepared yet. And I have a lot to do on the artifact we found."

"You'll have to go through the apartment at some point, too," Danny said. "I don't know when the lease expires. You'll need to talk to the super about arranging things. If you can wait until next week, I can help you. It might be hard being back in the apartment and going through his things. You don't have to do it alone."

Adam bit his lip. "It hasn't been easy for me being in that apartment for a long time. Not since Grandma died. This probably won't be much worse."

The day of his grandmother's burial flashed into Adam's mind. He missed her terribly in that moment. Adam remembered standing in front of the stereo speakers in the living room in their apartment after the funeral. The absence of music felt so wrong to him. He remembered that vividly. She had always had music going before she got sick: Count Basie, Artie Shaw, Benny Goodman. And Ellington. Especially Ellington. Adam remembered how gently he had placed the needle in the groove of her favorite record, "Sophisticated Lady," and how he watched as it moved up and down in the old, warped vinyl. He remembered how he would have given anything to have her there with him. He could still recall the flash of anger he felt then when he couldn't hear the song over the chatter of all the people there who were treating the day like a party or a reunion.

Danny seemed oblivious to Adam's reverie. "She seemed to know everything, didn't she?" Danny asked. He turned to Steven. "She used to talk about history, and politics, and art while she did her crossword puzzles. She had something to say about almost every clue."

Adam smiled through his tears. "She was a real talker."

Danny nodded. "Hank loved her so much," he said. "God, he was a wreck when she died. I was really worried about him."

"I don't know if it was conscious or not," Adam said, "but after a couple of weeks, my grandfather always had the radio on, or a tape going after she died. There was a lot of silence to fill. We never spoke about it, but it seemed like he would listen to just about anything with a woman's voice. He loved dance music and whatever was popular at the time. I remember laughing when I caught him listening to a Destiny's Child tape he bought. He went through a Madonna phase for a while. He was a little defensive about it. 'I don't know why, but it moves me,' he would say. Or 'she has a lovely voice. A real artist.' It was just a coincidence, I guess, that everyone he listened to was sexy as hell."

"He never dated after your grandmother died?" Steven asked.

"No." Adam said. "I don't think he ever got over her loss. As far as I know, he never dated anyone even before my grandmother."

"You know, that's not exactly true," Danny said. "He told me some stories . . . he had his share of wild times before he met your grandmother. He got into some trouble before Korea. He said the army helped straighten him out, you know." Danny smiled. "He told me about one time, right after he got out . . ." He let his voice trail away. "Sorry, Adam. Another time."

Adam couldn't hide his surprise. "He never told me anything about that," he said. "What did he tell you?"

Danny gestured at the grave. "It's not for today. I'll tell you some other time. It's not a big deal, just kid stuff, but it was a funny story. I used to ask Hank for stories all the time when I came over. You know how I idolized him. I asked him about everything he did. I wanted him to teach me plumbing, but he pointed out that I'd probably be better off learning the family business. I could always hire a plumber, he said. When I found out he was a professional boxer for a while, I wanted to take lessons from him, but my parents wanted me to go to a dojo like every other boy in my class. He understood. 'It's a different world now,' he told me. 'But some things never change. Some time you might find yourself in a situation where violence is your only option, and you'll need to know how to handle yourself.'"

"He was a boxer?" Steven asked. "I didn't know that."

Danny nodded, the pride radiating from his eyes. "'Digger Drascher' they called him. He got that nickname in Korea."

Adam shook his head. "I don't think it was from Korea, Danny," Adam said. "It was probably just a play on the name. Drash means dig; like when you interpret a Torah story, that's a drash. You're digging beneath the surface."

Danny fixed Adam with an incredulous look. "Do you think the guys in his unit spoke Hebrew? I doubt if Hank even knew that. He told me they started calling him 'Digger' when they saw how fast he could dig a foxhole. They said, 'Look at Digger go!' and then they put him on latrine duty." Danny smiled. "Maybe that's how he got interested in plumbing."

Adam decided to let it drop. If he had a nickel for every time he'd managed to teach Danny something, he wouldn't be any richer than he was now. "He taught me how to box," Adam said. "He started when some of the kids were giving me a hard time in middle school. For a couple of years, we went to the gym every Saturday and once a week after school. He told me the same thing he told you: 'A man has to know how to handle himself.' He must have told me that a hundred times. He said just learning to take a punch would be good for me, because if I weren't afraid of getting hit, my confidence would show and I'd be able to avoid most fights. He was right about that. I remember he once told me 'When you box a man, after a few rounds you know how he acts when he's tired and what he does when he's scared. If you surprise him, you can see what he defends first, what he wants to protect.' He said, 'There are guys I've boxed and never said a word to, and in some ways, I know them better than I know anyone else. Better than I know your grandmother after all these years.'"

"Why did you stop?" Danny asked. "He must have been a terrific teacher."

Adam shrugged. "We stopped before you started coming by. I didn't like it. It changes the way you look at people, the things you notice without thinking about it. I'd walk into the gym and immediately start sizing people up. Their reach, how they stood . . ."

"That's just what guys do," Danny said. "You should have stuck with it."

Adam shrugged. Maybe he and his grandfather would have been closer if he had. Maybe then Danny wouldn't think it was his place to tell Adam what he should and shouldn't say about his own grandfather . . . Adam cut himself off. He was working himself up over nothing, he told himself. All Danny had done was take better care of Adam's grandfather than Adam had. Arguing with him wouldn't change that. But when Steven asked if his grandfather had been a good fighter, Adam spoke over Danny's quick assent.

"No," Adam said. "He only had five fights. He was two and three. Thank God he stopped before he got hurt."

Danny said nothing. The cemetery felt very still. Even the birdsong had quieted. A gentle breeze brushed Adam's cheek and he watched his shadow play over the grass as he moved his hand back and forth.

Steven asked, "Are you going to work, tomorrow, Adam?"

Adam nodded. "I have to. I'll go crazy if I just stew. Anyway, no one's going to teach my classes if I don't."

"You can stay with us tonight," Steven said. "Todd would love to see you. He'll be done with his last patient in time for dinner."

"Thanks for the offer," Adam said. "But I need to prepare for class, and I've barely even been home." He stood up stiffly. He realized he was going to be very sore the next day. "Look, guys, Thank you. I really appreciate your giving up the whole day like this, digging with me in the heat . . ."

"Adam, stop, please," Steven said. "There was never any question."

"Seriously," Danny said. "Stop. Stop talking."

Chapter 3

Adam woke up slowly and for a moment, he half-thought he was still in Tel Arad. He put on his glasses and then let his head fall back onto his pillow. No. He was back in his one-bedroom apartment, surrounded by his books, his framed maps of the ancient world, his CDs. His grandfather was gone. He checked his phone. It was six in the morning, Labor Day. He considered going to his grandfather's apartment to get started on packing the place up, but he told himself he didn't have time. His classes weren't ready, and he had to do his laundry and go grocery shopping.

Adam got up sore and stiff. His limbs felt heavy, heavier than he remembered they'd ever felt, as if his grandfather had been buoying him up for his whole life and now he had been left to sink. He took a couple of ibuprofen, showered, and put on some clothes, including the Mets cap that, along with his unshaven beard, would mark that he was still in the earliest phase of mourning.

The cupboard was nearly empty, Adam saw, which saved him the trouble of making a shopping list. He started his laundry in the small washer/dryer he had in his apartment. Then he opened a can of tuna and ate it over the sink for breakfast before he settled in to try to get some work done. He sat with his lesson plans for a couple of hours, but made little progress. It was a relief when the ringing of his phone, his landline, interrupted him.

It was the rabbi at his grandfather's temple, Rabbi Mira. Adam didn't know if Mira was her first or last name. He had seen her only once, at High Holiday services with his grandfather.

"I'm so sorry for your loss," the rabbi said. "Danny Blumberg gave me your number and I wanted to call. So many of us in the community will miss Herschel. He was really special."

Adam stiffened. Herschel, she called him. Everyone called him Hank. Adam pictured her sitting in her office, reading off a card, checking another mourner off her list for the day. "Did you know him well?" Adam asked. He just managed to keep the bitterness out of his tone.

"Of course," she said. "Herschel was very active in the Temple Brotherhood and he was on the social action committee this year. He talked about you all the time." She paused, but Adam didn't respond. He was trying and failing to picture his grandfather selling raffle tickets and helping out at barbecues. "I wanted to let you know that we have a prayer group that visits houses of mourning," the rabbi said. "Most of our congregants are here in Queens, of course, but we'd be happy to come up to Westchester. You're in Larchmont, right?"

It was a kind offer, Adam realized. He pictured a dozen or so senior citizens coming up in a bus from Little Neck to pray in his apartment, a field trip for the underemployed. He would offer them something to eat and they would accept some token, probably a cookie each, maybe some warm water with lemon. Then they'd get down to business, reading from their prayer books in unison, not comprehending the Hebrew words. On their way out, they would make the appropriate sad faces at him and one of them might offer some Yiddish aphorism about sad times.

It was too horrible. "That's very gracious of you, thanks," Adam said. "I'm okay. I don't know how much praying I'll be doing, but there are temples near here if I get the urge."

Rabbi Mira was undaunted. Adam wondered how often she had this exact conversation. "Of course, we'd never want to intrude," she said. "But you can change your mind any time. Just let me know. I also wanted to remind you that Rosh Hashana is practically here. I can't believe it, but it starts Wednesday night, so the *shiva* period will end early. I don't think I can get to you before the holiday, but I would like to stop by sometime soon if I could. I also wanted to invite you to our temple for High Holiday services this year. I know you usually came with your grandfather. Please be our guest."

Adam hadn't thought about Rosh Hashana without his grandfather. His throat constricted. He needed to get off the phone. "Thank you, Rabbi. I can get your number from Danny if I need it."

The afternoon passed like a fever as Adam stared unfocused into space. Only the occasional stab of grief prodded his consciousness to awaken, like some swamp creature surfacing for air before sinking back down into the mud. It was after five when the phone rang again. This time, it was his cell. It was Danny.

"How are you doing, Danny?" Adam asked. He held his breath. He could hear it coming.

"Not so good, Adam." The whine in Danny's voice set Adam's teeth on edge. "I need a favor."

Adam knew his grandfather would have been Danny's first call. Evidently, he was next in line. He exhaled slowly. "Yeah?" He moved his laundry over to the dryer as Danny spoke.

"I'm at a trade show in Jersey. Rose has known about it for months, but she got called into work. It's an emergency, she says, and I can't get home in time even if I leave now." Danny paused, waiting, Adam knew, for an offer of help. After a couple of seconds, Danny asked, "Can you cover for me?"

"Cover what?" Adam was still in a fog.

"Henry. Can you watch Henry for me until I get back?"

Adam couldn't claim to be too busy, he thought, not after pissing away the whole day. And he had to admit to himself that the thought of spending some time with Henry was appealing. He could read him a couple of books, maybe sing him a song or two. The change of venue might even help him get something done. And his grandfather would have been very pleased, Adam knew. He loved that boy.

"Do you need me to leave now?" Adam asked.

"Could you? I'm two hours away, but the conference ends soon. I'm making some important connections. If I could stay to the end and then rush over there, it would mean a lot."

"Yeah. I can come. Don't be late, okay? I still have work to do for tomorrow."

"Thanks a million, Adam!" Danny said. "I knew I could count on you. I'll tell Rose to expect you."

Adam packed his notes and his computer and headed out. He was on the expressway within ten minutes and at Danny's within thirty-five.

Danny's house was a Tudor on a quiet cul-de-sac, just a couple of blocks from the traffic and noise of Northern Boulevard. Rose was waiting on the front steps as Adam made his way up the long walk. She had changed a lot since high school, Adam noted. Her hair was darker, almost black, and it was cut in sharp lines to her jaw. The red of her lipstick still made a striking contrast against the milky white of her face, but she now wore a painted-on smile in place of her adolescent scowl. Adam wasn't a fan of either, but if he had to choose, he preferred the scowl. She must still have her tattoo, he thought, though it was hidden under her crisply tailored blazer. It was a rose, he remembered. She wasn't one to avoid the obvious. She was holding Henry. Adam thought the boy's light brown curls had grown longer since the last time he was there.

Adam grinned at Henry before he looked back at Rose. "Danny told me you had to run out," he said, hoping she might take that as a combined greeting and dismissal.

Rose nodded. She handed the baby to Adam. "He should be just about ready to go down," she said. "He just ate and he's wearing a new diaper.

There are more on the changing table in his room if you need them." She spoke over her shoulder as she entered the house. Adam followed her in. "I thought I had Labor Day off," she said, "but we have a new client, a very big name, and I got called in. It's still very hush hush, so I can't talk about it."

Adam had no response. On his best day, he couldn't give a shit about advertising or marketing, whichever Rose did. There was a difference, apparently, but he'd never figured it out. "We'll be fine," he said.

Rose glanced up at the clock again. "Shit, I'm late," she said. "I need to run." She grabbed a black leather purse and snatched the keys off the hook by the door on her way out. Everything was fine until Adam heard her car pull out. That's when Henry started fussing, growing more and more agitated so that he was crying loudly within a couple of minutes.

"Are you hungry?" Adam asked. Are you thirsty? There was no answer, of course. Henry's diaper wasn't full. "Maybe there's something in the cupboard," Adam said. He checked, but most of the food there needed chewing and Henry had one tooth. Crackers and pretzels weren't going to work.

Henry made it clear that the bottle of formula Adam found wasn't going to cut it either, but some digging uncovered a pint of peach ice cream in the freezer. Adam figured there was only so wrong you could go with fruit and milk. He scooped a couple of generous teaspoons into a small bowl and fed Henry the ice cream with the tiniest spoon he could find in the silverware drawer. Henry looked at Adam with such surprise and delight that Adam almost laughed.

Adam hummed to him while he ate, and by the time the ice cream was gone, Henry was struggling to keep his eyes open. Adam put the bowl and spoon in the sink, and then he wet his finger under the faucet and used it to clean Henry's tooth before he took him upstairs. There was a rocking chair in Henry's room and Adam sat in it, holding Henry against his chest. He rocked Henry for a long time, willing his own muscles to relax as he lulled the boy to sleep. It was a trick his grandfather had taught him the last time Adam had watched Henry, the night of his grandfather's birthday.

It had been raining for hours that day, and they were at his grandfather's apartment. Rose was away at the time, on a business trip. Adam had arrived on time, he remembered, in the afternoon. But when he had walked in, it looked like Danny and Henry had already been there forever. Adam could still picture his grandfather bouncing the boy in his lap, singing him nonsense songs while Danny stood alongside him. He remembered the pang of loneliness he felt then, the feeling of being an outsider in his own home.

After dinner, Danny had been called into work to deal with a part of the cemetery that had been flooding. Adam didn't know what happened when a cemetery flooded, but he imagined it was bad news. That's what the look on Danny's face suggested at the time, Adam thought.

Adam smiled as he remembered how, when it was time to get Henry to bed, he and his grandfather rearranged the cushions on the living room couch to make a crib for him. They must have used a hundred feet of duct tape to hold it all together, but after his grandfather went to sleep, Adam still wasn't sure that it would hold. When Henry had finally conked out in the makeshift bed they had assembled, Adam settled himself down onto the floor right beside him so that if Henry did fall, he would fall on Adam. In the end, Danny was away most of the night. When he finally came home at about four in the morning, he woke Adam and shook his head at all the duct tape, "For God's sake," he said, "Rose doesn't need to hear about this." As far as Adam knew, she still didn't know.

Henry was asleep. Adam laid him in his crib and went back downstairs to the living room. He worked productively there for more than an hour, though a phone buzzed several times. After the first few calls, Adam tracked the sound to Rose's office. Her phone was in the purse lying on her desk, but Adam certainly wasn't going to go in and get it. He worked for a while longer before Danny texted to say he was on his way home and making good time. Adam dove back into his work, but half an hour later, he was startled by the sound of breaking glass and a scream.

Then he heard Danny's voice. "You son of a bitch!" He heard more glass breaking and another scream, not Danny. A terrified, inhuman sound.

Adam ran outside. He saw a tangle of legs, four of them, kicking against the shards of glass that littered the street. They were hanging out the driver's door of a red coupe Adam didn't recognize. Danny's car was parked behind it.

Adam sprinted over as Danny slid out from the coupe and onto his knees, pulling the other man after him by his belt. Adam could hear Danny's grunt over the man's screams as Danny ground the face of the other man into the asphalt and the glass. Adam shouted and Danny looked up at him for less than a second, but there was no recognition in his eyes. Danny stood up and kicked at the man once, twice, grunting like an animal each time. Adam tried to drag Danny away, pulling at his shoulders, but Danny shoved him, knocking Adam to the ground.

Adam screamed, "Stop it, Danny! Let him go!" But Danny didn't respond. There was no indication he even heard. Adam got up off the ground and tried to grab Danny's shoulders again, but Danny twisted away and then turned back toward the man on the ground. Adam saw an opening, and he took it. He punched Danny, connecting hard enough with his cheek that Danny rocked backward. "Let him go," Adam said. "Let him go."

For a moment, Adam wasn't sure what Danny would do, but Danny held up his hands and walked in a tight circle, breathing hard. The man was stirring, Adam saw, but he was in bad shape. The light from the streetlamps was enough to illuminate streaks of blood in the street and in the driver's seat of the car.

Danny looked untouched except for the bruise that was already rising on his cheek from where Adam had hit him. Only his hands were bloody. He was bent over now, breathing heavily, his hands on his knees.

The other man moaned, and Adam turned to see him roll over onto his side. His suit jacket was bunched under his armpits and his pants had twisted so that his belt buckle was a few inches to the right of center. The man turned his head as Adam knelt down toward him; Adam stared, open mouthed, at the man's battered face and at the blood running from his nose down to his collar, staining his white dress shirt. The man looked young, Adam thought, just a few years out of college. He had probably been handsome a few minutes before.

"We've got to get this guy to a hospital," Adam said. "Call an ambulance."

Danny shook his head. He was kneeling in the street now, just clear of the glass, panting. Adam thought he looked like he might cry. "We can't," he said. "We can't. Adam, please." He implored Adam with his eyes. "You could say you found him in an accident at the side of the road, couldn't you? You could put him back in the car and drive him to the hospital yourself."

The man had raised himself to his hands and knees. His face was low to the ground.

Adam shook his head. He wondered if Danny had lost his mind. "Help me get him inside," he said. "You can call from inside." He pointed to a house across the street where a light had just turned on." "Come on, Danny. Any second, people are going to come out here to see what's going on. It's going to look a lot better if you're the one who calls the ambulance."

Danny hesitated for just a second before he nodded his assent. He lumbered to his feet, and he and Adam each took an arm and helped the man up. They walked him inside, bearing most of the man's weight between them. Adam closed the door behind them after they deposited the man in an easy chair in Danny's living room.

Danny dialed 911 and paced back and forth to the kitchen as he spoke to the operator. Adam asked the man his name and if he needed anything. The man just held his hand up and turned away. When Adam went to the kitchen, Danny was already off the phone. "They should be here any minute," Danny said. "I don't feel good about this. I wish you'd listened to me. I wish you drove him yourself."

"And I wish you didn't make a bloody mess of his face, so I guess we're both disappointed, Danny." He tore a few paper towels off their roll, wet them under the sink, and squeezed them out.

"Hey, don't be sarcastic with me!" Danny said. "He got off easy. He had a lot of balls coming here." They were both silent for a few seconds before Danny said, "I'm going to check on Henry."

"Great. I'm going to see if your buddy will let me help him clean up before the ambulance arrives."

Danny stopped on his way out of the kitchen and turned to look at Adam. "He's not my buddy. He's Rose's boyfriend."

A police car arrived before the ambulance. Adam opened the door when he saw the car pull up, lights flashing and sirens at full blast. Two officers were inside the house moments later, and Danny came downstairs. The panic in Danny's eyes when he saw the police in his living room tore at Adam. But Danny's expression quickly changed. It was as if a tremendous weight had been lifted from him.

"Tommy!" he said to one of the officers. "Am I glad to see you! You remember Tommy, Adam. He was in my class."

There was another siren, and then a wail from upstairs. "Henry's up," Adam said. "No one could sleep through all this. I'll try to settle him."

"Are you the one who phoned in the complaint?" Adam heard Tommy ask as he ascended the stairs.

"Yeah, but it's okay. I'm all right," Danny said. As Adam entered Henry's room, he heard Danny say, "That guy attacked me. Take a look at this bruise. We had some words and he took a swing at me."

Adam closed the door behind him as he made his way to Henry's crib, glad to be upstairs, in the dark, far from Danny's disaster downstairs. He picked Henry up and rocked him for about ten minutes until he was sound asleep.

When Adam had made his way back to the living room, he saw paramedics examining the man in the chair, asking him questions, checking his vision, feeling his bruises.

Tommy, the police officer Danny knew, was asking, "Are you saying he didn't have a weapon of any kind, Danny?" He and Danny were standing close to each other, too close, Adam thought. Tommy's tone was all business now.

Adam said, "Danny, stop for a second. Maybe you should call your lawyer. Do you have the number in your phone?"

Danny shook his head, truculent, defiant. He didn't take his eyes off Tommy. "I don't need a fucking lawyer, Adam. This is my home. I didn't do anything wrong."

The paramedics had finished their examination. The one who seemed to be in charge came over to where Danny and the police were standing and said, "Concussion. Broken nose for sure. Some abrasions. Minor cuts . . . we removed some small shards of broken glass from his head. He's lucky. It could have been a lot worse."

"What about me?" Danny asked. He pointed at his cheek.

The paramedic took him by the chin and turned his head a few degrees. "A bruise," he said. "Put some ice on it." He turned to the police officers. "Can we take Mr. Calloway to the hospital?"

"OK, take him," Tommy said.

The other officer said, "You're in serious trouble, Mr. Blumberg. We're going to have to take you into the station."

"He came to my house!" Danny said. "He attacked me! What the hell country is this where I can't defend myself right in front of my own house? In my own home?"

"You can file a complaint against Mr. Calloway if you want to, Mr. Blumberg, but even if he hit you first, with your injuries that's a misdemeanor assault. Smashing an unarmed man's head into a car window, breaking bones . . . you're looking at a felony. We're going to have to take you in."

"You're arresting me? No! Come on, Tom. You know me! We went to school together."

Tommy said, "I'm sorry, Danny. I have no choice." His tone softened. "Look, I suggest you bring your checkbook. If you're lucky, you might have a chance to post bail tonight and sleep in your own bed."

The other officer took out his handcuffs. "Please put your hands behind you, Mr. Blumberg," he said.

Danny looked up at Adam. "You have to stay with Henry until I get back, okay? Rose could be out all night for all I know. I'll get back as soon as I can." He turned to the police. "Can I let Adam know when I'll be home?"

Tommy nodded. "We'll call him if we have to hold you overnight."

Adam watched, half in a daze, as they led Danny out the door, his hands cuffed behind his back. It all seemed so unreal. He was too shaken to get any work done. He tried reading and even watching television, but he couldn't sit still. Steven called when it was almost eleven.

"Is it too late to talk?" he asked. "I'm sorry. I meant to check in earlier and see how you're doing. I'm in the lab and I lost track of time."

"No, it's okay. I'm up. I'm at Danny's, actually."

"Danny's? Why? Let me guess. He needs a favor."

"He's been arrested," Adam said. "I'm with Henry. He assaulted his wife's lover."

There was silence for a second, and then, "Holy shit."

"I know."

"Very classy."

Adam wasn't ready to talk about it. "I'll call you tomorrow, all right? I'm keeping an ear out in case Henry wakes up."

A little after midnight, Danny walked in. "How is Henry?" he asked. "Still asleep?" His eyes fell on the bowl and spoon that Adam had left on the coffee table. "What's that?"

"Henry was hungry before bed, so I gave him some ice cream."

"He's not supposed to have sweets, Adam! Rose is going to pitch a fit."

Adam just looked at him.

Danny picked up the bowl and spoon. "Not now, Adam, okay? I've been arrested and interrogated. I just spent an hour and a half in a jail cell with a drunk, crazy homeless guy. I waived the right to an attorney so I could get released tonight, but it took me fifteen minutes just to explain why I'm not a flight risk and they should give me a reasonable bail. Where do they think I'm going to run with a kid and a house and two funeral homes? I'm a partner in a cemetery, for crying out loud." He walked the bowl and spoon over to the kitchen sink.

"How did this happen, Danny?" Adam asked.

There was no response as Danny turned on the faucet and scrubbed at the dishes.

Adam sat down at the kitchen table. "Did you hear what I asked you, Danny?"

Danny sighed and turned off the water. He laid the bowl and spoon to dry by the side of the sink. "I heard," he said. "I heard. The guy's name is Richard Calloway. I've known about him for a long time. I've never seen him in person, but I knew. Rose isn't as clever as she thinks she is, and she's been seeing him for a while. He works in Rose's department. I think he even reports to her." Danny dried his hands. "Pathetic piece of shit. Couldn't get promoted on his own, so he started fucking the boss."

"He works for Rose?"

"I know, right?" Danny said. "I didn't think women were supposed to have a midlife crisis. At least I've never heard of it. Rose being Rose, you'd think she'd be banging some rich bigwig, not some pretty boy with a fancy car he can only afford because of her."

Danny sat down across from Adam. He looked down as he spoke "This marriage has been over for a long time," he said. "We both would have walked a long time ago if it weren't for Henry. But there are rules, you know? Unspoken rules . . . when I saw him pull up in that fucking sports car, I just lost it."

"But you knew he was seeing Rose . . ."

Danny's looked up into Adam's eyes. "This is my house, Adam. My kid sleeps here! Do you understand? It was instinct. A man has to protect his family, right? He got out of the car and I saw his face under the streetlamp, and I just lost it. Rose isn't even home tonight. I thought, 'Is he trying to see Henry? Does he think he can just come over and read my son a fucking bedtime story?' and that was it."

Danny took a breath and let it out slowly, quietly. "I was on him before he shut the car door. The whole thing only took a few seconds. I punched him once in the gut and he doubled over. The car window was half open, and I guess I pushed his head through it. I heard the glass crack."

"I saw you pull him out of the car."

"He must have tried to scramble back in. I don't remember."

Adam looked at him in horror. "But there was no argument? He never hit you?"

Danny felt his swollen cheek. "No. That was you. You hit me pretty hard, you know. It hurts like hell."

"I was afraid you were going to kill him!"

Danny shook his head. "Don't be stupid. I wasn't going to kill him." He shrugged. "I was pretty mad, though. I don't think I've ever been that mad."

Adam's temples were throbbing. He cradled his forehead in his left hand. "Do you know how much trouble you're going to get into if the police figure out you were lying?"

Danny's voice was a high-pitched whine. "I panicked, Adam. What could I do? I had to say something, didn't I? If they thought I was violent, do you think they'd even let me see my son after we split up? And my cheek was throbbing where you hit me. It was too perfect." He shook his head.

"Tell them, Danny. Maybe it isn't too late."

Danny stood up and walked over to the sink. He stopped for a second before turning around to face Adam again. "It is too late. If they find out I lied about this, I'll lose custody. I could go to jail." He paused. "Look, you were right about the lawyer, Adam. I'll call tomorrow, first thing. I already filled out a complaint against Calloway. Maybe that will give me some leverage. Maybe he'll drop the charges. But we have to stick together. You have to help me."

Adam cursed under his breath. He got up. "I can't talk about this now, Danny. I've got to go. I have class in the morning. I need to get out of here."

Danny took him by the shoulders. His eyes glistened with tears. "Please, Adam. For Henry. For Hank. I need you."

Chapter 4

Adam didn't remember saying goodbye to Danny. He didn't even remember driving home. He did remember the impact of Danny's cheekbone on his fist, and the adrenalin that ran through him like an electric surge. He didn't sleep much. Throughout the night, Adam's mind kept racing back to the scene on the ground, to Calloway's bloodied face lying among shards and particles of broken glass catching the light of the streetlamp where they weren't stained dark red.

Adam felt underprepared and underdressed when he arrived at work, just before the start of his class. A tie had seemed out of place with his stubble and baseball cap, so he wore a dress shirt and jeans. He took a deep breath and forced himself to put everything else out of his head. He had taught this lesson before, he reminded himself. He'd be okay. But this wasn't the impression he wanted to make on the first day of the semester.

Adam counted twenty-four students in the room, none familiar. Almost all were sophomores majoring in another field. Two others on his list might have already changed their schedules or else they'd be coming in late.

As the students' voices died down and the rustling of paper gradually faded, Adam said, "Welcome!" His voice sounded clear, he thought. Authoritative. He could pull this off. "In case anyone is in the wrong room, I'm Professor Drascher, and this class is called Hebrew Scripture Through Jewish Lenses. This class fulfills a theology requirement for the core curriculum. More important, from my perspective at least, this course is designed to introduce you to the different ways in which Jews have read the Hebrew Bible, from early Jewish sects, through the rabbis and mystics to modern scholars. If you are looking for Christian perspectives, this class won't help you, but our department offers plenty of other courses that also fulfill the core."

There were a few scattered questions. Students asked questions about the course requirements. Adam pointed them toward the syllabus he had posted online. One student said that as a Christian, he believed the Bible was God's word, and he asked if he should take a different class. Adam told the student he would expose him to different perspectives and that he if he stayed, he would be expected to apply the tools he learned in the class.

Adam looked around the room. There were no more raised hands. "OK," he said. "Now, this isn't a language class, and we don't have time for you all to become conversant in Hebrew before we begin, but you will need some basic knowledge of how the language works if you are going to look at the texts the way Jews have always looked at them. The first thing you need to understand about Hebrew is that the language is really different from English or Latin or Greek. Accurate, unambiguous translation is impossible. Translating any language has its problems, but that's especially true for Hebrew. Let me show you why."

Adam went to the white board and drew a square root sign. "The Hebrew language is based on roots that are built from two or three consonants. The root gives the basic meaning of the word, but we get the specific meaning and a lot of grammar from vowels. The trick is, vowels weren't part of the written alphabet in early Hebrew. For the most part, they still don't appear in a Torah scroll. There's no punctuation there, either. So you often have to make inferences about who is speaking and in what tense before you can even pronounce the words. Where one sentence ends and another begins is also up to the reader to determine."

Adam gave the students a couple of moments to absorb what he had said before he continued. "Here's an example," he said. He wrote the word *qds* under the square root sign. "This root, *qadash*, has to do with separation or holiness." He saw the students, most of them, anyway, copying his words into their notebooks. Next to the root, Adam began writing a column of words down the board. He was falling into a rhythm. He could feel the rising energy of the class.

"All these words appear the same in a Torah scroll and in ancient documents, but the vowels give them very different meanings," he said. "*Qadosh* means holy. *Qadesh* means to be separated out for a sacred purpose. Be careful how you use it, though: the same word pronounced with a longer 'd' sound refers to the male prostitutes who worked the Canaanite shrines." Some of the students laughed, not sure if he was serious. Adam put up the Boy Scouts' salute and continued. "*Qidush*, with the long 'd' again, is either the wine drunk on festivals or the blessing over the wine. *Qadish*, the sanctification of God's name, is the traditional prayer of mourning. If any of you took Professor Esposito's composition course last year, you read Ginsberg's "*Kaddish*". That's the same word."

He stepped away from the board and walked toward the students in the front row. "I haven't even touched on another aspect of the problem: let's say I decide based on the context that the word means 'sanctify.' Is the text a command to make something holy? Is it a description of something a man did in the past? You can often make a sensible call, but just as often there are a number of choices that have different meanings. The rabbinic commentators played with this a lot. They saw this ambiguity as a virtue of the language, not a deficiency. They believed that by using Hebrew, God was able to impart multiple meanings in each word and in each phrase. An engaged and clever reader could discover something new on every reading, but that requires judgment and interpretation. Despite what many fundamentalists claim, there usually isn't one plain meaning for a passage in the Hebrew Bible."

A student raised his hand and Adam called on him. "Did the rabbis ever explain why God didn't just reveal scripture in a language people could understand?" A few people in the class laughed.

Adam smiled. "What qualities would you expect to find in the language of a sacred text? A computer language is perfectly clear and subject to only one interpretation, but it is very limited. Hebrew is a language of ambiguity and nuance. Unfortunately, too many translators see ambiguity as a problem to solve rather than a complexity to preserve. They say 'A' and 'Not A' cannot both be true, and so they lock in one meaning. That's not the traditional Jewish approach. For Jews, the different readings are in conversation with each other. None of the readings is viewed as excluding all the others. For Jews, the obligation isn't to memorize Torah or submit to Torah, but to engage with it. It's more like a wrestling match or maybe a dance than anything else. That actually gives us a good transition to looking at our first text. Turn to the first page of your handouts. We'll look at the first words in the Torah and explore how they have been translated and interpreted . . ."

The rest of the class passed quickly. The class seemed like a strong group, Adam thought. A few of them had already asked good questions, and Adam had already learned some of their names. Back in his office, Adam wrote himself a few quick notes on which prompts sparked the best comments and where he wanted to pick up at the start of the next class. He also left himself a reminder in his calendar to write a quiz based on the week's reading. It was best to start off the semester letting the students know he wasn't bluffing about keeping up with the syllabus.

When he was done, Adam leaned back in his chair and took a breath. He sent Claudia a quick email asking her to get in touch with him as soon as she could. He was anxious to hear about the tablet, and he didn't want to wait, but he knew better than to expect Claudia to call him on her own. What he wanted or needed was never going to be uppermost in her mind.

Before he left, Adam looked up the number of the superintendent of his grandfather's building and called to ask about clearing out his grandfather's apartment. The super asked if Adam could come by before one o'clock, so Adam grabbed a couple of books he needed from his office to prepare for the next day's class and he headed out.

He poked his head into the departmental office on his way to the stairs. Teresa, the department's administrative assistant, was there, ensconced at her desk between a picture of her granddaughter and a small Puerto Rican flag. She was in her early fifties, confident and capable. She had worked in that office for decades, running it day-to-day as department chairs had come and gone. Teresa was the first person Adam had met when he interviewed for his job, and she helped get him oriented after he was hired. He still often relied on her advice when he had to deal with departmental politics.

"Welcome back, Adam" Teresa said. She smiled, but didn't look up from her typing. She had on a blue V-neck sweater and the gold crucifix she always wore. "How was your class?"

"Not a bad start," Adam said. "Listen, I've got to head out, but I'll be back tomorrow morning for my class if anyone needs me, okay?"

Teresa must have heard something in his voice. She glanced up at him, stopped typing, and pulled a strand of her gray-streaked hair from her face. She leaned back from the typewriter. Adam could see the concern in her eyes. "Are you all right, Adam?"

"I'm fine. I've just got an errand to run. No big deal."

"You didn't shave. And I don't think I've ever seen you teach in a baseball cap before. What's going on?"

"Oh." Adam felt the brim of his cap, embarrassed. "I'll shave soon. Tomorrow night. It's a Jewish custom. I buried my grandfather this week."

"I'm really sorry, Adam. I had no idea. I'll let John and the others know."

"Please don't, okay? I don't want to make a thing about it. I'll be back to normal after tomorrow. Let's not make a fuss."

She tilted her head as if to get the measure of him from a different angle. She nodded. "If that's really what you want, okay, Adam. But I think people would want to know." After a moment, she asked, "Can I pray for you and your grandfather?"

Adam smiled. "Thanks, Teresa. I'm pretty sure that he's all right, but I'll take whatever help I can get."

Dealing with the super didn't take long. Rent on the apartment was paid through the end of the month, but the super let Adam know he'd appreciate it if Adam closed it out early. He was sure he could rent it out for the first of October if he had time to paint it and fix it up a bit.

Adam took the elevator to the third floor and got out his keys as he walked down the long hallway. The ceramic tile hadn't changed in at least thirty years—not since Adam had first moved in with his grandparents, anyway. The walls had been painted, but in almost the same color every time. Even the sound of his footsteps felt familiar. When he unlocked the door, Adam had to resist the impulse to call out to his grandfather. The apartment was silent, of course, but nothing looked different. His grandfather had changed almost nothing since Adam's grandmother died, back when Adam was still in high school. Everywhere was the same wallpaper, the same furniture, the same pictures in the same places on the walls.

He went into his old bedroom. Many of the books from his adolescence and even from his childhood were still there: the worn copies of d'Aulaire's books of Greek and Norse myths his parents had bought for him when he was still much too little to understand them, the illustrated children's Bible stories, *The Boy's Book of Poems*. Adam smiled at the memory of his grandfather reading those to him before bed: "A Man's A Man For A' That," "Invictus," "Gunga Din" . . . Adam always thought of them as The Manly Poems. He opened the book to "Death Be Not Proud," and as he read the words, he could almost hear them recited in his grandfather's voice, strong and low and reverent. Adam put the book into his bag. The bookcase was filled with treasures: King Arthur stories, a bunch of science fiction and fantasy, a semi-scholarly book of Irish myths and folklore that Adam had tried and failed to read when he was a teenager. He took that one, too.

Adam went to the living room. His grandmother's beloved books had been given away long before, and Adam still had quite a few of them. The top shelf of her bookcase was filled with photos now. Adam, Danny, and Henry were all well represented. The next two shelves now held videos. On the bottom there was a shelf of old-time detective stories by Spillane, Hammett, and Chandler. Those had been his grandfather's. Adam smiled. When he was a kid, before his grandmother died, his grandfather sometimes went around the house narrating his life like a noir detective . . ."As soon as my wife came out of the bathroom, I knew she was trouble. She wore pink fuzzy slippers and a robe that barely covered her knees. I took one look at the expression on her face and I realized right away that I had forgotten to take out the garbage . . ."

At the end of the bottom shelf was an ancient prayer book, all in Hebrew, that Adam's great grandfather had brought with him from Ukraine. Adam's grandfather would never have used it. He rebelled against his orthodox family when he was very young, and he never learned much Hebrew.

When Adam saw the book, even before he picked it up, a wave of memories flooded over him. He used to sit on the floor, just staring at the shapes of the letters, wondering what mysteries they could reveal to someone who knew how to read the magical writing. He remembered the feel of the soft, worn leather binding and the smell of the pages. That book might have been the single biggest reason Adam later studied Hebrew, though he had rarely opened it since he had learned enough to read it. Adam took the prayer book from the shelf. The binding was loose. He would have to have it re-done. He felt something hard and lumpy inside the front cover and when he opened the book, an audiocassette fell out of it. He picked it up off the floor. It was labeled "Adam."

"What's this?" he asked out loud. He wondered it if might be a practice tape for his *bar mitzvah* or some songs he'd recorded from the radio when he was ten years old. His grandfather's cassette player was on top of the bookshelf. Adam popped the tape in and pressed play.

He jumped at the sound of his grandfather's weary voice. He had never expected to hear that voice again. "Adam," the voice said, "it's me." Adam's knees felt weak. He sat down.

"I've been thinking a lot about dying, Adam," the old voice continued in a low rumble, "and I'm embarrassed to admit that I'm afraid. Not of dying. My life has been . . . well, there's been a lot of good and a lot of bad and I never thought I'd last forever . . . I've been pretty sick for a while now. The doctors say I have advanced heart disease and they aren't sure how much time I have left. I asked about surgery, but . . . anyway, I didn't say anything. You should be living your life, not worrying about an old man." There was a pause. Adam's grandfather cleared his throat. "I'm afraid because there are some things I should have told you, things you should know." He paused again. "I hope you don't think I'm a coward, Adam. I've never thought of myself as a fearful man. I have to admit I don't like it. But here I am talking into a machine instead of calling you on the phone." The voice paused. "I love you, Adam. That's not news, I hope. I've always been able to tell you that, thank God. But I wanted you to hear it from me again, for the last time, I guess. Your grandma and your mom and dad loved you too, you know. So much . . ." The voice grew thick and choked for a moment. "We haven't talked much about them in a long, long time. It's still very painful. But I wanted to say that straight off."

Adam stopped the cassette player. It was too much to take in all at once. His mind flew back to the tablet they had found in Tel Arad. "Come to me, Healers," he thought, but he didn't feel ready for this. He hadn't invited this visitation. He walked to the kitchen and washed his face. He took his time drinking a glass of water before returning to the living room.

Adam held his breath as he pushed play again. The voice was distorted for a fraction of a second before the tape got up to speed. "I never told you, Adam, that your parents' marriage had problems." Adam swallowed hard. "Your mom was a terrific person. I really liked her from the very beginning, but she and your father were never very compatible. They argued all the time. It wasn't like how your grandma and I used to argue almost for fun. They really had trouble getting along. They even separated for a few months. You were less than two years old. While they were separated, your father made some choices he wasn't very proud of. There's no easy way to say it. He had a brief affair with Marsha Blumberg. Danny's mom. They had dated in high school. She had been married for a few years, too, and they were also having trouble. They ended things and your father went back to your mother and Marsha stayed with her husband, but when Danny was born, your father strongly suspected that he was his son. I don't think he told your mother. I told him he shouldn't. Marsha never said anything, and I didn't think either marriage could take the shock, anyway. I wanted you to grow up in an intact family. Danny too."

The voice paused again and Adam took a deep breath. "This is harder than I thought," the voice said. There was another brief silence where all Adam could hear was the hiss from the tape before the voice continued. "I watched Danny grow up over the years, and I think your father was right. Danny looks a lot like his mom, but his smile is a lot like your dad's, and he moves like him. He walks like him. He has the Drascher hands." Adam thought about his grandfather's immensely strong, thick fingers. He would sometimes bend copper pipes to impress Adam when he was a kid. "You've probably wondered how I started to take such an interest in Danny, so now you know. I've never told him. He knows I love him, and he knows I think of him like a grandson, but it's a hell of a thing to tell someone his father might not be his father. I guess it's a hell of a thing to tell you that you might have a brother, too. I'm telling you now because . . . I was going to say because I don't want you to feel alone in the world, but I don't know if that's really it. I guess it's just something I don't feel I can take with me. That, and I want you to understand how important it is that you look after Danny. I know you don't feel like you have a lot in common, but you have me and you have your father, and I hope that means something to you. I'm counting on that meaning something to you."

He cleared his throat again. He sounded exhausted. "While I'm un-burdening myself at your expense, there's another thing I've been meaning to talk to you about. I've mentioned Vivian a couple of times, but we never discussed her. You never asked about her. I got the sense you didn't really want to know. She's more than a good friend.

You've probably guessed that. She's a good woman. Danny knows her. He can tell you. I have some things that she might want in a box with her name on it in the closet. Just sentimental things, but they might mean something to her. She's been a real comfort to me. I'd like you to give the box to her so she'll have something to remember me by. I don't know how to say goodbye to her properly, either. I've tried . . . the words won't come.

"I love you, boy. I intend to keep keeping an eye on you. I hope you're not too upset with me. Think of me once in a while." And then there was just white noise. He pushed stop again and rewound the tape.

Adam stood in front of the cassette player in silence for almost a minute. For thirty-three years, whenever he had been lonely, or bored, or frightened, he had been able summon his grandfather's voice with a call or a visit, and now that voice was gone. No more comfort. No more lectures or jokes. No more love. The phone might ring, but it would never be him on the other end. He had only silence and this tape. Adam took a shallow breath and then took the tape out of the player and put it in his pocket.

He looked around the apartment. Most of one wall in the hallway was covered with framed photographs of Adam's family. Their hall of ancestors, his grandmother used to joke. Adam had always liked knowing the pictures were there, a heritage ready for him to claim someday, even though he couldn't put a name to several of the faces.

Probably Danny knew who they were, Adam thought. He probably knew stories about all of them. Adam felt sick as it occurred to him that Danny would probably want to have pictures of Adam's father.

Maybe it was just wishful thinking on the old man's part that gave him the idea Danny was related, Adam thought. What did he have to go on? Some body language? Thick fingers? It wasn't much. It hadn't been enough for his grandfather to say anything while he was alive, anyway. Not that Adam could blame him for wanting to bring someone else into their family. Adam certainly wasn't enough to fill his life. Danny idolized him. Danny listened to his stories. Danny was with him when he died.

Adam tried to collect himself. He had work to do. He needed to figure out how many boxes he would need to pack up the apartment and then he could get the hell out of there. He looked at the walls and the bookcase, measuring in his mind. Two boxes for the pictures. He could decide what to do with them later. He looked through his grandfather's music collection: vinyl, 8-tracks, cassettes, CDs. Maybe he would convert some of the analog stuff. He'd done that with some of his grandmother's music and he liked to listen to it sometimes. It reminded him of her. Three boxes. He looked at the books. Between the ones he had read as a child and the handful he wanted from his grandfather, that would be another three boxes. Maybe four. He wouldn't be able to wear his grandfather's clothes or shoes. Goodwill. Or Danny. Some of it might fit Danny. Why not? He might be a grandson, too, as much as Adam was. More than Adam was.

Adam shook his head as he walked into the kitchen. No more self-pity. He needed to focus. Most of his grandmother's things had been given away years before, but he found her favorite soup pot and ladle and a set of napkins she had embroidered. One last box.

Adam stopped at the office supply store on his way home to pick up the tape and boxes he needed, and he left them in the trunk of his car. His brought himself up short whenever his thoughts returned to the tape. He told himself that he had a class to prepare, that he should focus on that or on the tablet. He knew he needed to feel productive.

When he got back to the apartment, Adam made himself a turkey sandwich and checked his email and messages. Claudia hadn't gotten back to him. No surprise there, he thought. But maybe he didn't have to wait. Maybe he could get started on what he had now. He put on Ellington's *Far East Suite,* and took out his phone to download the pictures he had taken after the discovery of the tablet. There were only two and they were nearly identical. Claudia and Maggie, tired and exhilarated, held the tablet in front of them. Claudia's lips were parted in a jubilant smile. Maggie looked dazed, but happy, trying to take it all in.

Adam had never intended the images to document the find; they were only meant to be mementos, and it showed. Claudia's and Maggie's arms and hands obscured part of the tablet. Shadows hid most of the rest. Even after he enlarged the images, Adam could make out only a few lines of text. He cropped one of the photos to retain just those lines, copied them out, and then transcribed the text into modern Hebrew letters:

קרבו אל' רפאם
פקדו את' אלם
כ' נכרת' מ' ''רשנ'
ומשחת מ' 'גאלנ'

Adam forced himself to work slowly, to vocalize each word in multiple ways, testing the alternatives. "Start with the verbs," Adam always told his students. "That's where the action is." He read aloud the text he had copied over. They appeared to be two couplets. The first line, "*Qirvu elai Refaim*," was pretty clear. It was a simple invocation: "Come to me, *Refaim*," or "Come to me, Healers." Adam thought of his grandfather's voice, and he lost ten minutes staring out the window.

Adam shook himself out of his fog. His hope that the tablet would distract him from his grief had been badly misplaced. He forced himself to focus his eyes again on his computer screen. The second line, "*Piqdu oti Elim*," was only slightly more difficult than the first. The verb there, *Pqd*, had many meanings, but they all related to recompense for good or ill, and to the idea of personal accounting. *Pqd* implied a relationship where the individual mattered, where someone was known and accorded his or her proper portion. Adam translated the line as "Take account of me, Divine Ones." His heart raced as he typed the line in English.

The text called the *Refaim* divine. Adam knew, had known for years, that the Healers had been worshipped in the Syrian town of Ugarit, hundreds of years before the tablet was written. That was well established. That was part of what had gotten Adam so interested in the Healers back in graduate school. The *Refaim* were mentioned many times throughout the Bible, but proof that they were viewed as gods in Judea at the time of the monarchy, that was new. If it held up, that discovery alone would make the tablet the most important find of Adam's career.

The second couplet was complex: "*Ki nikrati mi yirasheni / UmiShahat mi yigaleni*." The first line was a cry of anguish, "I am cut off," followed by a question: either "who will succeed me?" or "who will inherit from me?" The final line meant "Who will redeem me from *Shahat*?" *Shahat* was tough to translate. Sometimes it referred to the underworld, but it had more literal meanings, too. In the story of Noah, God flooded the world because it had grown "corrupt." That was the same root as *Shahat*. The first-born in Egypt were killed by "the Destroyer." Same root again. Was the speaker crying out for redemption from the underworld? From corruption? From destruction? There was no way to tell from just those few lines. Context would help, but for that, he would have to wait for Claudia to get back to him.

Adam saved his work and got ready for bed, repeating the lines to himself in Hebrew and in English, trying different translations. He brooded over the text like a mantra, the syllables burying themselves beneath his conscious mind as he sank into sleep:

Come to me, *Refaim*!

Take account of me, Divine Ones!

For I am cut off; who will inherit me?

And who will redeem me . . . from *Shahat* . . . from the underworld . . .
from corruption . . . from destruction . . .

Chapter 5

The next morning, Adam got to work early to make copies of the handout he had prepared for his senior seminar. He chatted with Teresa while the machine spat them out.

"John was looking for you yesterday," she told him. "I said you'd be back this morning."

Adam grimaced. John Gallo was his department chair and Adam found him to be an officious pain the ass. Adam glanced at the closed door to Gallo's office. "Is he in now?"

Teresa shook her head and offered a conspiratorial smile. "I'll tell him you tried to find him," she said.

Before Adam could respond, Gallo strutted into the office, his chest held out like a pigeon's in mating season. Adam noted that sometime over the summer, Gallo's beard, always precisely trimmed, had crossed the line from affectation to full-blown hobby.

"I hope you had a good summer, Adam," Gallo said in his most sonorous voice. It was more a pronouncement than a wish. "You were on that dig with Renaud, right? Was it productive?"

"It was all right, John. How about you?"

Gallo ignored the question. He looked at Adam over the little round glasses he wore perched halfway down his aquiline nose. "I don't have to tell you that your tenure application is due this year, Adam."

Adam said nothing. Gallo couldn't really think they should talk about this now, right before his class and in front of Teresa.

"Another article or two could make a big difference for you, Adam. With another book, well . . . but I guess that ship sailed long ago."

"Why don't we talk about this later, John," Adam said. "I have to get to class."

Gallo shook his head. "I'll be in meetings most of the day. We'll have to talk another time." He tapped Adam's chest with his index finger. "We take tenure very seriously in this department," he said. "Don't think you can just coast to the finish line."

Adam slid his gaze down to Gallo's hand and then up, past Gallo's fitted, pinstriped shirt and red bowtie to the bridge of his nose. With some effort Adam unclenched his jaw, but he said nothing.

Gallo looked up at the clock above the photocopier, his face set, expressionless. He said, "Don't be late for class." Then he walked into his office and closed the door behind him.

"Did I imagine that," Adam asked Teresa in a whisper, "or did that asshole just touch me? And since when did you need two books to get tenure in this department? He's been riding me ever since he became chair."

Teresa whispered back. "You know he's insecure, Adam. You might have an easier time if you just acted a little afraid of him once in a while."

Adam forced a shrug as he gathered his handouts. "Yeah, maybe. We'll never know."

To forestall any questions, Adam took off his cap and left it on his desk when he entered the classroom. There were only five students there, and Adam knew them all. Maggie, who had worked with him at the dig, and Paul, a slightly older student who was on his way to becoming a priest, were easily among the best in the department. The others—Greg, Aisha, and André—were solid as well. André was known to be quiet, but by the end of last year's class, he had been participating almost every week.

"I hope you all had a good summer," Adam said. "As you've probably figured out from the course title, we're going to be exploring ancestor cults and cults of the dead in the ancient world, and I wanted to start with an invitation. I'd like this class to be collaborative. I have an outline of a syllabus in mind, but your questions will drive a lot of what we do during the semester. My expertise is in the Semitic cultures, but I'm sure we'll be looking more broadly than that. I have friends I hope to bring in at some point, including a historian of ancient Egypt and an archaeologist who works on Confucianism and beliefs about the afterlife in ancient China. But for the first few weeks, we'll be looking closer to home, or at least closer to where I feel most at home." He paused to check for reactions, and he was pleased to see they looked excited. "The syllabus is online, and that will explain the assignments and grading for the course. Do you have any questions before we start?"

There weren't any. "OK. Good. So we'll be dealing with religion and the dead. Let's start by brainstorming the types of questions we will want to ask. Any thoughts?"

There was silence for over twenty seconds. Adam counted the time out in his head as he looked from student to student. He had learned long before that you have to be willing to wait the class out if you want them to engage, especially in the beginning of the semester. Once they get the idea that you'll speak for them when they're quiet, they won't do any thinking for themselves.

When Maggie finally jumped in, she had a long list of questions. "What happens at burials? What clothes are people buried in? What objects are buried with them? What words do they say at burials?"

Adam nodded and stood up to write the questions down on the whiteboard under the heading "burials." He underlined the word "what" in each question.

"What about mourning customs?" Aisha asked.

"What about them?" Adam asked.

"Well . . . what do people do? You know, are there rituals, or do they avoid doing certain things? That sort of thing."

Adam wrote "what rituals / what taboos" on the board.

"Do they have myths about the afterlife? What are they?" That was Greg.

Again, Adam wrote the questions. "Anything else?" he asked. He looked at Paul and then at André, but they shook their heads.

Adam looked at the board. "You're all very disciplined," he said. We've trained you well, I guess. All of those are good, solid, 'what' questions. They'll all have answers we may be able to learn directly by reading ancient texts or by interpreting artifacts. But I have some questions of my own that won't be so easy to answer." He paused, waiting for them all to look up. Adam asked, "How did the rituals and the myths we'll be studying help mourners cope with their loss?" He wrote "loss" on the board. Then he wrote "living" and "dead" with a double-headed arrow connecting them. "Did the living believe they were helping the dead? Did they think the dead would help them? How did they relate to each other?"

"That sounds pretty dicey," Maggie said. "If you want to answer those, don't you have to assume all the people we'll be studying have the same psychology we do?"

Adam nodded. "You're right. We have to be really careful about our assumptions. That's why we'll spend most of our time on 'what' questions like the ones you've come up with. But sometimes, I might push for us to do a little more." He paused to glance at his students' faces. "This may not sound very rigorous," he continued, "but for what it's worth, I believe people are people. All societies have had to come up with some kind of response to the fact that their loved ones die. Many of them came up with ways for their relationships with people they cared about to persist beyond the grave. I wouldn't be studying this stuff if I didn't think we could rely on our shared humanity to understand people who lived long ago and far away." He gave each of the students the handout he had prepared and returned to his place at the front of the room.

Adam took a deep breath. "OK." He said. "That's enough of an introduction for now. The papers I just gave you have all the readings you'll need today. We'll start with the cult of the dead in ancient Hebrew and Canaanite culture. The texts I gave you are the translations of every mention we have of the *Refaim* in the Hebrew Bible. It's a very poorly understood term. Some of the translations use the term 'Healers' instead of *Refaim*. That's because *Refaim* comes from the word, '*rafa*' which means 'heal.' Some of the texts use the word 'shades' instead. You'll see why shortly. You also have the most relevant Ugaritic texts, but in Ugaritic the word is *R'pum*. And for fun, I threw in a curse found on a Phoenician tomb. Remember, the Phoenicians were later, but culturally they were closely related to the people of Ugarit. I'd like you to read through all these together and try to break them down into categories we can study further. You can look up the Hebrew for the quotes in your Bibles to get a better sense of the original."

The class took a long time reading and cataloging the texts, but Adam didn't interfere. He wanted them to have the experience of analyzing the text for themselves first, before they heard from him. "What have you got?" he finally asked them, when they seemed to have reached consensus.

Aisha volunteered first. "There was a place called the Valley of *Refaim*," she said. "Many of the quotes refer to the valley, but they don't say much as far as I can tell."

Adam nodded. "Good. That's seven of the quotes. Eight if you count Jubilees. That isn't a canonical book in most traditions, but it is more than two thousand years old.

What else?"

Greg looked like he was taking a quick count. "Eleven of the quotes mention a group of people called *Refaim*. Apparently, they lived in the Holy Land long before the Israelites got there. Maybe afterwards they were restricted just to one valley, or maybe that valley was their capital or their religious center or something."

Adam smiled. "Maybe. What else?" He called on André.

"The other quotes are really complicated," André said. He sounded frustrated. "They all have something to do with dead people, but sometimes the *Refaim* are dead and sometimes they aren't. Eight of the quotes are about spirits in the underworld. And the Phoenician one is a threat that grave robbers will have "no home with the Healers," whatever that means. So maybe that has to do with the underworld, too. But the quote from Isaiah says, the earth will give birth to the *Refaim*, so they obviously aren't dead there."

Adam looked at him with encouragement. "What does the whole quote say, André?"

"It says, 'Your dead shall live, their corpses shall rise. Sing out, you who lie in the dust! Your dew is aglow and the earth will give birth to *Refaim*.' Oh." He looked embarrassed "It's about coming back from the dead . . . sorry. I didn't think Jews believed in that."

"OK, first of all, we should reserve the term Judaism for rabbinic Judaism or this is going to get very confusing very fast. Judaism grew out of the culture of the people we're studying: the Israelites and people from the kingdom of Judah," Adam said. "The dating on that Isaiah passage is controversial, but it's definitely older than rabbinic Judaism. For what it's worth, for over two thousand years, most Jews have believed that the dead would be resurrected someday. As for what the Judeans and Israelites believed, quotes like these are our best sources."

Adam thought for a moment that Maggie had a question, but when he turned in her direction, she looked away. Aisha raised her hand. She said, "In the Ugaritic texts, sometimes the *Refaim* are the king's ancestors and sometimes *Refaim* is in parallel with 'Divine Ones.' Are you sure these are all supposed to be the same *Refaim*?"

"That's a valid concern," Adam said. "*Refaim* the indigenous people and *Refaim* the dead, for example, could be homonyms, though I tend not to think so. But there's no consensus on that."

"People in many ancient cultures thought their dead ancestors were gods," Paul said. "Roman families offered sacrifices to their dead ancestors. They called them *Manes*. Virgil talks about them. I think maybe Ovid did too."

Adam nodded. "We can be pretty confident that during the reigns of Hezekiah, Manasseh, and Josiah, the Israelites were sacrificing to the dead, because prophets refer to it and Deuteronomy 26 goes to the trouble of prohibiting it."

"Why would they sacrifice to their ancestors?" Greg asked. "What did they want? Did they think their ancestors could help them?"

"We don't know," Adam said. "But be careful. Don't lose sight of the fact that a sacrifice is more than an opportunity to ask for something. A sacrifice is also a shared meal. Imagine how powerful that might have been, to be able to share a meal with the people you had lost, to be able to feel like you were in communication with them."

Adam paused. He thought of his grandfather's voice on the tape, so present, so real, saying, "Adam, it's me . . ." He swallowed hard. He said, "It makes you think about what we've lost, doesn't it? Imagine a culture where you would never feel that final separation when someone dies, where you could still contact them, call them at will . . . How did we give that up? What do we have. . . what could we possible have that was worth trading for that?"

Adam flushed as he realized he had been speaking too loudly. He cleared his throat and tried to regain his focus. He dropped his voice and turned to Paul. "Do you think you could do the first of our class presentations on the *Manes* for next week? Maybe that will give us some insight into how different societies have viewed their dead."

Paul smiled. "Sure, I can do that," he said.

Maggie had her hand up. "Can we go back to the translation of *Refaim*?" She asked. "You said that comes from the word '*rafa*,' but does that have to mean they were healing people? Couldn't the Canaanites have called the dead 'Healers' because they are supposed to be recovering from something, maybe from whatever killed them, or even from the trauma of dying? Maybe that's why they have to wait before they rise up in that Isaiah passage." She spoke quickly and her voice rose with excitement. "Or maybe they're healing from all the things that happened to them during their lives so that they can have a fresh start."

"I really like that." Adam said, smiling. "Sort of a combination of purgatory and therapy for the dead."

Maggie looked deflated. "But you don't believe it," she said. "Why not?"

Adam was almost apologetic. "The grammar. The word *Refaim* is constructed out of the form of the verb that refers to healing someone else. If you wanted to talk about someone who was *being* healed, the verb would have the same root, but it would be from the *nifal* form: '*nirfa*' rather than '*rafa*.' If you made a noun from that you'd get '*Nirfaim*,' or convalescents, not *Refaim*. It is a cool thought, though."

"What disease were the dead supposed to be healing, then?" she asked.

"You've got me. There's no shortage of pain in this world. It would be nice if it were someone's job to heal it."

"Amen," Paul said. A couple of the other students laughed.

After class, Maggie stayed behind while Adam erased the white board. "What's up, Maggie?" He asked.

"I just wanted to ask if everything is okay. You left the dig in such a hurry."

"I'm all right, Maggie. Thanks." He finished cleaning the board and turned around to find she was looking at him. She seemed skeptical, he thought, and concerned. "I needed to get back to see my grandfather," Adam said. "He died a few days ago."

"I'm really sorry," she said. She looked genuinely sad for him.

For a moment, Adam could almost see himself through her eyes, a wounded mentor in need of consolation. She was a sweet kid. "I'm really okay, Maggie. It's not my first loss. I just got a little too wrapped up in my subject today, that's all. It's probably a good thing, right? A scholar should be personally invested. Maybe I'll learn something useful." Maggie didn't respond. Adam tried changing the subject. "You know that tablet we found mentions the *Refaim* . . ."

Maggie's eyes grew wide. The excitement was obvious in her voice. "It does?"

Adam smiled. He nodded. "I've been trying to reach Claudia to get better photos. Do you have any?"

"No. Dr. Renaud insisted on documenting everything herself. She said she had to keep all the raw data because she's the Principal Investigator on the dig."

That made no sense to Adam. "I left a message for her," he said. "If she hasn't replied when I get back to my office, I'll bug her again. You and I can go over the photos when I have them."

Adam returned to his office, unlocked his door, and sat at his desk. He brought up a Mingus album on his computer. There was no message from Claudia. No email. It was starting to get to him. Adam left a terse message on her phone that he needed to talk to her and hung up. She could have let Maggie take photos of the tablet. For that matter, she should have emailed the photos to him days ago; it would have just been common courtesy. He had enough stress without having to chase her down, he thought. He had never really been able to count on her. She had always been too self-absorbed and too overcommitted, but this was really over the line.

Adam started a list of topics for student presentations and jotted down some notes on the seminar, but before long, his phone buzzed. It was Danny. Adam froze for a second and then he declined the call. The thought of hearing Danny's whining voice begging him to support his lies about the assault repelled him. He felt a flash of resentment at his grandfather's foisting Danny on him from the grave and then a surge of guilt that almost induced him to call Danny back.

He needed to clear his head. He got up to go to the bathroom. He'd probably see Danny in temple in a couple of hours anyway, he thought. He could talk to him then. He'd have to talk to him, then.

As he approached the water fountain on his way back from the bathroom, Adam saw a man and a woman having a heated discussion right outside his door. They were an unusual pair, Adam thought. The man was Asian, probably in his late twenties. He was clean-shaven and built like a wrestler: stocky, and strong. He wore a dark suit and a red tie. The woman was white and older, in her mid-sixties, Adam guessed. Her hair curled in yellow wisps almost to her shoulders. She wore a beige, patterned pants suit that reminded Adam of an upholstered chair that used to sit in his grand-parents' apartment. When he was little, he used to trace the designs in the fabric with his finger.

Adam heard the man speak first. His voice was low, but sound traveled well through the tiled hallway. Adam took a long, slow drink to give himself a chance to hear their conversation.

"I hate wasting our time, is all," the man said.

"And I told you this isn't a waste of time." The woman had a hoarse voice and a strong Queens accent.

"The guy teaches in a Catholic school. Are we going to interrogate a nun next?"

Adam lifted his head from the water fountain. His first instinct was to head for the staircase that lay just a few steps behind him and drive home as fast as he could, but he knew that if the detectives found him here, they could find him at home, too.

The woman shook her head. Adam couldn't make out most of what they said after that, but the condescension in the woman's body language was clear, and he did catch "thank you for your very fresh perspective" and "maybe you'll learn something." Based on the man's posture as he stared a hole into the floor, Adam guessed he was seething.

Adam took a deep breath and walked as calmly as he could toward his office. He offered the detectives what he hoped was a casual nod as he took out his keys and unlocked his door. The music was still playing on his computer.

"Are you Adam Drascher?" the woman asked. "Could we speak with you, please?" In spite of her rasp, the woman's tone was animated, almost playful.

"Of course," Adam said. "Who are you?"

Adam felt that she took him in with a glance. She said, "I'm Detective Levy and this is Detective Cheng." The man stepped forward to stand beside her, but he didn't speak. "We're from the 111th precinct in Queens," she said. She showed Adam her badge. "Do you mind if we come in?"

Adam took his second folding chair from behind his door and placed it alongside the one he always kept out for students who dropped by during office hours. He sat at his desk and gestured for the detectives to sit down just as a burst of woodwinds, brass, and human voices speaking over each other burst from the speakers on Adam's computer. Adam saw Detective Levy raise an eyebrow at him, and he smiled by way of apology as he pushed pause.

"Mingus," Adam said, gesturing at the screen, "from *Blues and Roots*. Are you a jazz fan?"

Detective Levy shook her head and smiled. "Not even a little." she said. "It sounded like a traffic jam to me."

Detective Cheng remained standing, but she sat down across from Adam, her ankles crossed and her hands clasped on her lap. "Please tell us what you know about Richard Calloway and the events of last night," she said. From her tone, she might have been asking about the weather.

Adam spoke slowly. He tried to sound casual. "I don't know much," he said. "I was inside the house when it all started. I'd never even heard of Mr. Calloway until after it was all over."

Detective Levy's eyes were like shields of polished bronze. Adam couldn't meet her gaze.

Levy was silent for a moment, as if she were debating whether to press the issue. Finally, she said, "All right, let's get there a different way. What were you doing in Mr. Blumberg's house last night?"

"Danny asked me to come and babysit. He had some kind of meeting and his wife, Rose, had a work emergency. I was working on my classes when it all happened. I had already put Henry to bed. That's his son."

Detective Cheng interrupted. He had been looking at Adam's bookcase. He must have noticed Adam's name on the spine of his book and he pulled it off the shelf. "You wrote this?" he asked. He read the title aloud: *Canaanite Iconography in Ancient Israel's Conception of the Divine.*

Adam nodded. "I study archaeology. I'm in the Religious Studies Department here."

Cheng seemed to find that very amusing. He shot Levy a look. "I want to make sure I'm getting all this down . . . teaches religion . . . works on ancient Israel."

Levy showed no reaction. "May I see the book, Ronald?" she asked. He passed it to her, and she opened it to the title page and flipped through to the table of contents. Adam was silent. If Cheng opened it, too, Adam thought, he would probably have doubled his readership.

"Are you married, Adam?" Levy asked. "Any children?"

Adam shook his head. "No. I'm single." He forced a smile. "Why, have you got someone in mind for me?"

Levy didn't react. "There aren't many single men who babysit eight-month-old babies. Why did Mr. Blumberg ask you?"

Adam shrugged. "I don't know who else he would have asked. I don't think he has a lot of friends." He exhaled slowly. "I've known Danny forever. We grew up in the same neighborhood. My grandfather raised me, and he and Danny meant a lot to each other."

"And what about you and Mr. Blumberg?" she asked. "Are you close?"

Adam bit his lip. "Not really," he said. "We saw a lot of each other, growing up, but Danny and I don't have a lot in common apart from my grandfather. We just buried him a few days ago."

"I'm sorry," she said. Her voice was softer. "I'm very sorry for your loss."

Adam nodded. "My grandfather and I watched Henry a few times before. Henry knows me. And he's an easy kid."

Levy put on a puzzled expression that Adam didn't find at all convincing. "So. You had work to do, and you just buried your grandfather. You aren't close to Mr. Blumberg. But when he asked for your help, you came over. Why?"

"He sounded desperate. He said he needed me."

"So?"

Adam looked at her, not sure if he understood what she was asking. "So, that's what you do."

Levy met his gaze, her head at a slight tilt. She was silent for a long time. Adam's phone buzzed in his pocket. In the silence of his office, the sound was obvious. Adam mumbled an apology to the detectives and silenced his phone with his left hand without taking it out.

"Maybe you should get that," Levy said.

"What? No. That's fine. Whatever it is can wait."

The phone buzzed again, and she said, "Seems like whoever it is really wants to get in touch with you. Go ahead, Adam. Take it."

Adam took out his phone. It was Danny. Adam struggled not to groan.

"Adam! We've got a problem. You wouldn't believe what's been going on."

Adam pressed the phone as close to his ear as possible. He prayed that the detectives couldn't hear Danny's voice. "I'm pretty busy right now," Adam said. "I'll see you at services tonight, okay?" He saw that Cheng had leaned in to say something to Levy, but she waved him off. She got up and walked over to the framed eight by ten photograph of Miles Davis Adam had hanging on his wall. She took it down and examined it as if she thought Miles might have the answers to her questions written on his face.

If Danny heard what Adam had said, he ignored it. Adam couldn't get another word in. Danny didn't even stop for a breath. "There were cops here asking questions, Adam. You should have heard Rose shrieking at me after they left. Henry was crying. It was awful."

"I'm sorry, but . . ."

"She kicked me out, Adam. Can you believe that? After everything she did?"

It was all Adam could do to keep his voice level. "Like I said, I can't talk now," Adam said, slowly and deliberately. "I'm sorry, but I'm busy here speaking with some detectives in my office. I'll see you at temple." He hung up.

"You're going to Rosh Hashana services with Mr. Blumberg?" Detective Levy asked.

Adam nodded, chagrined. He wondered how much of Danny's end of the conversation she had overheard. "He still goes to the temple where I grew up."

She looked very thoughtful as she replaced the photograph on the wall. "Who played that song again? The traffic jam from when we came in?"

"Mingus." She wrote down the name.

"Are you sure you're not a jazz fan?" he asked her.

She sounded distant when she answered, "I'm sure." She asked, "When did Mr. Blumberg ask you to come over?"

"I don't know." Adam reached for his pocket. "I could check my phone..."

Levy shook her head. "I know the time. I'm asking you about the order of events. Mr. Calloway called and texted Mrs. Blumberg several times last night before he drove to the house. Her phone was in the house with you. Did you see those messages?"

"No," he said. He thought back. "I heard it buzz while I was working, but I ignored it."

"You didn't answer the phone?" Cheng asked. "You were just minding your own business and didn't even check to see who was texting?"

Detective Levy wrote something in her notepad. She asked, "And when Mr. Blumberg called you, that was after Mr. Calloway texted, wasn't it?"

"I don't remember." He didn't.

"Did you warn Mr. Blumberg that Mr. Calloway was coming over?"

"No! I told you I had no idea who Calloway was or that anyone was coming. None of this has anything to do with me."

Levy was still, but Adam saw Cheng writing in his notebook. He fought the temptation to ask what was so interesting about his not being involved.

Levy said, "Mr. Blumberg says he was attacked first and was only defending himself. He has quite a bruise on his face."

Adam said nothing.

"Did you happen to notice Mr. Calloway's ring?" she asked.

"His ring? No."

She looked up toward Cheng. "You either, Detective?" Adam thought she looked smug. "I took a look at it this morning," she said. It's a bit flashy for my taste. There's a cute inscription on the inside of the ring, though. 'With love and promises,' it's got a rose engraved at the bottom. That's a rose for Rose Blumberg, I'd imagine."

"I don't know," Adam said. He didn't see where this was going.

"The ring has several small sharp stones in the center. Mr. Calloway wears it on his right hand." Her smile was gentle. "I bring it up because it was Mr. Blumberg's left cheek that was bruised and swollen, so the blow must have come from the right hand of the man facing him. But there's no cut on Mr. Blumberg's cheek, and no abrasion. Strange, isn't it? It seems likely that a blow with that much force would have left more of a mark on the skin."

She looked up at Adam. "You were the only other person at the house, except for Henry, of course. Is there something you'd like to tell us about Mr. Blumberg's injury, Adam? Was that another favor you did for him, to make it seem like Mr. Blumberg was defending himself?"

Adam closed his eyes. He realized he had been holding his breath, and he forced himself to exhale. He should have spoken up, he knew, when Danny had first lied to the police about how he got the bruise on his face, but it had all happened so suddenly. He hadn't understood what was happening until it was too late. He could still come clean, though.

"Danny lied," he could say. "Danny lied, and I won't protect him anymore." He could tell them everything he knew, and he'd be in the clear. But he didn't know what would happen to Danny then.

The words poured from Adam's mouth before he had consciously decided what to say. "I already told you, I didn't see how it started, Detective. I never heard of Richard Calloway before last night. I didn't know about him and Rose. I never answered Rose's phone. I've never ambushed anyone in my life. And the only favor I did for Danny last night was babysitting."

Levy stared into Adam's face for a long time. Her expression was impenetrable. Finally, she put her notepad and pencil into her bag and she stood up. "I'll be in touch, Adam. Thank you for your help."

"I'm free to go?" Adam couldn't believe his good fortune.

She offered a faint smile. "You were never under arrest, Adam. We know how to find you if we need you." She signaled to Detective Cheng and the two of them walked out. She was still holding Adam's book.

Chapter 6

Despite the heat of the shower, Adam had to press his razor hard against his skin, rubbing his face raw as he drew the blade along his neck up to his jaw line. His thoughts were spinning in a tight circle of anger, grief, and fear. "Accomplice" was too dignified a word, he thought. Danny had made him his stooge. And his grandfather . . . even his grandfather's death couldn't free him. It just dragged him even deeper into Danny's seamy life, deep enough that now the police were investigating him. Adam had almost Googled "impeding an investigation," when he got home, but he stopped short when he considered how bad that would look if they ever confiscated his computer.

In the steam and lather, Adam's mind drifted back through the tape, deep beneath his grandfather's words, so that he was cocooned in his grandfather's voice, its low rumble deepening his grief even as it comforted him. He closed his eyes and he stood there, his back leaning against the wall, for he didn't know how long, breathing, hearing himself breathe, but feeling that he might suffocate.

He needed to get moving. He knew that. Services would be starting soon and he had to talk to Danny, to warn him about the questions the detectives were asking and to find out if Danny had further implicated him. Adam turned off the water and dried off. He put on his suit. He wouldn't be wearing the Mets cap again; he had already thrown it away.

Adam hurried. The traffic was always heavy at the beginning of Rosh Hashana, and he knew he would be lucky to be able to drive to Queens in under an hour. Sure enough, he reached his old neighborhood just a few minutes before services were scheduled to begin. The streets were already crowded. He had to park several blocks away from the temple.

Adam walked from his car in a throng of congregants, all in their gray suits and brightly colored dresses. Some of them pushed strollers or held a child's hand. It occurred to Adam that Danny might bring Henry with him—his nephew maybe, Adam thought. He'd never had family younger than his grandparents. Then he imagined telling Danny about the tape, and he had to fight the urge to turn back and go home. He wondered for a moment if the tape could have been just his grandfather's final gambit to bring him closer to Danny, but he knew that couldn't be true. His grandfather would never have dragged his father into this if he didn't mean every word. They both held his father's memory too sacred for that.

Ushers were checking the congregants' tickets as they entered the lobby. Adam had no ticket. He should have been on the list as the rabbi's guest, but he hung back, reluctant to approach the ushers and explain his situation. After a few minutes, Danny came huffing inside, his tie draped untied around his neck. He didn't have Henry with him.

"Adam!" Danny clapped him on the back. "Good timing." He pulled Adam toward the usher and said, "*Shana Tova*, Jeffrey! He's with me. Adam Drascher. He's probably on the rabbi's list, too."

Jeffrey smiled and shook both their hands with a warm "*Shana Tova.*"

"Come on, Adam. Let's get seats before we can't find two together."

The sanctuary was filling quickly. Danny pushed Adam toward a spot near the back where there were empty seats in the middle of a row. He gestured for Adam to precede him into the pew as he finished knotting his tie.

The rabbi rose to greet the congregation just as Danny sat down, and everyone fell silent. Even in her white robes and from so far away, Adam could see she was pregnant.

The rabbi said, "The mystics tell us that with our acclamation, God is crowned anew as ruler of creation every Rosh Hashana. All are commanded to rejoice at the festival. Blessed is the One who spoke, and the world came into being!"

Adam looked away. His mourning period was officially over, she meant, as if you could control a man's grief by fiat, as if you'd have the right even if you could.

Several times during the service, Danny leaned over to whisper something, but Adam shook his head and leaned away. When the prayers were almost over, the rabbi began her sermon. Somehow, Danny took that as a signal to try again to talk to him.

"I'm really sorry about the detectives, Adam," he whispered.

"Not now, Danny." Adam held his hand up between them.

Danny leaned back in his chair, cooling his heels, his lips pursed, his hands clasped together in his lap. He managed less than a minute in that pose. "Let's go," he said. Adam shot him a look, but Danny said, "I can't sit through a sermon. We need to talk." He took Adam's arm and asked the people in the seats to let them squeeze by. Adam blocked his face with his free hand as he left, praying the rabbi wouldn't notice him as Danny ushered him out of the temple and across the street.

"The two of them came to my house this morning, Adam," Danny said, oblivious to Adam's discomfort. "An Asian guy and an older woman. I didn't tell them anything I didn't already say on Monday. I wish you had been there, though. That detective was a piece of work. The woman. I felt like she was looking right through me."

Adam nodded. "I saw them both in my office," he said, "Levy and Cheng. Levy did most of the talking. I don't think she believes your story." He saw the expectant look on Danny's face and he didn't keep him in suspense. "I didn't tell her anything."

Danny wiped his hand on his cheeks, a nervous gesture Adam had seen him make hundreds of times over the years. "I thought I had everything figured out. I'm so stupid!" He put his hand on Adam's shoulder. "You could have turned your back on me, but you didn't, Adam. You came through for me when I couldn't have counted on anyone else. I'll never forget that."

Adam looked down at the ground.

Danny smiled at him. "It's good you came, Adam. Hank would have liked that we were together at services tonight," he said.

"I know he would have."

"Walk me back to the house, okay?" Danny asked.

Adam nodded. "All right." They walked in silence for a couple of blocks before Adam asked, "Did my grandfather mention to you that he was making a tape?"

Danny shook his head. "No. What kind of tape?"

"I was in the apartment yesterday, looking around, trying to get organized for the clean-up. He left a tape for me to find." Adam wasn't sure what to say next. He hadn't planned this far. "He said on the tape that he had been seeing a woman for a while. She seemed important to him."

"He put that on a tape?" Danny said. "That's Vivian."

"I didn't know he was dating anyone," Adam said.

Adam could see Danny's surprise by the light of the streetlamps. "That's what it sounded like from what you said at the funeral, but he must have mentioned her to you," Danny said. "Nice lady. She's a widow. She used to own a flower shop near here." Danny shook his head. "She was really broken up when I told her Hank died. They were really sweet together."

"I've heard her name a couple of times, I guess, but I had no idea they were a couple," Adam said. "I wish he'd told me."

Danny looked confused. "What do you mean you heard her name? Like if he said, 'I saw Vivian today,' wouldn't you have said, 'Oh, really?

Who's Vivian? What's she like? Are you two going out?' That's how conversations work."

Adam shook his head. "Maybe that would have made sense, but that's not what happened." Adam said.

"So, what then? He said, 'I saw Vivian today,' and you said, 'Gotta go. I have a soufflé in the oven?'"

Adam said nothing.

"Wow," Danny said. "Wow. Maybe he thought you didn't approve and that's why you didn't ask."

"I would have approved! I would have been happy for him." He could see that Danny was judging him and he found it infuriating.

Danny shrugged. "Maybe it's not such a big deal," he said. His tone was unconvincing. "I don't think they were about to get married or anything, and it's not like she was the first woman he dated after your grandmother died."

Adam didn't know what to say.

"You know women always liked Hank," Danny said. "Everyone liked him, but women especially. He was a very charming guy. He had a very easy way about him. Anyway, it's not like you ever talked to him about women you were seeing either, did you? He used to ask me. Like I'd know what you were up to."

"I didn't know he asked," Adam said. "I could never talk to him about that stuff. He was always so sad, so alone. It would have felt like I was abandoning him. What could I have said? 'I'm sorry, but I barely remember my dad, and I miss Grandma too, but I'm moving on . . .'"

Danny stopped walking. He locked eyes with Adam. "Do you think for a second that he didn't want that for you, Adam?"

Adam couldn't answer. There was no way he could make Danny understand. Danny couldn't know what it was like to grow up in his father's old bedroom, to sleep in his father's old bed. He never took a breath in that house that didn't feel like an act of grieving. They walked in silence for several blocks.

"Did I ever tell you what happened after my grandmother's funeral?" Adam asked. He knew he hadn't. He had never told anyone, not even Steven. "It was in the summer after my junior year, and I was working in that deli off of Little Neck Parkway. Do you remember it, Danny?"

"The deli? Sure. It closed a few years ago."

"We buried her in the morning," Adam said. "There was a big turnout. All these people showed up who meant nothing to me, nothing to my grandmother." He turned to the side and saw the expression on Danny's face. "Come on, you know I didn't mean you, Danny. It was all those strangers, with their clucking and jabbering. They all looked at me like we were members of some mourner's club. I couldn't stand it. I just wanted to be left alone."

"That's why you didn't want anyone at Hank's funeral?" Danny asked.

Adam nodded. "Would it really have been better the other way? We would have hired some professional we don't know to say a few words and your men could have done the burial while we drove home. That wouldn't feel right, would it? We took care of it ourselves, the people who cared about him and who he cared about." Adam almost wished Danny would put up an argument so he could defend his decision, but Danny didn't answer.

Adam said, "We all went back to the apartment after Grandma's burial, and most of the crowd came with us. The place was just packed. I couldn't take it. I felt like I would explode if I stayed there. So I left. I went to the deli to see if they could use any extra help. Shari was there. Do you remember her? She worked there while she was in college. She was probably nineteen at the time. It was just after her freshman year."

"Sure, I remember her," Danny said. "She was a pretty one. I wonder what ever happened to her."

"I don't know." Adam said. He had tried looking her up on Facebook once, but no luck. She might have changed her name. "We got to talking. I told her about the funeral, about my grandmother. I guess she felt sorry for me, or maybe she was bored, I don't know. We closed the place up early and went into the storeroom in the back and spent most of the next couple of hours fooling around. That was the first time I really kissed a girl."

"Yeah?" Danny said. "And . . ."

Adam tried to ignore the leer he thought he heard in Danny's tone. "And then I went home. Everyone was gone by then, except for my grandfather, of course. He never asked me where I had been. He didn't say anything. He went to his room, I went to my room, and we spent most of the *shiva* avoiding each other. I couldn't exactly tell him I was sorry I left Grandma's funeral but at least I looked so pathetic it helped me get into a girl's pants; or that I couldn't deal with grandma's death, and his mourning and my mourning, and I just needed to disappear for a while; or that I was horny and sad and didn't have the strength to deal with his pain?"

Danny rolled his eyes. "What do you have to make everything so complicated for? You had a good time. She had a good time. Maybe she had a thing for breaking in virgins, you don't know. For any other guy, that would be a happy memory, but somehow you turned it into this fucked up, guilty . . . I don't know." Danny shook his head. "You know who would have been happy for you? Your grandma. Miriam would have said, 'if I have to be dead, Adam should at least meet a nice girl out of it.'"

Adam laughed, surprising himself. "I could almost hear her say that, but she would have had something else in mind. I don't think she would have approved of my getting it on with Shari in the back room of the deli and then never going out with her again."

"No," Danny agreed. "Miriam had very high standards. She would have hoped for something a little more romantic. But Hank would have understood. He was a man, after all. His balls didn't fall off when your grandmother died. Besides, he probably would have liked Shari. She worked hard. She was going to college. Why didn't you see her again?"

"She was nineteen, Danny. I was a high school kid. She was just being nice to me. Anyway, she went back to school and I didn't see her until the next summer. It was a moot point by then."

"You still could have talked to him, Adam."

Adam was silent for a moment. He looked at Danny's face; he tried to see in it what his grandfather must have seen, but he couldn't. "The two of you talked about everything, right?"

"Yeah," Danny said. If he heard the bitterness in Adam's voice, he gave no indication of it. "I could tell Hank anything. He was my rock."

Adam nodded. He felt a pit in his stomach. "The apartment was so dark without grandma," he said. "I don't think he ever recovered. I guess it was one loss too many. He wandered around that apartment like a zombie for months. We both did."

Danny spoke quietly. "I remember, Adam. I was there. It was horrible. But he recovered."

Adam looked at him. "When? When did he recover? I didn't see it."

"Slowly," Danny said. "It took time. They were married for a lot of years. He wasn't really himself again until after you moved out. He was really worried about you, you know. He knew you were hit really hard. We talked about it a lot."

Adam's throat constricted. It had never occurred to him that his grandfather talked about him with Danny. He hadn't considered how much it must have helped him to have Danny there to talk to when Adam was off on his own.

"You were at least as much a grandson to him as I was," Adam said. He had to force the words out. He meant to go on. For an instant, he intended to tell Danny about the rest of the tape, but he couldn't bring himself to do it.

Danny stopped in his tracks and looked up at Adam. He placed his hands on Adam's shoulders. His eyes glistened with tears. "That's an incredible thing for you to say to me, Adam," he said. "You don't know what it means to me to hear you say that . . ." Adam looked away, embarrassed at Danny's display, but Danny was undaunted. "You know I named Henry after

Hank. I even thought about naming him Herschel, but Rose wouldn't hear of it. Too old fashioned, she said."

Adam felt hollow. It was just one more way that Danny had usurped his place. He was ashamed of his pettiness, but that didn't change anything.

They were walking again. After an awkward silence, Danny said, "I'm worried, Adam. If Rose and Carroway end up together, it could get really bad."

"Would it?" Adam asked. "Maybe it would be for the best. You said yourself the marriage was over."

"It's not about the marriage," Danny said. "I don't want her back. I'm done. I'm out." As they crossed under a streetlamp, Danny stopped walking and took out his wallet. "You don't get it," he said. He took out a picture of Henry and held it up for Adam to see. "Look at this kid. This kid means everything to me. Look at him. He's a handsome boy, right? Big for his age. Blue eyes. Look at that smile. That's a kid who knows he's loved."

Danny gazed at the photograph for a moment before putting it back in his wallet. "No one in my family has ever looked like that," he said. "I don't think anyone in my family has ever smiled like that, with that sweetness."

Adam nodded, confused. "He's a handsome boy."

Danny shook his head impatiently. He looked hard at Adam. "No! Adam, don't be so dense. Do I have to spell it out? Rose and I haven't had sex in almost two years, except once. I came home one night to find her all dolled up and acting like she couldn't wait to get into bed with me. About eight months later, Henry was born. When I found out about Calloway, I started piecing everything together. She wanted me to think Henry was mine until she was ready to tell me he wasn't."

"My God!" Adam said. "Are you sure? She really did that?"

Danny nodded. "She admitted it a few days ago when I confronted her." Adam could see the pain in Danny's eyes. "It doesn't work that way. He's my son. I was there when Henry was born. I feed him. I bathe him. I change his diapers. I'm going to teach him to play ball. I'm going to be there for everything."

"But what about Calloway?" Adam asked.

Danny bit his lip. "That's my point. Calloway has a biological claim, right? Who am I? Legally, I mean? If Calloway and Rose end up together, what rights do I have? If Rose wanted to move across the country with him, they could take Henry and I couldn't do a thing, right?"

"I don't know. Does Calloway know the kid is his? Why didn't Rose just leave with Calloway and Henry months ago if it were that easy?"

"I don't know," Danny said. "I don't know what game she's playing. Maybe he's not sure that he's the father. He only knows what Rose told him, and you don't have to know Rose for very long before you know she lies to get what she wants. But then I'm a paternity test away from being nobody. I can't sleep. It's driving me crazy . . ."

"You should never have attacked him, Danny."

Danny scowled. "I'll tell you what, Adam. When you care about something a tenth as much as I care about Henry, you get to judge me, okay? Maybe you can't understand it, but there's no way I could let him get between me and my son."

Adam was disgusted. "That's a great speech, Danny," he said. "Tell yourself what you want, but Calloway isn't the biggest threat to your relationship with Henry. You are. You lost control of yourself like a child. Like a fucking child! And now the police are involved. And they're investigating me, too, if that matters. They could charge me, too. They're already implying they think I was your accomplice. They asked if I knew he was coming, if I helped you ambush him!"

Danny couldn't meet Adam's eyes. He started to speak and then he looked down and swallowed hard. "I'm sorry, Adam," he said. "I am. I'm sorry. We just need to stick together, okay? We have a lot of credibility between the two of us. No one is going to believe some punk kid over us."

Adam looked down at the ground and tried to pull himself together. "Did you talk to your lawyer?"

Danny grimaced. "It's not great. He says Calloway and I could agree to drop our claims against each other, and maybe Calloway would do it if Rose wanted him to, which is a fat chance, or if I offered him enough money, which I have no idea about. If this goes to court, he said I should plead to a misdemeanor assault if the D.A. will let me. That won't look good if Rose wants a custody fight."

They were almost at Danny's house now. Danny put his hands in his pockets. "I guess I've got to go in there," he said. "I need clothes for tomorrow. She's going to pitch a fit."

Adam was silent. He didn't like where this was going.

"I was hoping you might be able to help me out," Danny said. "She told me not to come back when she kicked me out. We were arguing and I said some things that maybe I should have held back."

It would be so easy to walk away, Adam thought. He could be done with Danny's bullshit and his demands. Danny could clean up his own mess for a change. But he didn't go.

They were in front of Danny's yard now. Rose must have seen them coming up the sidewalk. She was standing in a white bathrobe in the open doorway, her hands on her hips. "I see you brought your friend with you,

you coward." Her voice carried well in the warm night air. "You both should be in jail."

Adam saw that one of Danny's neighbors was looking out his window at the scene. Rose had stepped onto her front walk and had crossed her arms. "Pathetic." He heard her mutter. "How did I marry that?"

Adam had a few answers for her: to piss off her parents; because his family had money; because deep down she was afraid she couldn't do better . . . because, at one time, when they were both angry, messed up kids, Danny had loved her. Adam remembered one time when he was home from college and Danny and Rose were seniors in high school. Rose had broken up with Danny after one of their fights, and Danny had locked himself in the bathroom for a long time. He didn't respond to Adam or his grandfather when they knocked or shouted, and Adam's grandfather was starting to panic. They kicked the door open and found Danny curled up on the bathroom floor with his headphones on, blasting a tape Rose had given him.

"I'm sorry you and Danny are having problems, Rose," he said, "I am. But that has nothing to do with me. I have nothing to do with this."

"Right. You were just minding your own business, right?"

"That's right."

"But you were there."

Adam said nothing.

Rose looked uncertain. She thought for a moment before she said, "You want your clothes, Danny? Send your friend in. If you set one foot in here, I'm calling the police."

Danny looked at Adam and then looked away.

"Come in or don't, Adam," she said. "You can talk to me or you can see me in court."

Adam took a deep breath and walked slowly toward the front door. "*Shana Tova*, Rose." He said.

"Fuck you." She walked into the house and Adam followed.

Adam cleared his throat. "Just give me his stuff and I'll get him out of here for the night, okay?"

Her stare was like ice. "Come upstairs. Don't wake Henry. I just got him down."

Adam followed her up the stairs and into the bedroom she shared with Danny.

She walked over to the closet and pulled out a large green suitcase and laid it open on the bed. Then she opened the top drawer of the dresser in the far corner of the room. She pulled out all the socks and underwear that the drawer contained and tossed them toward the suitcase. Most of them landed nearby on the bed. Adam retrieved them. "He only needs clothes for tomorrow," he said.

"He's not getting in tomorrow," she said.

Adam nodded. That wasn't his business.

She said, "If you helped Danny hurt Richard, you'll wish you were dead, Adam. I'll make sure of it." She went to the closet and pulled out several dress shirts and a couple of pairs of pants and threw them at Adam.

Adam folded them quickly and put them in the suitcase.

"I swear to you Rose, I didn't know about any of this. I didn't have anything to do with it. I was horrified. It was brutal."

She looked at him, weighing his words, he thought. She looked unsure. "I can imagine what Danny told you, the manipulative little shit," she said. She lowered her voice and exaggerated her accent to imitate Danny's. "'She's a goddamn whore! She was shtupping some kid right in my house!' Was that it?"

Adam closed his eyes. He was trapped. He just wanted to get out. "I'm sure you had your reasons, Rose," Adam said.

Rose gritted her teeth. "*I'm sure you had your reasons,*" she mimicked. "You can be a real bastard, Adam. You know that? You're a smug son of a bitch." Her voice caught in her throat. She turned around, and for just a second, Adam thought she might cry, but she took a breath and seized control of herself. "I may not have a PhD, but I'm not stupid, okay? You always thought you were better than us and now you're laughing at me. Why? Because Richard is younger and he works for me? Does that give you the right look at me like I belong on a fucking reality show?"

Adam thought a reality show wasn't out of the question given the Blumberg paternity issues. He said, "I'm not laughing at you, Rose, and I never thought you were stupid. I'm sorry you and Danny are so unhappy. That's all. He really cared about you, Rose. He loved you desperately."

She looked down. "He's needy," she said. "That's not enough. Not anymore. I can't live on that. People are supposed to change, aren't they? You aren't supposed to stop growing in high school. You aren't supposed to settle for the same shitty lives your parents had. I deserve more than that, don't I? Look at me! Don't I deserve more than that?"

Adam said nothing.

"I thought I had the day off," she said. She stifled a sob. "I told Richard I was off and Danny would be at a conference. It was Labor Day, and when they called me in, I forgot my phone. A little thing like that and everything changes . . . I know Richard and I would have worked out our problems . . ."

"You mean you and Danny," Adam said.

"What?" She looked startled, and then her voice was as hard as stone. "Go. Tell your friend not to come back here. I'll send things to his hotel if he needs them. And Adam—"

"Yeah?"

"—I almost hope you did help Danny attack Richard. I would love to make you pay. I would get a lot of satisfaction from that. A lot. Now get out of my house."

Adam zipped the suitcase and he let himself out.

Chapter 7

Danny was waiting for him across the street. He was shameless, Adam thought. He had no sense of the swamp he had made of his life and no compunction about dragging Adam into the mud with him. "Could you lie for me, Adam? Could you face down my wife for me, Adam?" And now, with his stooped shoulders and his downcast eyes, Adam could see that Danny was angling for an invitation to stay with him.

Danny must have intuited something of Adam's mood. He didn't press when Adam extended the suitcase to him. He just took it with a mumbled "thanks," and asked Adam if he'd be at services the next day.

"I don't know," Adam said. "I don't think so. I don't know." He walked back to his car and drove home in silence, feeling the sting of the wordless reproach his grandfather would have offered him if he had known Adam had let Danny stay at a hotel—had turned away from Danny as he stood outside his house, holding his suitcase with nowhere to go. "I am cut off," Adam thought, sneering at his own self-pity. "Who can save me from corruption? From death?"

The next morning, Adam woke up late, late enough that he could convince himself there was no point in going to services. Just after he got up to fix himself breakfast, there was a knock on the door. "Who is it?" he asked. "Hold on a second."

"It's us, Adam! Open up." It was Steven's voice.

Steven and Todd were standing there, looking self-satisfied. Todd, neatly bearded and bespectacled, was holding a white bakery box tied with red and white twine.

"Cannoli," Todd said, his arms outstretched for a hug. "We came for *shiva*."

Adam and embraced them both in turn. "Come in," he said. He almost smiled. "*Shiva*'s over, but I'm sure there's an exception for cannoli."

Todd handed him the box. "There's always an exception for cannoli. It's good that we came, right? Remind me where you keep your tea." He walked into Adam's kitchen and pulled three mugs down from their shelf.

Steven said, "I assured Todd that either you'd be delighted to see us, or this would be character-building for you."

Adam laughed. "It's good you came," he said. "Really good." He offered them a choice of tea bags and they each took one.

"I'm so sorry I couldn't be at the burial," Todd said as he filled the cups with water. "If I could have rescheduled my patients, you know I would have."

"Of course I know. It's fine." Adam cut the string on the bakery box and set the cannoli onto a large plate. "Change of subject. What's going on with you two?"

Todd smiled. "We have some leads on an adoption . . ."

"It's still much too early to talk about," Steven said.

"It's very exciting," Todd said. "The mom we've been talking to is healthy and she's very nice. She wasn't sure at first about the two dads thing . . ."

"And she still isn't sure," Steven said.

"She's coming around." Todd rested his hand on top of Steven's and turned to Adam. "We have a very good rapport. She's young. She wants to go back to school. She's drug-free."

"At least she has been during the pregnancy," Steven said. "Really, Todd, it's still too up in the air. We don't know what's going to happen with her."

The microwave had finished heating the water and they brought the tea and cannoli to the table.

"These look terrific," Adam said.

Todd nodded. "Mario's. Unbeatable. Try it. You'll see."

Steven said, "It's going to be a girl. What do the two of us know about raising a girl?" He looked at Todd. "It's not impossible that this is all just a plot of Todd's to get his mother to move in with us."

Todd had taken a large bite and he answered only with a dismissive wave.

Adam said, "You'll both be great. She'll be a very lucky girl."

"I hope so," Todd said. He looked at Steven. "I hope it works out. We've been waiting such a long time."

Steven studied Adam's face. "You look worse every time I see you, Adam. Is it your grandfather? It isn't Danny, is it? Did he really get arrested?"

Adam nodded. "He really did. He beat a guy up. He's out on bail. But that's not it. Maybe it is. I don't know."

Steven and Todd didn't respond. They waited Adam out while he gathered his thoughts.

"I found a tape in my grandfather's apartment the other day," Adam said. He was looking down at his tea. "He knew he was dying. He must have been a lot sicker than he let on. He said he left it for me because there some things he wanted me to know that he couldn't tell me in person. He said he thinks Danny is my brother."

"No!" Todd looked like he might jump out of his chair.

Adam laughed at how wide Todd's eyes were. "Yup. He said my father had an affair with Danny's mom when I was a kid. Danny has no idea."

Todd looked more serious. "Are you okay? That must have come as a terrible shock."

Steven laughed. "Now you sound like the psychologist I married," he said. "I was wondering for a second if you just sat there during your sessions, mouthing 'Oh-My-God' at your patients."

Todd shot Steven a look and then turned back to Adam. "So, you haven't told Danny yet?"

"I don't even know if it's true. It was just my grandfather's guess. He was going by the timing of everything and some family resemblances. I don't even know how Danny would take it."

"Probably he'll ask you for something," Steven said. "A kidney, maybe." Steven paused for a moment. "You could get tested, you know. If you have the same father, you'll have the same Y chromosome. It wouldn't be expensive."

"Great," Adam said. "I'll just ask him for a cheek swab and not mention it again unless it comes back positive." Adam paused. He ran his finger along the rim of his mug.

"What?" Todd asked.

Adam swallowed. "The guy Danny attacked is his wife's boyfriend. He came to the house looking for Rose, and Danny lost it. He put the guy in the hospital and then told the police it was self-defense. He said the guy hit him in the face, but that was me, trying to get Danny off the guy. Yesterday, two detectives came to my office to ask me about it. I think they suspect that Danny was lying."

"Danny must have pitched a fit when he found out you wouldn't cover for him," Steven said.

Adam didn't answer.

"You didn't tell them the truth? How can you let him manipulate you like this?"

Todd said, "They might be brothers, Steven. It isn't that simple."

"It's simple enough."

Adam said, "My grandfather would be heartbroken if anything happened to Danny, Steven. He loved him so much . . ."

"Your grandfather's gone," Steven said. "Cut Danny off. If you're not careful you could both end up in jail. He's not worth it."

Adam pushed his plate away. He had lost his appetite.

"Was there anything else on the tape?" Todd asked. "You said there were things he couldn't tell you in person. Was there more than one?"

"Nothing compared to the first thing," Adam said. "Apparently, my grandfather was in a pretty serious relationship with a woman I don't know. Danny knows her."

"You sound like that upsets you," Todd said.

"Not that he was seeing someone. That he didn't tell me. I don't know. It shouldn't be a big deal, but it still really surprised me. Now that he's gone, I guess it's really been hitting me that we could have been closer."

"You were very close," Steven said.

Adam shrugged. "Maybe I pulled away. Danny was always there, clinging to him . . ."

"Like a tick," Steven said.

Adam winced. "I was trying not to say that." He looked up at both of them. "Rose said I've always looked down on her and Danny. She thinks I'm a snob. She said I think I'm better than they are."

Steven rolled his eyes. "That doesn't make you a snob. You are better than they are."

Todd cleared his throat. "You might not be the best judge of snobbery, Steven."

Adam almost laughed, but he said, "I don't think it makes me a snob if Danny gets to me. He has no boundaries. He doesn't regulate himself. He's emotionally incontinent."

"Emotionally incontinent? Really? Is that a thing, now?" Todd asked.

"Come on. Look at his life!"

"But you're not a snob," Todd said.

"That was a cheap shot, Todd," Steven said. "Danny has objectively made a complete mess out of his life."

"I've seen a lot worse." Todd turned to Adam. "I still can't get over your grandfather's leaving you that tape. How many people get that chance, to hear what someone they loved most wanted them to know after they were gone? You must have been just reeling."

"He did go to an awful lot of trouble to make sure he got the last word," Adam said. "I never thought I would hear that voice again. I wish he'd told me all of it while he was alive."

"You've always described him as so wounded," Steven said. "He should have told you about his girlfriend. He should have showed you that he wasn't crippled by all that he'd lost. He healed. People can heal."

"Danny saw it," Adam said. "I don't know if my grandfather told him more or if he was just better at seeing it than I was."

Todd asked, "What if that wasn't the last word? What if you could talk to him now?"

Adam tried and failed to force a grin. "If he were standing right here? If he knocked on the door? I'd say 'It's been a long time. A person could call. Or you could visit once in a while.'"

Todd smiled, but he didn't reply.

"He'd probably say 'It's a long trip, boychik, and I'm not so young anymore,'" Adam said. "And he'd probably tell me to take better care of myself. He always told me that."

"He might tell you that a little emotional incontinence wouldn't hurt," Todd said. "You lock yourself up so tight . . ."

Adam was looking down at his plate. He shook his head. "Is a little incontinence one of the options?" he asked. He cleared his throat. "It's my understanding that there's either a cork in the bottle or there isn't."

"He'd probably tell you to get out more," Steven said. "That's what he did, right? He found someone."

"I do okay."

Steven looked skeptical. "When was your last relationship? Nine months ago? Ten?"

"Not that long," Adam said. And I've been on a couple of dates since then."

"Well, the clock is ticking," Steven said. "I've got a friend at Hopkins who found a chemical in men's sweat that lowers anxiety in women. It's just a matter of time before all you straight guys could be replaced with a spray can."

Adam muttered, "I can still open jars."

Todd shook his head. "They have tools for that now," he said. In a scandalized whisper, he added, "they have tools for *everything*."

Chapter 8

After Steven and Todd left, Adam's eyes fell on his grandfather's old prayer book. There was still a bulge in the cover where the tape had been housed. He didn't have to go to Queens to pray, he realized. He could find Claudia in her office, get the photos of the tablet that he needed, and attend services half a block away at the Fletcher University Hillel afterwards. Adam glanced at his watch. He'd have to hurry, but there was time.

He was on campus within the hour, taking long strides toward the archaeology building as he called Claudia's office on his cell phone.

He could hear the irritation in her voice from her first syllable when she answered the phone. "It's Adam," he said. "You haven't been easy to reach."

She paused for longer than he would have expected. "I'm sorry, Adam. I've been really busy. In fact, I can't talk now. I have meetings I need to get to this afternoon and more meetings tomorrow."

"I only need a few minutes," Adam said. "I can wait until after your meetings today if I have to."

She spoke quickly. "Today doesn't work. There's nothing I can tell you now, anyway. I'll call you probably at the end of next week, all right?" She hung up.

It wasn't all right. Not even close. Adam was almost at the archaeology building when he saw Claudia walking out. He noted with some satisfaction that she looked rattled to see him approaching.

"Adam . . . I didn't know you were on campus."

"I thought I'd try the Rosh Hashana services here," he said. "Where are you off to?"

Claudia didn't meet his eyes. "I need to be at a trustee's meeting," she said. "Some big donors will be there, and I guess the provost wants to see how I do at fundraising."

She started walking and Adam fell in step alongside her. "That's new for you, isn't it?" He asked. "Trustees and fundraising? I guess you're a real player now. How does it feel?"

"You know I'd rather be in the field," Claudia said. He could tell she was insulted. "Look, I told you I can't talk now. I can't be late for this." She quickened her pace.

"I won't take much of your time," Adam said. "I've been thinking a lot about the tablet we found. I need to see the text." He took a deep breath. "It's important, Claudia. I think it may refer to the *Refaim*."

Claudia stopped walking. "The *Refaim*? Adam, you know what a rabbit hole that is!" She looked into Adam's face and then at her watch. "I only have a few minutes," she said. She gestured to a bench a few steps away from them that looked out on a courtyard where students were playing Frisbee and she sat down. Adam sat down next to her.

Claudia looked at Adam for a moment as if she weren't sure how to begin. Then she looked down at her lap where her hands were clasped together. "How long has it been since I was your professor, Adam? Nine years ago? Ten?"

Adam looked at her, puzzled. She wanted to chat about the old days? "Eleven years," he said. "I was just out of college." Her knee was an inch or two from his. The sun came out from behind a cloud and illuminated her lap so that he saw her the outline of her strong, graceful legs beneath the translucent fabric. She had worn the same skirt, he remembered, the night she'd called him out of the blue a couple of years before to invite him to her apartment. She had said she wanted to celebrate her new book contract. It was late and she'd already had something to drink before he had arrived. The night had ended badly.

Adam knew he couldn't afford to let himself be drawn in. He shifted away.

Claudia didn't seem to notice Adam's slight movement. "When we met, that was only my second year as a professor," she said. "I had no experience, but I knew where I wanted to be and I didn't let myself get distracted by all the shiny objects that litter the side of the road."

She still wore the same perfume. Adam recalled how the skirt had clung to her hips when she had gotten up to pour them both wine. He remembered how her eyes had shone when she asked him to sit down next to her then.

"There's a lot on that tablet, Adam," she said. "Isn't it time you focused on the things that are going to further your career? I often think if I'd kept you as my student a little longer, things would be different. There's so much more you could be doing. If you had focused more on the political side . . . you didn't have to take your first job offer, you know."

Adam slid another few inches over on the bench. He remembered his grandfather's reaction when he had told him he was taking the job at Belmont over Claudia's objections. "You're doing the right thing, Adam," he said. "Put a couple of miles between you and Claudia." When Adam had started to object, his grandfather had said, "I know she's been good to you, and I know she's powerful, and I know you're too smart to get involved with a married woman. But I'll still feel better if you aren't seeing her every day." Adam had no response. He had barely acknowledged how he felt about Claudia to himself, let alone to his grandfather, but somehow the old man knew.

With some effort, Adam kept his voice even. "I am focused on my career. I need to see the tablet if I'm going to keep my job. I could only pick out a few phrases from the photo I took of you and Maggie at the site, and I need to start working on the rest."

"Ah." Claudia said. She looked down again. "That's not possible right now. The tablet isn't ready for public release yet, but if you wait a week or so . . ."

Adam felt as if he had been slapped. "Who do you think you're talking to, Claudia? You must have the complete set of photos and records of the find, right? Certainly, you can show me those!"

Claudia hesitated as if she were searching for her words. "There's a lot to sort out in terms of rights and privileges," she said. "I'm the principal investigator, so the legal department here still has to go over all our agreements with the Antiquities Authority in Israel to make sure everything is done properly."

"What? We always share whatever we find when we're on a dig together, but do I have to remind you that Maggie and I found the damned thing? What does the IAA have to do with it? I just need to see the photos."

She was silent for a moment before she met his eyes. "Bernadette is retiring, did I tell you that?" she asked quietly. Bernadette was Claudia's department chair. Everyone knew they couldn't stand each other. Claudia had often complained that Bernadette intended to be the last successful woman in their field. "The provost and the dean of faculty are very excited about the dig," she said. "They're particularly impressed with what I've told them about the tablet. They've been hinting that they want me to be the next chair. I think the department will go along. We've fallen a bit in the rankings over the past few years, and I think they see that I can lead us in the directions we need to go."

She turned toward Adam and her hand brushed against Adam's arm. Adam felt the heat rise in his face and the back of his neck. He said nothing. "Being chair will mean a lot of administrative work, but there are compensations. Are you really satisfied with your career, Adam? When I think of you teaching core classes in a Catholic school theology department . . ."

Adam didn't answer. Claudia never understood how he could feel fulfilled working at Belmont. She'd laugh if he reminded her that his department was religious studies, not theology.

"I can't make any promises just now, Adam," she said. "I had wanted to wait until next week before I spoke to you. Think about what this place could do for your work. You'd have graduate students and colleagues to collaborate with right down the hall. I'll be able to recruit the best young minds in the field here. You'd have world-class resources, a lighter teaching load with the chance to teach graduate courses . . . You'd need at least one more book, of course. Even a department chair has only so much influence. But if I knew you intended to join us here, I think you could get what you need. You could put something together from your last few articles, and you and I could collaborate on a chapter from our work this summer to round it out . . ."

Adam was too shocked to respond. Claudia had never even hinted that she wanted him in her department before. She had always wanted Adam's input on what she wrote, and she generally tried to keep the condescension out of her tone when they discussed Adam's career, but Adam knew she felt she was in a different class, professionally: the class with the famous names and the big grants.

Adam choked back his first, furious answer: that he didn't need her backhanded job offer, just the respect he deserved as a colleague and a collaborator. He took a short breath and said, "I left Fletcher a long time ago. I'm happy where I am. Just let me know when I can see the photos documenting what Maggie and I found."

Claudia's expression froze. She checked her watch, slung her bag over her shoulder, and stood up. She said, "I'm going to be late. I need to go. Think about what I said." Adam watched her walk away, sunlight reflected in her hair, her skirt brushing against the tops of her leather boots with each step. He walked to the commuter rail station at 125th Street and caught the train back home. He was in no mood for prayers.

Chapter 9

Monday's department meeting would drag on until every trivial gripe had been aired and echoed, Adam realized, whether he paid attention or not. So he didn't. After the last bit of official business had been brought to some conclusion, he went to his office to grade the stack of quizzes and response papers he had waiting for him.

He had gotten about a third of the way through when his phone rang. "Dr. Drascher?" Adam froze at the sound of his name, though at first he couldn't place who was on the line. The man spoke again. "Mr. Drascher, this is Detective Cheng."

Adam had to resist the strong urge to hang up. "What can I do for you, Detective?" he asked. He wondered why it wasn't Levy calling. She had done almost all the talking when they had met in Adam's office.

The detective sounded ill at ease. "I have something to discuss with you," he said. "Where will you be this evening?"

Adam hesitated. "I'm really behind on my work," he said. "Couldn't we just talk on the phone?"

"I'd appreciate your cooperation, Dr. Drascher," Cheng said. "Don't make this unnecessarily difficult."

Adam held the phone away from his mouth and let out a long breath. "All right, Detective," he said. "I'll come down to the station. Just let me know when to be there."

"Not the station," Cheng said. "Your apartment. Eight o'clock." He hung up.

Adam cursed under his breath. Cheng would be coming to his home. He knew the address, apparently. Adam glanced at the grading he hadn't finished. He couldn't concentrate now. And he hadn't cleaned his apartment since he returned from Israel. He threw the papers and quizzes into his bag and kicked his desk before he headed out.

It didn't take Adam long to get his place in reasonable shape. He got back to his grading for a solid couple of hours before his phone rang again.

"Hello?" He said.

"Adam? This is Rabbi Mira, do you remember . . . ?"

He remembered, of course. He half expected her to ask why he and Danny left in the middle of the service on Thursday night. "Of course, Rabbi," he said. "What can I do for you?"

"I've been meaning to come by, Adam. I'd like to meet with you. Normally, I would have come during *shiva*, but it was so crazy before Rosh Hashana. I hope you understand. I did look for you at services, but I didn't see you."

That was a relief, anyway. "No, Rabbi. I'm sorry I didn't get a chance to thank you for having me. Danny and I were way in the back."

"Of course. I understand," she said. "When could I see you? Do you ever work from home?"

"I'm home now grading papers, actually, but I guess it's getting kind of late in the day," Adam said. He thought he if he could put her off just for a bit her attention would fall on someone else and her interest in him would blow over. "Maybe in a week or two? You could call me when you have a sense of what would be good for you."

"No, today is good," she said. "I can be there at four-thirty if that works for your schedule." Adam sighed silently.

It was four thirty-five when the rabbi rang his doorbell. Adam took a breath and reminded himself that she was just being kind. It was basically a *shiva* call, even if *shiva* was over. What would it be, ten, fifteen minutes of pleasantries, tops? Maybe she'd leave him a small fruit basket or something and say a kind word about his grandfather. He could be gracious.

The rabbi smiled and looked up at Adam when he opened the door. She wore a white blouse with a red scarf, and her curly hair was dark brown with streaks of silver. Adam thought she looked like she might give birth at any second. When he offered his hand, she took it warmly. "I'm not sure we ever got the chance to meet in person," she said. "I'm Rabbi Mira. I was a big fan of your grandfather's. We all were."

Adam took two steps back so she could enter. "Please come in, Rabbi." He gestured toward his couch. "Do you want to sit down? Can I get you something?" He glanced at his fridge. What did he have to offer her? Not a beer, obviously. "Chips? Tea?"

The rabbi looked at him intently. "I'm good for now, Adam, thanks." She looked amused. "You seem a little flustered. Have I come at a bad time?"

"Sorry, Rabbi. It's been a rough week. Please sit down. Are you sure I can't get your something?"

"Just water would be great." She smiled. The rabbi pointed at Adam's desk chair. "How about over here? The couch is a little low for me these days."

Adam strode quickly to the chair and cleared off the ungraded papers that he had stacked onto it. "Of course," he said. "Please make yourself comfortable. How—" he glanced at her belly and broke off, not sure if it was too personal a question.

She smiled. "A hundred and seventy pounds," she said. She laughed at Adam's horrified expression. "I'm kidding, Adam. I knew what you were asking. Thirty-four weeks." She nodded knowingly when she saw Adam's face and she added, "I know. Six more weeks, give or take! How enormous am I going to get?" She slung her leather bag over the back of the chair and sat down.

Adam got her a glass of water. "How did you know my grandfather, Rabbi? He wasn't much of a temple-goer."

"I wouldn't say that," she said. "I came to the temple about a year and a half ago. I met Herschel at a Brotherhood-sponsored softball game: confirmation class against staff. He was one of the umpires." Her face lit up as she recounted her story. "I hit a line drive and Herschel called me out while I was sliding into second under the tag. I was a hundred percent safe, you'll have to take my word, so I argued the call with a certain amount of conviction. Herschel played to the crowd. He tossed me out of the game." She shook her head, smiling. "The kids thought it was hysterical, and he and I were friends from then on." But there was no humor in her voice when she added, "I was clearly safe."

Adam said, "When I was growing up, my grandfather was strictly a twice-a-year Jew. My grandmother lit candles for Shabbat and we would sometimes go to temple, but my grandfather always said his parents had forced him to go to enough services when he was a kid to last a lifetime. You changed that by arguing a call in a softball game?"

"I think you underestimate my charisma," she said. "He didn't usually come to services, but he was on the Social Action committee, which I work closely with, and the Brotherhood, which I can't take any credit for. Sometimes he'd come to other events. We all loved Herschel. He was a very special man. He had a tremendous heart." The rabbi took a sip of water. "He was very charming, you know. I'd even say he was courtly but in a rugged kind of way. He called me Madam Rabbi." Her smile grew even brighter at the memory. "He was very sweet, but you could feel his strength when he looked at you. He was very popular with the ladies of a certain age." She saw the expression on Adam's face and said, "Don't look so surprised. He wasn't bad looking! Anyway, I don't think he ever saw any of them outside of temple, but there was always a lot of buzz about him after a meeting. I think he knew. He seemed to enjoy the attention."

"Danny Blumberg told me he had a girlfriend in the neighborhood," Adam said. "I never met her. Did he ever tell you about her?"

Rabbi Mira looked thoughtful. "No. He never mentioned to me that he was seeing someone. Neither did Danny." She put down her glass. "It was very touching to see how devoted Danny was to Herschel. They were quite a pair."

Adam changed the subject. "How come you call him Herschel? Everyone called him Hank."

"I called him Hank when I first met him, but he corrected me. He said when he was growing up, rabbis were old men with gray beards, and they always called him Herschel. He hated it, he told me, but to him a rabbi who called him Hank was a non- starter. He said he could get used to a lady rabbi half his age, but a man can take only so much change." She took another sip of water and looked up at the maps on Adam's wall. "You study ancient Jewish history, right, Adam? Your grandfather told me. He was very proud."

Adam raised an eyebrow. "Proud, or bewildered? I don't think he ever really got what I saw in this stuff."

Rabbi Mira looked surprised. "No, he was proud. He told me he was a plumber, but his grandson was a historian who made a living with just his thoughts."

Adam smiled. That sounded like his grandfather. "I'm not really a historian; I get my hands dirty. I'm an archaeologist."

The rabbi pointed to her belly. "You'll have to imagine that I'm leaning in to hear better because I'm interested in what you're saying," she said. "I loved archaeology in college. What are you studying?"

"I'm interested how Canaanite religion shaped Judah and Israel during the monarchy," he said. "I'd like to help recover what we lost when we rejected Canaanite culture."

"What we lost?" Rabbi Mira shook her head in disbelief. "I can't see that we lost much. They worshipped violent, bloody gods. They sacrificed their children, didn't they?"

"Not everyone agrees on that," Adam said. "It might have been propaganda, though I tend to think it happened. The Canaanites committed repellant crimes, but that's not all they were. They were still human beings. We can still learn from them. They were our most important influence, after all. You'd be willing to learn from the Greeks and the Romans, right? Their hands weren't exactly clean. The Canaanites lived with us. They were our neighbors."

The rabbi gave him a skeptical look.

"You've only read what the people who hated them wrote down," Adam said. "I don't think the Canaanites were so different from us. I think the Canaanites might have had a lot to teach us. I'm especially interested on their views of the afterlife."

"Didn't the Canaanites think the dead became chirping ghosts who drink blood?"

Adam shrugged. "Every culture has rituals and superstitions that look foolish from the outside. I'm studying a text now," he said quietly, "an invocation to the dead. 'Come to me,' it says. 'Take account of me!' When the Canaanites lost the people they loved, don't you think it hurt them as much as it hurts us?" He felt suddenly self-conscious and he lowered his voice. "Isn't it possible that they found something that gave them peace, something we could learn from?"

The rabbi spoke softly. She looked into his eyes. "Have you said *Kaddish* today, Adam?" she asked.

Adam just stared at her.

"Don't look at me like that, Adam. It's not chutzpah. This is literally my business. Do you want to see my rabbi license?"

Adam looked at the floor. "My grandfather wouldn't care if I said *Kaddish*."

"I think he would care. And it's not for him." She held out her arms. "Come on. Give me a hand up."

Adam smiled despite himself. He extended his hands toward her and she pulled herself up.

"Thank you," she said. "Sometimes I feel like a stuffed pepper; I really do. It's the first commandment in the Torah: 'be fruitful and multiply;' it's also our most basic biological function. You'd think there would be more dignity in it." She leaned against the back of the chair as she spoke. "Look, Adam, when someone dies, a lot of the time it feels wrong. We feel in our bones that life should be about increase, about more life. Something about death feels obscene, unnatural." She met Adam's eyes. Her gaze was kind and resolute.

"How do you respond to the loss of someone irreplaceable?" She asked. "Do you give in to despair? Do you stop living? Our faith says no. It pulls you in. You have relationships, whether you want them or not, and those relationships come with obligations. You're part of a community, and supporting each other is not optional." She kept her eyes locked on his. "You're not the only one who has lost someone recently, Adam. Come say *Kaddish* with me."

Adam looked down. "I tried on Rosh Hashana," he said. "It was awful."

"We'll try again. I can find a *minyan* very easily."

Adam grimaced. "What do I need a *minyan* for? Even if I wanted to pray, I wouldn't need a crowd. We could be our own *minyan*."

The rabbi picked up her handbag from where she had slung it on the back of her chair. She shook her head. "This isn't a *minyan*. You need at least ten for a *minyan*. This is just a conversation, which I'm winning, by the way." She smiled.

"You're winning?" Adam asked, amused. "You're winning a conversation?"

"In a blowout. It's like seventeen to two," the rabbi said. She opened her purse and fished out her smart phone. Adam watched as she moved through several screens with a few deft movements of her fingers. "This is a great app," she said. "I use this all the time. Give me a second . . . okay. There's a Conservative temple just a couple of miles away. I'm very proud of being a Reform rabbi, but let's face it; you can't count on us for a daily *minyan*. The Orthodox are very efficient, but they wouldn't let us sit together and they wouldn't count me as one of the ten. I prefer to count. Let's go. If we leave now, we can make it in time."

"Look," Adam said. "You're obviously used to getting your own way, which is my nice way of saying you're pushy as hell, but I don't want to go."

"Go anyway," she said. "The son redeems the father."

Adam couldn't have been more stunned if she had started speaking Ugaritic. His mind raced over the text of the tablet: "I am cut off . . . who will redeem me?"

"Wait," he said. "Wait a minute! What do you mean? Are you quoting something? Where's that from?"

She seemed about to answer when she took a step back and wagged her finger at Adam as if she had caught him at something. "You're trying to distract me, and it won't work. There's no point in arguing. We both know in the end you'll come with me. I'm seven and a half months pregnant in a strange town, I haven't said *Kaddish* yet today, and dusk approaches. You won't make me go by myself."

"You're in mourning?"

"I say *Kaddish* for the people in my congregation who died recently or who have lost someone close to them. I haven't missed a day in years." Adam met her eyes again. To be mourning, every day, forever, for a whole community . . . She looked up at him with a sympathetic smile, and after a brief moment, the whimsy was back in her tone. "Put away the long face. I also celebrate with them when they marry or have children. It's like having a huge family. Let's go."

"You may be the bossiest person I ever met," Adam said.

"It's for a good cause. Do you want to walk or drive? Probably we should drive." She shot Adam a mischievous glance. "They say walking can stimulate labor."

"You don't scare me," Adam said. He grabbed his keys from where he had left them on his counter.

"A little bit I do." She said "That's okay. You're in good company."

Adam held the door open for her and followed her through. He opened the passenger side door of his car for the rabbi and shut it after her before he went around to his side.

As Adam pulled out of his parking space, Rabbi Mira said, "OK. A promise is a promise. Here's why you need a *minyan*: In the Torah, it says God will be 'sanctified among the children of Israel.' So already, there's a connection between prayer and community. In Isaiah, even the angels were calling out to one another when they said, 'Holy, holy, holy . . .' They couldn't do it alone. So, understandably, the rabbis in the Talmud concluded that certain prayers, at least, the ones that proclaim God's holiness, require a congregation. Okay. So they had to determine the minimal number for a congregation. If you look through the Torah, the smallest group of people ever referred to as a congregation are the ten men Moses sent to spy out the Land. True, they were called 'a wicked congregation,' but there you go. Ten makes a *minyan*."

"That's absurd," Adam said. "Our model is ten wicked spies?"

"All of a sudden, you have standards?" The rabbi asked. "You want to learn from the Canaanites, who murdered their children, but you're not so sure about your neighbors who want to praise God's name with you in memory of your grandfather?" She patted his arm. "Look, Adam, of course the individuals matter. Of course they do. We don't even assign numbers to people when we count for a *minyan*. We count their hats or books or anything else, because a person is not a number. And yet we need ten. We're bound to God more strongly, more intimately, as a community, even a flawed community. Families are like that too, right? One-on-one the feelings aren't the same as they are when we encounter each other together."

"I couldn't say. It was just me and my grandfather for a long time."

"You'll have to take my word for it, then." The rabbi said. "When I see my sisters and my parents all together, there aren't just the people in the room and their own individual relationships. It's like the family is an extra participant, above and beyond the people in it. The mourner's prayer is like that, but even more so, because when we say the *Kaddish*, we're bound to our ancestors as well as to God and to our neighbors. That sounds like something an archaeologist should be able to appreciate, no?"

They were at the temple now. Adam parked across the street and helped the rabbi out of his car. She looked at her watch. "We still have a few minutes," she said. I'm going to run to the bathroom, and I'll meet you in the chapel. It will probably be a smaller room off to the side of the main sanctuary."

Adam nodded. The Rabbi joined him just as prayers were starting. There were fourteen people there, counting Adam and Rabbi Mira. The combined afternoon and evening services took less than half an hour. At one point, after the first few minutes, Adam was brought up short when he realized he had been actually praying. Rabbi Mira nodded encouragement as Adam stood with the other mourners and forced out the words of the mourner's *Kaddish*.

Adam drove them back to his apartment building. On the way, he said, "I never noticed the blessing about the resurrection of the dead before. How could I have missed that?"

"The Orthodox and Conservatives have always had that prayer. The Reform have it as an option now too, but until a few years ago, the Reform didn't think it was in keeping with our modern, rationalist sensibilities. The Enlightenment was good for a lot of things, but inculcating a sense of mystery wasn't one of them. Or humility, either."

"I would have guessed the Reform didn't mention resurrection because it's only in the prophets and not the Torah."

The rabbi shook her head. "I don't think that's it. Jews have found the promise of resurrection in the Torah for as long as they've looked," she said. "If you want to see it badly enough, it's there. Do you remember Jacob's blessing? 'Rueben shall live and not die?' They found it there. There are a lot of examples. For example, God promised to return Jacob to Israel even if he went down to Egypt. Only, Jacob died in Egypt, so when will God keep his promise? I think that's really where the idea of an afterlife comes from. People die with their expectations unfulfilled, but we don't give up hope in God's promises."

Adam could almost relate to that. He certainly understood it. He parked in his old spot and helped the rabbi out on her side. They walked together toward her car. "Tell me why you said that before about the son redeeming the father," he said. "It reminds me of something in the text I've been working on."

"From the Canaanites?"

"Eighth century Judah," he said. "It's quite a text. I've only focused on a few lines, but there's so much there . . ."

Rabbi Mira looked dismissive. "There couldn't be any connection," she said. "The story I referred to is from medieval Europe. An illiterate orphan has a dream where Rabbi Akiba, who has been dead for a thousand years, tells him that his father is suffering in the afterlife. Akiba says, 'the son redeems the father.' And he tells the orphan he needs to learn to say *Kaddish* to ease his father's suffering. That's where the custom of saying *Kaddish* for the dead originated."

She looked at Adam's face and laughed. "Don't look so disgusted. It's just a story. Let me guess: it doesn't sound Jewish to you to pray for the dead to relieve their suffering in the afterlife?"

Adam nodded.

"Don't worry, it's not my Judaism, either. To me, the Akiba story is about a boy who needed to find a way to honor his father, and he found one, that's all."

"I prefer the text I'm working on," Adam said.

The rabbi said, "I guess you can dig down into any text and find meaning in it. You can always find what you bring with you, at least." She adjusted her bag on her shoulder. "Actually, Cantor Moser and I were just having a discussion about this very thing."

Adam was surprised to hear the rabbi mention Cantor Moser. Since he hadn't been at Rosh Hashana services, Adam had assumed the cantor had retired. Adam remembered him well from his childhood. He had been huge and terrifying, and he had taken it upon himself to chase Adam and his friends out of the hallways numerous times during Hebrew school. "Is Cantor Moser still at the temple?" he asked.

"Oh, yes," Rabbi Mira said. "He's a lot of fun. And really sharp. Last summer, I told him I was thinking about giving a sermon where I never mention any of the traditional sources, just to surprise people a little, get them talking." She smiled. "He suggested I use only pop song lyrics. He dared me, actually."

"That sounds like a really terrible idea."

She shook her head. "It wasn't. I did it for three weeks in a row. People still quote those sermons to me."

They walked the short block to the rabbi's car. Adam offered Rabbi Mira his hand and she took it in both of hers. "Thanks for the conversation," he said. "I'm not even going to ask what the score is."

She nodded. "Best not. Will you join us for Yom Kippur?"

"I don't know," he said. "I haven't thought that far in advance."

"I'll be looking for you." She turned to him as she opened her car door and added, "May your grandfather's memory be a blessing." She gave his hand a gentle pat before she got into the driver's seat. Adam closed her door after her and he watched her drive away.

Chapter 10

Cheng arrived at eight sharp. Adam invited him in, and the two men sat across from each other at Adam's kitchen table. When Cheng leaned forward, Adam could see the detective's gun in his shoulder holster.

"I'm going to get right to the point out of courtesy, Dr. Drascher," the detective said. "You could be in a great deal of trouble, but if you're straight with me, I'll do what I can to help you out."

Adam didn't respond well to intimidation, even genteel intimidation. "I don't know why you're here, Detective," he said. "I haven't done anything, and I already told you and Detective Levy everything I know."

Cheng sighed. He looked almost apologetic. "You think you're safe, Dr. Drascher. Take it from me. You aren't. Now that Mr. Calloway has had some time to recover, his memory of the events at Mr. Blumberg's house are coming back, and he says your role in the assault is getting clearer. He was ambushed, he says. The next thing he remembers is you pulling him out of the car and then dragging him into the house."

"That's not true! I never touched him except to help him into the house to wait for the ambulance!" Adam said. "Should I have left him where he was?"

Cheng shrugged. "Mr. Calloway and Mrs. Blumberg think you and Mr. Blumberg might have planned the attack together, or possibly that you joined in with him when you heard the fight start out in the street. They want satisfaction for what happened. They're very passionate about that. They want Mr. Blumberg punished and if you helped him, they're determined to take you down, too." He shook his head. He looked Adam in the eyes. "You seem like a decent man, Dr. Drascher. You've got a stable job, a clean record . . . if you're innocent, now is the time to talk to me. Tell me what you know."

Adam began to object, but the detective interrupted him. "You could go to jail for the assault. You could go to jail for obstructing my investigation. And if Mr. Calloway and Mrs. Blumberg don't think they could prove your guilt beyond a reasonable doubt, they could always sue for damages with a much lower burden of proof. One way or another, they're going to get a piece of you if they can. You could lose everything."

Cheng sat back in his chair. "It's Mr. Blumberg they really want," he said. "He's responsible. I know that. And your testimony would be very useful. I think I could talk them into leaving you out of this if you cooperated with me."

Adam fought to control his emotions. He tried to keep the expression from his voice and from his face, and he could feel himself fail. He could hear his voice cracking under the strain. "And what if I won't cooperate, Detective?"

Cheng shook his head. "You'd find yourself at the center of this investigation," Cheng said. "Journalists will pick it up. I'll guarantee it. The *Post* would love a story about a Catholic school teacher and a local businessman caught in a love triangle and an assault. Your life could be ruined before Mr. Blumberg ever got to trial."

Adam felt sick. He tried to look Cheng in the eye, but his gaze kept returning to the gun. Adam could feel his future slipping away from him like the drops of sweat sliding down the sides of his ribs. He didn't ask for this, he told himself. The detective threatening him in his own home, at his own kitchen table—that was Danny's fault, not his. Danny fucked up, and it was Danny Cheng wanted. And there were only two answers. He could tell Cheng "yes" or he could say, "Fuck you."

Neither man saw Levy enter the apartment. Adam could feel the words forming on his lips when he heard her speak. It was only then that they turned to see her. Her voice was low, but menace crackled in the air around her like an electric charge. She said, "What the hell kind of bullshit stunt is this, Ronald?"

Cheng shifted sideways in his chair to face her. Adam thought he almost managed to look unsurprised.. Cheng said, "Let's try to keep this professional, all right, Detective?"

"Don't talk to me about being professional. You've been a detective for what, a month? Do you know how it looks when you go sneaking around behind my back after hours, not telling me what you're up to? It's a good thing I have friends who keep me informed, because I obviously can't trust you."

Cheng flushed. "Maybe you should do your job and then I won't have to go off on my own!"

She glanced over at Adam. "I apologize for this," she said. "We have a nice, collegial precinct at the 111th. Sleepy. Quiet. Detective Cheng had been hoping for a more glamorous place to start his career, like the 110th, maybe." Her tone implied Adam should understand the significance of the 110th. "Maybe he thinks this sort of thing will get him transferred. What are you hoping for, Ronald? Narcotics? Homicide? I know a lot of people, Ronald. Cops who don't stick together don't get on the fast track. Their careers don't go anywhere."

Cheng gave her a dead smile, cold and stiff. He said, "Dr. Drascher and I had just finished our chat when you arrived, Sue. I'll see you at work tomorrow. We can talk then." He turned to Adam. "You know how to find me. I know you won't forget what we've talked about." Cheng stood up and walked calmly toward the door, nodding to Levy as she stepped aside to let him out.

Once Cheng was gone, Levy flopped down on Adam's couch. "The aggravation in this job can be unbelievable," she said. "How about a glass of water?"

Adam poured her a glass and dropped three ice cubes into it. She nodded her thanks and took a long sip. "I understand why he came here," she said. "He must be very frustrated about your case. Mr. Blumberg's case, I mean. I've been very deliberate. I've been intentionally slow, frankly. I've taken an interest."

Adam didn't speak.

"When I came up about a million years ago, there weren't a lot of women detectives," she said. "I spent years earning the respect of my partner, my captain, everybody. I had to wait behind everyone else for promotions until I had been passed over so many times they stopped even considering me. I put up with all kinds of bullshit that no one would try to get away with today. And along the way I learned that I don't need them to like me. I don't even need their respect. I know how good I am." She glanced back at the door and shook her head and then she finished her drink and handed the glass to Adam. He put it in the sink.

She considered for a moment. "Let's go for a drive," she said. "I think better in the car."

Adam looked at his watch. It wasn't even eight-thirty. "Where are we going?" he asked.

"The supermarket. Ronald's antics interrupted my shopping. He shouldn't have come here on his own like that. That wasn't right."

She walked out without looking over her shoulder. Adam took a breath. He didn't have much choice. He followed.

Levy waited to start the car until they were both buckled in. "You direct me," she said. "Whatever is open." Adam nodded. At the next light, Adam gestured that she should go around the corner to the left.

"I don't want you to get the wrong idea," she said. "Ronald's okay. He'll get there. A lot of the young cops, especially now, they think this job is about the technical stuff. You know, forensics labs, DNA, like on TV. But that's not what it's about. It comes down to noticing how things fit together, common sense. The most important thing is knowing people, understanding how they work. I wasn't on this case ten minutes before I realized you were the key," she said. "I just knew. That's experience; you don't learn that in the academy and you don't wake up with it after a month or a year. But who's going to learn from me? Ronald has only been my partner for a month and in another few weeks I'll be retired." She pointed at her head. "What's going to happen to all this when I'm gone?" She looked at Adam quickly and then turned the corner as the light turned green.

Adam kept his mouth shut, afraid that anything he might say could just make his situation worse.

She turned to look at him as she drove.

"It's a right just up there," Adam said. "Then it'll be three blocks or so on your left."

"Do you understand what I'm getting at?" the detective asked.

He didn't. Not at all. He shook his head.

"It's the people more than the facts, Adam" she said. "The people more than the facts. You have to understand people. You know I didn't come here to talk philosophy, Adam, right? This isn't some abstraction. I want to understand you better. It's important." She pulled into the supermarket parking lot. It was nearly empty, and she parked close to the building, just next to the handicapped spaces. Adam followed her inside.

"We don't need a cart," she said. "I just need a couple of things."

She turned into the produce section and picked up a yam before putting it down. "I don't like these," she said, absently. "I never have." The watermelons were nearby, and she thumped at one. "I have some things I'd like to clear up about the night Mr. Calloway was attacked," she said. "I'm pretty sure I know what happened in the big picture, but there are some details . . . they might not seem that important for the case, but they could reflect on you very strongly." She handed him the watermelon. "Hold onto this for me, all right? We're nearly done here."

Adam took the watermelon. He looked around. They were almost alone in the store. It began to dawn on him that Levy might be crazy.

Levy spoke slowly, as she navigated the aisles of the store, if she were working her thoughts out in that moment. They turned into the Mexican foods section and she picked up a bottle of hot sauce and beckoned him to follow her to the front of the store. She said, "Let's say Mr. Calloway told the truth from the beginning. Let's say he just drove up to the house, looking for Mrs. Blumberg and Mr. Blumberg attacked him without warning."

Adam opened his mouth to speak, but she said, "No, Adam, don't interrupt. You haven't lied to me yet. Let's keep it that way. Let's say that's what happened."

Adam inclined his head toward the cashier in a silent plea for her to change the subject until they got out of the store, but she gave no indication that she'd noticed. He hefted the watermelon onto the scale after she handed the hot sauce to the cashier. "Are you having a party?" he asked.

"No." She seemed surprised at the question. She paid in cash, exact change, and she put the hot sauce in her handbag. "Let's go," she said. They walked out to the car. Adam held the watermelon on his lap with one hand as he fastened his seatbelt, and she started the car.

She took several turns until she pulled into an alley Adam didn't know. It was very dark. Levy said, "I don't think Calloway ever saw Blumberg coming. I don't think Calloway threw a punch. The ring, right? The bruise. But then, that means you were the one who hit Mr. Blumberg. There was no one else it could have been."

Adam was silent. It was all he could do not to scream.

She parked the car and turned off the ignition. She turned toward Adam. He could hardly see her in the darkness. She said. "Mr. Blumberg called you to babysit, but it wasn't just babysitting to him. In his mind, he had a crisis, and you were going to help him through it. You were the one person he was counting on, weren't you Adam? And he was right to count on you. He called and you came. It's like you told me the other day. 'That's what you do,' you said." She locked eyes with him. "You really don't like to let people down, do you?"

Adam shook his head. He had to control his urge to bolt, to run as fast as he could, back to the supermarket, back to his house, anywhere but here in the dark, in an empty lot.

"Now what was the crisis?" She asked. "Did he just have to stay late at a meeting, or was it his marriage falling apart because his wife was involved with someone else? What kind of help did he need from you?" She didn't wait for an answer. "Believe it or not, Adam," she said, "the most important thing to me right now is your character. I like to think I'm a very good judge of character, but I need to hear it from you. Where were you in all this?"

Her face was inches from his. She took his chin in her right hand. "When did you hit Mr. Blumberg?" She asked. Her voice was low. "Was it to stop the assault on Calloway? Maybe. But there's also a very dark possibility. I don't even like to consider it, but it's there." She let go of his chin and lightly brushed his cheek with her hand. "You could have helped Mr. Blumberg to attack Calloway. You could have told him about Calloway's texts and the two of you could have planned the whole thing together. You could have hit Mr. Blumberg yourself before the police arrived to make it look like it was Mr. Calloway who attacked him. I have to say, Adam, that would disappoint me. I'd like to think you're better than that."

She was studying him, Adam thought, testing out her hypotheses by feel, or smell, maybe. He felt that he shouldn't answer, that he could only hurt himself by talking, but he couldn't stop himself. He had no more self-control. He had spent it all.

"You want to know about my character?" Adam asked. "You're asking if I'm a good man? Let me explain something to you. I never attacked Calloway. I don't know him. I don't even know how I got here. This is a nightmare, but not even my nightmare. It's like it belongs to somebody else, okay? My life is simple and it's quiet. I teach. I study. I write. That's it. That's what I do. I don't break bones and put people in the hospital. I don't conspire. I don't ambush. I don't get interrogated by the police, or kidnapped, or whatever the hell this is. But somehow, I'm waist deep in this shit. I'm mired in it. Let me tell you something else. No one asked me if Danny and Rose should get married, or if Calloway and Rose should start fucking each other. I would have said no. No to all of it. And no one asked me if I wanted to be Danny's go-to guy when he thinks the world is crashing in on him and he needs to be rescued. That just happened. It's a nice inheritance from my grandfather. I'm just trying to get through this with something like a clear conscience and some self-respect. Do you understand what I'm saying, Detective? Does that answer your fucking questions?"

Detective Levy sat in silence for a long time. Adam almost wondered if she could read his thoughts. His heart was pounding. It was difficult to breathe. But then Levy patted him on the thigh. "I've done some checking on you, Adam. You're as clean as can be. The police in this town never even heard of you. You have no history of violence, no record, no moving violations, even. But I needed to hear you say it, do you understand? And it shows me something, it does, that a big boy scout like you would jump into the middle of a fight and stop it, even punching his friend in the face to do it." She smiled at him as if that were meant to be his reward for bravery. "But I have one more concern. Loyalty is a good quality, but there are limits. Who have you been defending, Adam? Mr. Blumberg obviously has a temper, to say the least. Mr. Calloway's injuries attest to that. Has Mr. Blumberg hit his wife? Is she in any danger?"

Adam let out a breath. "Never. Not Danny. I know him well enough to say that unequivocally. He would never hit Rose or any other woman."

Levy turned toward the windshield and settled again into her stillness. She was calculating, Adam thought, weighing all she had heard, deciding his fate. He found himself counting his own heartbeats. He got to seventeen before she spoke.

"I've got a niece," she said. "Irene. She's beautiful. She's smart. She's very talented . . ." She reached into her purse and pulled out a piece of paper and pressed it into his hand. "Call her."

Adam was too shaken to speak. He thought he must have misheard. But there he was, holding the paper. "You want me to call your niece?" he asked. "You're serious? This is your way of setting me up on a blind date?"

"I'd never joke about something like this," she said. "Trust me, I have a strong feeling about this." And then there was an edge to her voice, just the suggestion of a threat. "Call her, Adam. I hate when guys don't call." She turned the car on and drove him home. She didn't ask him for directions. When they arrived in front of his apartment building, she unlocked the car doors. "I know you'll do the right thing," she said, as if he had asked her for advice. "I'll be in touch."

Adam entered the lobby of his building before he opened his hand. The paper had a phone number and a website written on it. He ascended the stairs to his apartment half in a daze. He took three ibuprofen and then spent almost half an hour pacing, trying to process what had happened. Were both detectives in this together, he wondered, putting on a show for his benefit, trying to manipulate him somehow? But manipulate him to do what? Levy seemed to have guessed everything. She might be crazy, but she certainly wasn't stupid. Was he really supposed to call her niece? Adam knew the answer to that last one, at least. The detective was definitely not joking.

Chapter 11

Adam's alarm woke him the next morning from a night of troubled sleep. He scanned the *Times* online while he ate his cereal. Skipping the political stories at the top of the page, he scrolled down to the Science section. Adam's stomach tightened as he clicked the link to the short article titled "Artifacts Reveal Jewish Life in the Time of the Prophets."

> Archaeologists working in Tel Arad, Israel uncovered a clay tablet and other artifacts that may unlock key mysteries of ancient Hebrew culture. The objects date to approximately 800 BCE, around the time of the prophet Elijah, and they offer a rare glimpse into religious and political life at the time, according to the leader of the team at the site, Claudia Renaud, Professor of Archeology at Fletcher University: "These artifacts show that although the people of ancient Israel spoke Hebrew and had their own government, they were very much a part of the larger civilization that stretched at least from the Mediterranean to Babylon. They traded with each other, they knew the same stories, and they worshipped the same gods."
>
> David Solokov, Director of the Middle Eastern Studies Program at Harvard University stressed the need for caution, saying that "until the academic community has had the opportunity to examine all the objects uncovered at the dig, any conclusions about their importance is premature and inappropriate," but, Renaud stressed, the artifacts she found are exceedingly fragile and will require the utmost care before they are restored sufficiently for study. "When they are ready," she said, "we will, of course, invite scholars from other institutions to study them."

There was no photo of the tablet. The graphic accompanying the article was a map of modern Israel with the Tel Arad site marked in large print. Adam cursed as he read the story again. Every sentence added to his anger. He asked himself how Claudia determined that she was running the dig by herself or how she could have persuaded herself to forget the he and his student were the ones who actually found the tablet. Adam knew Solokov, of course. The man was a relic and a pompous jackass, but he was absolutely right about this.

He was about to call Claudia at home to let her know what he thought of the article and about her ethics in general, but he controlled himself. He was too close to this, he thought, too furious. He needed an outside perspective before he did or said anything. He texted Steven: "Free for dinner tonight?"

He read the story again, parsing Claudia's words as carefully as he could. "We will invite," she said, as if she had the tablet and the other objects on hand—but then she would have had to have gotten them out of Israel. That's exactly the sort of thing the IAA existed to prevent. He couldn't imagine the IAA ceding control to Claudia.

Steven texted him back. "Our place. 6:30 or 7. Never fear. I'll cook. Bring wine." It was a running joke of Steven's that he thought Todd incapable of making toast.

Adam showered and dressed quickly. He just caught the train. He was still stewing over the article when he walked up the stairs of the religious studies building, hoping to spend a few minutes alone in his office before heading to class.

Gallo found him of course. The man was a walking irritant. "Adam! Did you see the paper this morning? We need to talk about that article."

"I'm teaching in a few minutes, John." He said. "Can it wait until later?"

Gallo shook his head. "I'm busy all afternoon. That was your dig, wasn't it? Why didn't you tell me they found something so important? You knew about it, right?"

"Yes, I knew about it. Maggie and I are the ones who dug up the tablet!" Adam was fuming. He had enough to deal with without being pestered by this puffed-up titmouse.

"Then why weren't we in the *Times* article?" Gallo asked. "I only saw Fletcher mentioned, not Belmont. Five years from now, you know who'll get credit for the discovery? The people in the article." Gallo stood so close, Adam thought he might poke him again. This time, he promised himself, if it happened, he wouldn't let it go.

"I want you to call the *Times* and have them make a correction," Gallo said. "Today. This morning. Make sure they mention Belmont and our department by name. Tell them to include that we had our undergrads on the dig. I want people to see the kind of opportunities we give our students."

"They're not going to print a correction, John." Adam did his best to keep his voice even. "Leaving us out wasn't an error; it was just in bad taste.

If you ask them to correct that, we'll only sound petty. The article had lots of inaccuracies, but they're subtle enough that the *Times* won't listen and I'll feel ridiculous for complaining."

"You're so naïve," Gallo said. "This was a strategy. Fletcher's P.R. department didn't want to share. I don't blame them, but we need publicity even more than they do. Don't worry about the problems being small. If we can build it into an academic controversy, people will start talking about this. We'll get our P.R. department on it. We'll place stories in other papers with our interpretations of what the artifacts mean. Maybe we can get you on NPR."

"What are our interpretations, John?" Adam asked. "I hope you have some, because I haven't had a chance to analyze the tablet yet, and I'm not speaking to anyone until I do."

Gallo shook his head at Adam. "Don't be stubborn, Adam. You're coming up for tenure in a year. Getting your name out there could save your ass."

Adam forced himself to speak slowly, to maintain control. "I have a book, two articles, and a chapter, John. You know that. And I'm going to get at least one book out of the tablet, but it's going to take time."

"Don't tell me. Tell it to the deans. I heard they're really going to be cracking down this year. And every one of them listens to NPR." Adam could see the disappointment in Gallo's face. "You know what's wrong with you, Drascher? You're a nice guy and you're bright, and you think that's enough. It isn't. You aren't hungry. There's no fight in you. If you want this, you're going to have to fight for it."

Adam stared at Gallo. It wouldn't take much; Gallo's weight was back on his heels. One punch and Gallo would be on the floor, hopefully with his beard facing down where Adam wouldn't have to look at it.

Adam let out a slow breath and counted to five in his head. He was overreacting; he knew that. He reminded himself that he hadn't slept well in days. The loss of his grandfather was still fresh. The stress of dealing with Danny and the police and Claudia was getting to him. He checked the clock on his computer screen. He had less than a minute to get to his core class on time. He said, "I've got to go, John. Class is starting." Then he strode out of his office and toward the stairwell as fast as he could, leaving Gallo to close his door behind him.

Adam shut himself into his office after class. He was still smarting from his conversation with Gallo. "No fight," he thought; "Idiot. Like it's a fucking boxing match." He told himself not to get distracted. He had too much work to do to spend the day stewing. He just needed to focus. His next class related closely to the tablet. He could work on his research and prepare his lesson at the same time if he just bore down.

Adam pulled *First Meditations* up on his computer and set it to re-peat. There were days when he would listen, really listen, to the suite, and then Coltrane's saxophone was a searchlight probing the darkness. But now Adam used the music as a work song, and he was swept along almost insen-sibly by the rhythms of the piece.

Adam made steady progress until late in the afternoon, when he was too exhausted to continue. He set his phone to wake him after a twenty-minute nap, and he slumped down in his desk chair with his arms folded across his chest. Before the alarm went off, Adam was awakened with a start by a knock on the door. "Come in," he said, as he readjusted his glasses. Maggie was standing there, clutching a sheet of paper. She was so angry she was shaking.

"Maggie—" Adam started.

"Have you got a minute, Professor?" Maggie's voice trembled. He could see the paper she was holding was a printout of the *Times* article.

"Yeah, of course, Maggie. Come in. Sit down." Adam left the door open a crack and sat in his desk chair. Out of instinct, he rested his hand on the desk drawer where he kept his box of tissues.

Maggie offered him the article. "Have you seen this yet?"

Adam nodded. "I read it this morning." He tried to tamp down his an-ger and keep his tone neutral. He didn't want to stoke Maggie's fury. Maggie needed someone to steady her, and his raging wouldn't help.

"It didn't even mention us! How did this happen? Why didn't they talk to us? Did Dr. Renaud do this to us on purpose?"

Adam nodded. "She must have. Claudia and the public relations people at Fletcher. I didn't see this coming at all. I just spoke to Claudia a few days ago, and she didn't say anything." He spoke quietly, one phrase at a time, as if he were carefully releasing excess pressure through a valve. "It's okay, Mag-gie. It's just a newspaper. We haven't been scooped. We can still publish." He tried to smile. "We could just think of this as a really inconsiderate way of letting us know we aren't on the same team."

Maggie wasn't having it. "No offense, Professor," she said. "But that's fine for you. I'm applying to graduate schools this year. I was counting on that find. We discovered that tablet! I thought that would really set me apart from the other applicants."

"Do you really think it's fine for me, Maggie? Do you have any idea what the tenure process is like?" Adam's voice was shrill. He was half out of his chair when he sat down, bit his lip and started again. "Forget that. It doesn't matter. That's not your problem." He took a breath. "I'll explain what happened in your recommendation letter. You'll be okay. I still think you should apply to all those schools we talked about . . ."

Maggie looked straight at him. "How can you say that I'll be okay?" She asked. "You don't even know if you'll be okay!" Adam saw her eyes welling up, though she was fighting the tears back. He opened his drawer and offered her a couple of tissues, but she didn't take them. "I'm sorry," she said. "You're a victim in this, too. I know that. It's just my boyfriend is going to law school and we're applying to schools in the same cities so we can be together. We need all the options we can get."

"I know," Adam said. She had told him a long time before, in a much happier conversation. "Maggie, it's going to be okay. I still know some people at Yale. I keep in touch with my senior thesis advisor and I'll email him as soon as your application goes out. I used to have a contact at Georgetown, but he didn't get tenure. Still, it's a Jesuit school. I'll call the head of the department there. I'll explain."

He could see that Maggie wasn't satisfied. She thought he was letting her down, letting Claudia steamroll him. "Look, Maggie," he said, "I'll get access to the tablet. That's a promise. And I'll make sure people know your part in the discovery. You're going to be okay."

She was looking down at the crumpled paper.

"Maggie, look at me," Adam said. "It's going to be all right."

Maggie forced a dismal smile. "It's going to look bad that I don't have a letter from Dr. Renaud, isn't it? Everyone will know it was her dig."

A part of Adam wanted to tell Maggie to forget about Claudia, but he fought with himself to keep a clear head. "You should ask her for a letter," he said quietly. "I don't know what she's thinking, Maggie, but it has nothing to do with you. Claudia knows how good you are."

"Are you serious?" Maggie asked. Her voice broke, but her expression was defiant. "After what she did, I'd rather not get in anywhere than ask for her help! You should have heard her after you left, acting like she was my friend, telling me what a bright future I have . . ." She muttered, almost below hearing, " . . . *maldita embustera . . .*"

Adam continued to speak quietly. He was so, so tired. "Don't make this your fight, Maggie. It doesn't have to be and it shouldn't be." He let out a long breath. "I think she meant what she said; you impressed her. Ask her for a letter. Claudia has a lot of influence, and she's very smart, not just academically—politically too. Especially politically. She could open doors for you." Adam caught himself biting his lip again. His only ally was a twenty-year old undergraduate, and he was sending her away. But that was one way, at least, that he would be better than Claudia. Not everything had to be about him.

"You can't trust her after what she did!" Maggie said.

He laughed. "No. Do I look stupid?" He smiled as he saw her bite back a response. "Well I'm not, anyway," he said. "Look Maggie, you're just starting your career and you're not in her way; that's how you should keep it. She won't agree to write for you if she won't write a strong letter. I still think she's better than that. Just be sure to apply to Fletcher, too. If you don't, she'll be insulted, and that would hurt you." He cleared his throat and looked at his computer screen, hoping Maggie would get the hint that he needed her to go. He could see that she did; she dropped the article in his garbage can and stood up.

She looked at him intently. "Are you going to be all right, Professor?" she asked. Adam nodded, touched once again by her concern. Maggie turned to leave, but she stopped and looked over her shoulder at Adam. "I just don't understand why she did this. I thought she was your mentor. I thought you were friends."

Adam closed his eyes. "I thought so, too."

Adam forced himself to finish his lesson plan, and then he took the subway down to the Steven and Todd's apartment on the Upper West Side. He arrived on time, wine bottle in hand, and they buzzed him in. When the elevator opened at the 8th floor, Todd was standing in the doorway. He was buttoned into a snug green cardigan and his arms were extended in joyous welcome.

"Come in, come in!" He said. "Have a seat on the couch. Help yourself to some appetizers. Steven is just finishing dinner, but he can hear us and join in the conversation." Todd held the door open with his foot so he could give Adam a hug as he entered the apartment.

As Adam passed by the kitchen, Steven called out a hello. "My hands are full of onion," he said, "but I'll be out as soon as I can."

Adam held up the wine bottle he had brought. "The guy in the store said this would be good," he said. "He was wearing a corkscrew around his neck, so I listened to him."

Todd took the bottle and read the label. "Perfect!" he said. "This will go great with the fish."

Adam sat down and Todd pulled up a seat facing him. Assorted bruschetta were out on the coffee table and Todd took some on a small plate. Adam followed suit. "How are you?" Todd asked. "Are you doing okay?"

"It hasn't been a great week for sleeping," Adam said. "Actually, I've got a problem at work and I was hoping to talk to you both about it. It's about the tablet we found in Israel."

Steven poked his head out from the kitchen. "Have you figured out what you found yet?"

"It's from eighth century Judah. It's covered in Hebrew writing."

"He means BC," Steven said to Todd.

Todd rolled his eyes. "I know, Steven. Adam thinks the Roman Empire is modern history." He turned to Adam. "What's the writing about?"

"That's the thing," Adam said. "I've only read some of it, but I think it relates to the cult of the dead."

Todd said. "Well, that's what you get when you go rummaging around in ancient tombs. Isn't your whole profession basically a cult of the dead?"

"Please stop being clever," Adam said. "These aren't the insights I need from you."

Steven shouted from the kitchen, "Go on, Adam. I'm listening. I'm very focused. Dead people. No cleverness. Only the insights you ask for. Go."

Adam shouted a sarcastic "Thank you" before he went on. "So, first you have to know that my student and I dug up the tablet before I left for my grandfather's burial." As he said it, he remembered that at the time he had still hoped to see his grandfather again. "When Claudia got back to New York, I left her a few messages because I wanted to talk about what we found, but she didn't answer. After a few days, I surprised her at her office and she was really evasive. She wouldn't show me her notes or photos or answer any of my questions. Then, out of the blue, she basically offered me a job. Or really, she invited me to apply for a job and suggested if I worked really hard and I wrote another book, maybe I could get hired with her help."

"Nice," Steven said. "Very nice."

Adam nodded. "We didn't really finish our conversation. She had to run off to a meeting with some very important people, she said. Okay. Fine. I figured we could sort it out in a couple of days. I had a lot to do for my classes, anyway. But this morning, the *Times* printed an article on our dig. Did you see it?"

Steven shook his head. "Sorry. I haven't looked at the paper today."

"I didn't see it," Todd said. "Where was it?"

"Third story in the Science section on the web," Adam said.

"Why the Science section?" Steven asked. "Archaeology isn't science." He got out his smart phone and searched for the article.

"Don't start again," Todd said. He reached for his iPad on the shelf below the coffee table. "They put it there because the same people who like to read about science like to read about archaeology." Todd found the article first and he read it out loud.

Steven whistled. "Claudia screwed you," he said. "This is really bad."

"Why would she offer me a job and then do this?" Adam asked.

"Did you give her an answer on the job offer?"

Adam shrugged. "I told her I'm happy where I am. Why? Do you think she was insulted? She thought she was doing me a favor and I turned her down. I can't imagine that she would care enough about that to steal my work."

"Don't look at me," Steven said. "I don't know why anyone does anything. Sometimes I think I understand zebrafish genetics, but that's only on a very good day."

"Do you think she knows how you feel about her?" Todd asked.

Adam bristled. "I don't feel any way about her except pissed off." He saw the look of skepticism on Todd's face. "We've been through this, Todd. I had a crush on her a million years ago. That's all."

"Neither of you even acknowledged it, right?" Steven asked. "Nothing ever happened."

Adam looked away. He hadn't ever talked about that night, not even with Steven. "Once. Sort of. Nothing happened. I kissed her, but that's all. One time."

Steven looked horrified. "You never told me that! What did you do?"

Adam sighed. He would have preferred to talk about anything else, but there was no way they were going to let this go. "I didn't do anything, okay? She invited me over. I thought she was sending pretty strong signals and I was wrong. It was almost a year after her husband died. Anyway, I kissed her and she started to cry."

Steven tsked. "That doesn't say a lot for your technique, my friend."

Todd said, "Shut up, Steven! I want to hear what happened. What did she say?"

Adam felt sick at the memory of it. "She apologized for crying, but she couldn't stop. She'd had some wine before I arrived. She spent the next hour telling me about Theodore and how much she still missed him. He was a famous artist, really talented. She just kept crying, and the whole time she was telling me about his paintings. They were all over the apartment. She must have told me the stories behind half a dozen of them that he'd made for different birthdays or anniversaries. Finally, I convinced her that she needed to go to sleep and I left. We never talked about it again."

"I'm really sorry, Adam," Todd said.

"It's fine," Adam said. "It's for the best. It was hard enough getting over her when it was just a fantasy; if we had gotten involved it would have really messed with my head. The point is, whatever there was between us was only in my mind and it's been over for a long time. I figured out the deal with Claudia back in graduate school. There's a certain distance I need to maintain, and then I'm fine. Getting too close was a problem, but I always kept my distance except for that one night. I'd never let that happen again, I promise you."

Steven nodded slowly. "And you're sure she isn't interested in you?"

Adam tried to smile, but he couldn't manage it. He sipped his wine. "She never was. We're colleagues, that's all. Or I thought we were."

Todd looked thoughtful as he chewed on a piece of bruschetta. "OK," he said, with some reluctance, "let's say that's right. Let's leave any romantic angle out of it. Why would she offer you a job and try to steal credit for your discovery in the same week?" He wiped his hands on his napkin and looked to Adam and Steven, but they offered no response.

Todd thought for a moment more. He steepled his hands in front of his face.

"Maybe she never really wanted to hire you. Maybe she knew from the beginning she was going to do this to you, and she only offered you the job in her department to soothe her conscience or to keep you off balance." He looked at Adam and Steven, but got no response. "Or maybe Steven was right," he continued; "maybe she really did want you in her department and she took credit in the *Times* story because she was offended that you didn't take her up on her job offer." He looked at them again, but they offered nothing. Todd shrugged. "I don't know. I'm sorry. I have no idea."

Steven shook his head. "This is why psychology shouldn't be in the Science section, either," he said. Adam noticed he was tapping his index finger against the tines of his fork, a reliable sign that he was agitated. "Is this standard in your field, Adam, to claim you found something great, but no one can see it because it's too fragile? Because that definitely wouldn't fly in biology."

"No," Adam said. "It's not typical. And it wasn't true, anyway. I held the tablet myself. That was bullshit. Anyway, she shouldn't have the tablet at all. We were supposed to leave all the artifacts in Israel."

"Whoa!" Steven said, "Wait a minute! You think she smuggled the tablet out of Israel? That sounds really illegal. How would she even do that? And if she did, why would she tell the *Times*?"

"I don't know," Adam said. "I have no idea. But one way or another, she thinks she can control who gets to see it. The surest way would be if she had it in her possession. Maybe she has friends in customs. I don't know. I know she has friends in the Antiquities Authority."

Steven looked skeptical.

Adam shrugged. "Maybe I'm just being paranoid. But I need to publish on that tablet if I'm going to keep my job. Gallo made that very clear."

"You're not being paranoid," Steven said. "She's definitely writing you out of the discovery. She's probably going to put a whole misery of grad students on the project to squeeze all the data out of it before anyone else has a chance at it."

"How many grad students are in a misery?" Todd asked.

"Almost all of them," Adam and Steven said at the same time. It had been a joke between the two of them for years.

"I meant," Todd said with exaggerated patience, "how many of her students are you going to be competing with?"

"It's pretty specialized stuff," Adam said. "I don't think Claudia has that many people she can throw at this."

Adam thought of the look on Maggie's face when she showed him the article. All day, angry as he was, he'd been holding himself in check, telling himself not to overreact. But he was done. "I'm not letting this happen," he said, "I can't."

"Do you really think Gallo would vote against you for tenure? Your teaching is good, right? And it isn't like you haven't published. You've done pretty well, haven't you?"

"If he voted against me, enough of the others might fall in line to torpedo my chances," Adam said. "I don't know what his problem with me is, but he's all but told me he doesn't think I have enough to stay. He blames me for not being part of the *Times* story. And he wants to see at least another article, or ideally a book. The tablet is all I have going right now. I don't know how, but I need to see that tablet."

They talked about Todd's work while they ate. His practice was growing, and they were thinking of taking on a fourth partner. Adam asked Steven about his experiments, and Steven held up his hands in mock resignation.

"I don't know," he said. I might be on to something, but I don't know." He refilled Adam's water glass. "The fish I engineered are aggressive and territorial and I don't think they're attracted to each other at all. It's like I'm back living with my parents."

"Why don't you seem more excited? Isn't that great news?"

"We'll see if it holds up," Steven said. "If it doesn't, I should just quit academia. I could open a pizza parlor, I guess. My zebrafish would probably make reasonable anchovies."

When the dishes were done, they went to the living room to sit down. Steven asked, "What ever happened with Danny, anyway? You haven't even mentioned him. You haven't gotten any more questions from the police, I hope."

"I wouldn't say that," Adam said. He told them about his encounter with Detective Levy.

"She wants to set you up with her niece?" Steven said. "That seems really off, doesn't it?"

"Off? Yeah. Everything about her was off. I think she might be genuinely crazy. It's the nicest compliment I've had all week, though."

"Where do you think she got the idea?" Todd asked.

"I don't know," Adam said. "Either she tries to unload this woman on everyone she interrogates, which almost makes me curious just to see how bad she could be, or else there's something in the answers I gave to her questions, I guess. The detective said she had a strong feeling about it. I don't know. She's very intuitive, I'll say that. I wouldn't want to play poker with her."

"You sound almost intrigued," Steven said. He seemed amused.

Adam shrugged. "I can't call her. What would I say? 'Your aunt was investigating me in connection with a crime and thought we'd hit it off?' That's a little awkward, isn't it?"

Todd looked thoughtful. "She just gave you her phone number and said to call?

"Pretty much. Just her name and number and her website."

"Well?" Todd asked.

"Well, what?"

Todd was obviously exasperated. "Well, did you check out her web page?"

The question surprised Adam. "No."

"We have to look," Todd said. "Aren't you curious?"

Adam shrugged. From his pocket, he fished the paper the detective had given him and read the small, neat handwriting. "It's irenelevymusic. net, all one word," he said. He put the paper back in his pocket.

Todd got his iPad and typed the URL. "She's a composer!" he said. He clicked something. "She might be cute. The video is from too far away to tell. Do you like her voice?"

Adam listened for a few seconds. "Yeah. She's got a nice voice," he said.

"I'm trying Google images," Todd said, "but there are a million Irene Levys in New York."

"It doesn't matter what she looks like," Steven said. "He just needs to make some excuse if the detective brings it up again."

Todd shook his head. "I disagree, Steven. I think he should call her."

Steven's jaw dropped. "Why? Because we want him spending even more time with the detective who's investigating the crime he covered up?"

"What if you had never called me after we met the first time?" Todd asked. "What if the detective really saw something? What if she's really right for him?"

Steven rolled his eyes. "You just think it's sweet that a crazy lady wants to play matchmaker with Adam. This is serious, Todd."

"I know it's serious, Steven. Look, if the detective is going to put anyone in jail, do you think it's going to be the guy who called her niece, or the guy who didn't?"

Steven nodded thoughtfully at that. He said, "The world is run by—"

"—hostile and arbitrary forces," Adam finished. "I know. You have a very unhealthy world view, Steven." Neither of them responded. They just looked at Adam. "You both think I should call?" he asked.

Steven's and Todd's eyes met for a moment before they responded. "Just be real nice to her, Adam." Steven said.

Todd's tone was emphatic. "Bring flowers!"

Chapter 12

Adam began his class by projecting his picture of Maggie and Claudia holding the tablet onto the white screen at the front of the room. Adam noted Maggie's surprise with some satisfaction as the photo came into view. If Claudia didn't know how to share credit, he did. First, he would teach his class. Then he would finish his business with Claudia.

"Maggie and I dug this out of the desert in Israel this summer," Adam said. "You can count on your hands how many people have seen it in the last twenty-seven hundred years." Maggie flushed as the students looked at the screen and then back at her.

"What does it say?" Aisha asked. "That's not Hebrew or Arabic or any alphabet I know."

"It's Hebrew," Adam said. "But it's the ancient script. I've only been able to work on a few lines of it so far, but they directly impact our work this semester." Adam skipped to his next slide, which showed his transcription of the lines he had studied into the modern alphabet, without vowels. "Do you want to take a stab at it, Maggie?" He asked. Adam didn't have many students with the Hebrew skills for this, but Adam thought Maggie might be up to it.

She spoke the words slowly, one by one. "Draw near, my God, *Refaim* . . ."

"*Refaim* and *Qirvu*, 'draw near,' are both plural," Adam said, "So it probably isn't *Eli*, 'my God'; it's probably *elai*, 'to me,' right?"

Maggie nodded. "That flows better . . . 'Draw near *to me, Refaim*. Visit me, gods . . .'" She struggled, then. "I don't have the vocabulary for the rest," she said. She let out a deep breath. "I can see the root of one of the verbs is *yarash*, but I don't remember what that means." Adam saw Aisha flash her a thumbs-up.

"That's a really good start," Adam said. "I would translate the line with that verb as: 'For I am cut off; who will succeed me?' That will give us plenty to discuss today. I want you to keep the verb 'to succeed' in mind during Paul's presentation. I can see he's suffering and wants to get this over with. True, Paul?" Paul nodded. "OK, then, come on up. The floor is yours. Tell us about the *Manes* of ancient Rome."

Paul spoke well, as Adam had expected he would. He had asked him to present first because he knew from experience that Paul was comfortable in front of a classroom, and Adam wanted to set the bar high for the others.

Paul spoke for about twenty minutes, which included questions and interruptions from the other students. The *Manes*, the dead ancestors of ancient Rome, had two annual festivals, he explained. One reinforced the ties between the living and the dead in general. The other was meant either to placate or to drive out malevolent spirits of the dead.

Adam split the class into groups. He asked them to review the *Refaim* texts from last time and to compile a list of observations about how the *Refaim* seemed to compare and contrast with the *Manes*. "When you're done with that," he said, "draw up a list of questions you have about the roles the *Refaim* played in the lives of Canaanites."

After Adam had let them work for a while, he reassembled the class. Greg raised his hand. "I don't understand these malevolent spirits," he said. "Why would people who looked after their families while they were alive suddenly turn nasty after they died?"

"Maybe they were nasty when they were alive too," André said.

"There is that," Adam said, "though I don't get a sense from most of the texts that it was the malevolent people who became malevolent spirits. Let's return to that question in a bit. I think we'll have more to say about it after we discuss a couple of other points."

He paused for a moment to collect his thoughts and he glanced around the room.

They were all looking at him expectantly. He had succeeded in piquing their interest, he thought, for what that was worth. He knew he was making an unusual move, but he had taught them all before, so he was willing to take a calculated risk. Over the course of the week since Adam had visited his grandfather's apartment, he had flipped through several of the books he had brought home with him, just to reminisce. The opening chapters of the book of Irish myths made a strong impression on him and had inspired him to further study. Adam wanted to explore the connections he thought he saw between the myths of the conquest of Ireland and his own work.

"Last time," he began, "we wondered if all the uses of *Refaim* in the Bible refer to the same people. In some texts, the word *Refaim* seems to refer to the spirits of the dead. In others, the word seems to refer to the indigenous inhabitants of the land of Canaan who were conquered, according to the Bible, by the tribes of Israel and Judah. Several of you wanted to know if these are just homonyms or if there is a relationship between these two seemingly unrelated meanings for *Refaim*.

"For a long time, I've suspected that the indigenous *Refaim* and the underworld spirits were either the same or really closely related, but how could that be? What could link those two ideas? So I had a thought. According to myth, the ancestors of the Irish were invaders who conquered the earlier inhabitants of their land. But even though the Irish defeated the people who preceded them, they revered their memory and attributed supernatural powers to them. In fact, that's the origin of the 'wee folk' of Irish folklore.

"To me, the parallels to the *Refaim* seem strong. The Israelites told the story of entering Canaan from outside and vanquishing the Canaanites, utterly dispossessing them according to some stories, driving them into a few outposts according to others. I wonder if maybe, like the Irish, the people of Israel and Judah venerated the spirits of the people they had conquered."

Maggie raised her hand. "You aren't saying that one group got their stories from the other?" she asked. "They were thousands of miles apart."

"True, and the Irish stories were probably much later. No, I'm talking about the way the human mind works, the way culture works. Maybe we can understand one group by studying the other, even though there was no direct influence."

Maggie said, "That goes against a lot of what we learned about methodology in my anthropology classes . . ."

Adam nodded. He smiled an apology. "I know. It's very Structuralist, very Lévi-Strauss." He saw only blank faces looking back at him. "No? I'll post a reading online tonight for next week. There are problems with it, but it should make for some good discussion." He stopped for a moment to find his train of thought. "You're right, Maggie, that the Healers aren't *Manes*. We can't draw explicit conclusions from one to the other, but there are interesting parallels that may help us figure out what questions to ask. Go along with me for a bit, okay?"

Maggie nodded, but Adam expected it wouldn't be long before she had another objection to offer.

"OK," Adam said, addressing the class, "why would the Irish venerate the people their myths say they defeated?"

"Maybe they felt guilty for taking land that didn't belong to them!" Aisha called out. "Or maybe they were afraid the spirits would take revenge."

Adam guessed from the heat he heard in her response that Aisha saw modern geopolitical parallels to the biblical narrative, and he saw in retrospect that it was an obvious reaction that he should have anticipated.

Before he could respond, Maggie raised her hand high in the air and began speaking.

"I think there's a problem with your hypothesis, Professor. In Genesis, the Canaanites and Israelites are descended from different sons of Noah. If the *Refaim* were Canaanites, they couldn't have been considered ancestors of the Israelites."

Adam tapped his pencil against his thigh. He thought he might be able to answer Maggie and Aisha at the same time. "Good," he said. "OK. Let's think about how these stories most likely developed. One: if you look at the languages, Hebrew is pretty much a dialect of Canaanite. Two: there isn't any archaeological evidence of a mass conquest or genocide in ancient Canaan. Those are just two of the reasons that most scholars doubt the biblical narrative. It's a lot more plausible that Israelite culture grew out of Canaanite culture. And if that's the case, it might have been the most natural thing in the world for the Israelites to call their dead ancestors and the Canaanites by the same name. Their ancestors were Canaanites! So that's one explanation for how the term '*Refaim*' came to apply to both. The story of the conquest and the idea that the Canaanites were descended from a different, cursed lineage would have developed later."

Adam looked around the class. There were no objections, anyway. He took that as license to continue. "OK," he said, "since we're back to the idea of dispossession, let's talk about the word I asked you to keep in mind from the tablet, '*yarash*'. In the Bible, the word usually refers to the victor taking spoils from the conquered. One might '*yarash*' one's enemies, meaning you would dispossess them. Does that sound like the meaning in our text?"

"No," Aisha called out after a brief pause. "The person in the tablet asks '*mi yirasheni*', which means, 'who will *yarash* me. He wouldn't be waiting for someone to dispossess him."

"I agree," Adam said. "I think, the use of the verb here is close to what we see in Genesis 15, when God promises Abraham that he will have a son who will '*yarash*' him. They usually translate that as 'inherit.'"

"You translated *yarash* as 'succession,' before," André read from his notes.

Adam nodded. "I was trying to get at both meanings with one word. You succeed your predecessors, which could just be inheritance. But the word sounds triumphalist to me, too. Did you notice that the object of the verb '*yarash*' refers to the people who used to own whatever stuff we're talking about? 'We will *yarash* them' means we will take their stuff. 'They will *yarash* us' means they will take our stuff. It's very personal. That feels very different from the English word, 'inherit.' You inherit money or a piece of furniture. It's about the stuff. Think about how it might affect your view of inheritance and your view of the dead if inheritance and despoiling a defeated enemy were described by the same word. Maybe the people of ancient Canaan were afraid that the dead might not always be pleased that the living inherited their world and lived in their houses and ate from their land. Maybe they were afraid the dead might resent them or even try to take revenge."

"That's pretty dark," Greg said. If I had a kid, I'd want them to have a life after I died. Don't all parents want that?"

Adam lost his train of thought as he remembered Danny's question to him on Rosh Hashana—"Do you think for a second Hank didn't want that for you?"—but he quickly recovered and finished his lesson.

Maggie hung back after the rest of the class left. She gestured with her head at the transcription that was still projected there. In a small voice, Maggie said. "I'm sorry about what I said in your office. I know there was nothing you could do. I shouldn't have taken it out on you."

She turned and walked out quickly, her footsteps resonating in sharp, staccato beats on the floor of the hallway outside the classroom. Adam wanted to call after her, to tell her he was going to confront Claudia, that he would get back their photos, but he knew his promises would sound hollow. He didn't want to expend his anger on words.

Adam caught the subway and got off at the Fletcher stop. Wrought iron gates marked the entrance to the campus. Within, most buildings were in the classical style or Gothic. All were oversized. McMonuments, Adam thought. Pretentious New World striving. In the main quad, several broad, paved paths converged on the library, a new Parthenon bearing mottos in Greek, Latin, and English inscribed above its pillars. As Adam ascended the steps to the main entrance, he ran his hand along the robe of the statue of Benjamin Fletcher that stood guard outside the library doors. He had given the college its charter back when he was governor of colonial New York. Rumor had it that Fletcher had raised the money for the college's first library from pirates who needed a safe haven from which to practice their trade. At least back then everyone knew who the pirates were, Adam thought.

Adam showed his Belmont ID to the security guard and entered the library. If Claudia had brought the tablet back with her, it might be here in Fletcher's collection of antiquities. If the tablet were here, Adam thought, he wouldn't have to confront Claudia at all; at least, not today.

Adam went down two stories to the dimly lit antiquities repository. He had written most of his thesis there, surrounded by Fletcher's collection of ancient artifacts. He tasted the still, stale air, and immediately felt as if he had come home.

He found Dr. Popadopoulos, the librarian in charge of antiquities, just where he always was, sitting at his small desk several feet back from the counter where people could wait to ask him questions. There was never a line. Hours would go by, Adam remembered, sometimes even a whole day, when he and Popadopoulos would be the only people down there. Adam hadn't seen him in years, but he looked just the same. What were a few years to Popadopoulos? He measured time in centuries.

Popadopoulos was almost bald except for the closely cropped silver hair on the back of his head. His skin was pale and unwrinkled, unblemished by sunlight. He was dressed in gray slacks, the same as always, with his soft eyeglasses case clipped to his oxford shirt pocket. Like the room's carpet and its furniture, Adam loved Popadopoulos impersonally and completely.

Adam walked over and the librarian looked up from his book and nodded in greeting. Although no one else was nearby, they spoke very softly.

"Dr. Popadopoulos, how are you doing?" Adam asked.

The librarian thought for a second, maybe two. "The same," he said. Adam smiled a little.

"I was hoping you could help me," Adam said. "I'm looking for the artifacts Dr. Renaud brought back from Israel at the beginning of the month. Have you catalogued them yet?"

Popadopoulos shook his head. "Dr. Renaud hasn't been here." The librarian said. "I heard she found some wonderful objects. I wish she had brought them here." He had a wistful look in his eyes. "Of course, she probably had to leave them in Israel. They're very strict, I'm told, and they must be working to preserve the objects before they can be moved. They have wonderful chemical engineers there. Still," he said with some pride, "we aren't without resources for dealing with fragile artifacts here at Fletcher."

Adam nodded. "I don't doubt it," he said. "Thank you."

That left open the question of whether Claudia had the tablet. She had control over it, anyway. That was clear from the newspaper article and from their conversation. As to whether Popadopoulos might not be telling the truth, Adam had no concerns on that score. Popadopoulos couldn't lie about an ancient treasure any more than he could fly. If he said they weren't in his collection, they weren't.

Adam steeled himself. If he had to talk to Claudia, things were likely to get very ugly. He glanced once more at his old study carrel before going upstairs into the sun.

It was a short walk from the library to the archaeology building. Linda, the department's administrative assistant, was at her desk in the main office there. She was a slender African American woman, just a couple of years older than Adam, elegantly dressed, her hair in tight braids. Linda," he said, "it's good to see you!"

She looked up from her computer screen and took off her reading glasses. "Adam Drascher, is that you?" Her decades in the city had hardly eroded her Tennessee drawl. She stood up and gave him a hug, then pulled back to look him over. "It's been years!" she said. "Now why is that? You're still at Belmont, aren't you? That's just a few miles away, last time I checked . . ."

"I know, I know," Adam said. "I mean to come back and visit, but you know how it is. How are you doing? How are things here? You must be close to graduating, right?" Linda had been taking one or two classes each semester for as long as Adam had known her.

Linda smiled. "I've got just three classes to go. I'm hoping for this May. Anyway, we're all just fine! Are you here to visit Claudia? She went home early to change. She's having dinner with the provost."

"Derrick, you mean?" Adam asked. Robert Derrick had been Dean of the Graduate School when Adam was a student there. Adam remembered hearing that he'd been promoted.

Linda nodded. She looked very pleased. "I think your old mentor's moving up in the world."

Adam nodded. Yes, she was. "I'm sorry I missed her," he said. "When you see her, just tell her I said hello."

Adam turned to leave, but he didn't go far. He had made too many promises: to himself, to Maggie. His career was at stake, he told himself. He couldn't go away empty-handed.

Adam walked down the corridor and turned the corner. He had been Claudia's teaching assistant for years when he was a student and she'd sent him back to her office many times to retrieve forgotten books or objects she had needed for class. He knew where she kept her spare key.

Adam didn't allow himself to consider what he was doing or to ask how he had let himself get to this point. He dismissed the questions before they coalesced fully, before he would have felt compelled to answer them. He focused instead on the tablet and on Claudia's thievery. When he reached Claudia's door, Adam looked around to make sure no one was there to see. He slid her nameplate to the side and took the key down from where she had taped it. Then he let himself in and closed the door behind him with a faint "click."

Over the sound of his throbbing heartbeat, Adam moved though Claudia's desk drawers and then through the drawers of her filing cabinet one after the other. The tablet wasn't there. He looked through her bookcase and even behind it. Nothing. Maybe Steven was right and she left the tablet in Israel. But even if Claudia hadn't brought the tablet back, she would have the photos.

Her desktop was password protected and Adam had no idea how to get in. He typed "Mycenae," the site that had inspired Claudia to study archaeology. He tried "Claudia1." He typed "Theodore," with several combinations of lowercase and capital letters. Nothing.

That left only one grim alternative. He let himself out and replaced Claudia's key behind the nameplate on her door. It was still early enough to catch her before she left for dinner. "All I need is the photos," he told himself. "I'll get them, and I'll get out." He repeated that to himself as he strode uptown and west.

Claudia's apartment was a ten-minute walk from the Fletcher campus. Adam made it in eight. He hadn't even considered what to tell the doorman. He only realized that as he entered her apartment building.

"Can I help you, sir?" The man asked. He was wearing a navy-blue blazer and a solid matching tie. He sat behind a desk that held a telephone and several security screens.

Adam cleared his throat and said the first words that occurred to him. "I'm here to see Dr. Renaud. Robert Derrick. She knows me. We're scheduled for dinner later this evening, but something has come up and I need to explain."

The doorman nodded. He picked up the phone and punched three numbers from memory. "Mr. Derrick to see you, Dr. Renaud. Yes. Yes." Adam tried not to look nervous. "I'll send him up." He looked at Adam. "Twelfth floor, sir. Apartment C."

Adam took the elevator to the twelfth floor, walked toward Claudia's apartment, and rang the bell. She opened the door with a brilliant smile. She was in a dark suit and she wore a lapis pendant around her neck. Adam noted the look of horror that flashed briefly across her face as she realized he was the one standing at her door.

"Hello, Claudia," Adam said. "May I come in?"

"No, you can't come in! What the hell are you doing here, Adam? I'm heading out." She looked over his shoulder as if she expected to see the provost right behind him. Adam saw that she was in her stocking-feet, her makeup half-applied.

"Sorry, Claudia. It's just me," Adam said. "I won't take up much of your time. I came to see the tablet. Then I'll go."

Claudia crossed her arms in front of her door. "Adam, get out," she said. Her voice was sharp and low. "Now. Go home. I don't have time for this. I'll call you later."

"Sure you will, Claudia," Adam said. "You've just been too busy until now." Claudia looked shocked as he pushed his way past her into the apartment.

Good, he thought. Let her be off balance for a change. "I noticed you weren't too busy to give interviews, were you, Claudia? Would it have killed you to mention that to the reporter that Maggie and I found the tablet? Did that just slip your mind? Did it slip your mind that I helped you edit your grant? Or that I brought my own money from Belmont to pay my way and Maggie's?" He let the disgust show on his face. "She really looks up to you, by the way. Did you know that? Did you consider her at all?"

Adam noted that she closed the door behind him. Evidently, she didn't want to make a scene.

"I'm not impressed by your self-righteousness," she said. Don't try to make this about your student. She dug where we told her to dig. A few weeks ago, she didn't know one end of a spade from the other."

Adam kept his tone even. "Not many undergrads would have done as well as she did," Adam said. "I know. I trained her. But if you want to make this about you, fine. It's not complicated, Claudia. You told the reporter the tablet was your find. That was bullshit. You said it was too fragile for anyone to look at. That was bullshit, too. Stop playing games with my career. You know I'm coming up for tenure. You know that! I need to publish on that tablet. I've worked too hard for too long to get ripped off."

"Your career?" Her tone was dismissive. "At Belmont? Why are we even talking about that? You don't understand what I'm offering you. It isn't just the tablet; there are other artifacts as well. For the next few years, all articles and books on the artifacts from that dig will come from Fletcher. I'm meeting with the provost tonight to talk about plans for after I take over as chair. I'm going to attract a cadre of first-class people here: the best students, the best faculty. With all that talent concentrated in one place, Fletcher is going to be the number one place in the country to study the Middle East." Her expression was importuning. "Don't blow this, Adam. This is an important opportunity for you. I'm offering you the chance to stop wasting your life and be part of something important."

Adam shook his head. "Really, Claudia? No one else can study what we found? I can't study it unless I follow you to Fletcher?"

Claudia brushed that off. "Don't be snide, Adam. It's beneath you. Who am I hurting? You? I'm doing you the biggest favor of your career. Solokov? He hasn't published anything worthwhile in years."

"And what if I'm happy where I am?" he asked. "What if don't want your favors, Claudia?" He looked in her eyes and he felt almost sorry for her. "I just don't get it. Where are your ethics? Are you this desperate for more success? What can they even promise you at this point? More accolades? A tiara? Is Derrick going to name you homecoming queen?"

Adam exhaled slowly. His eyes fell on a painting on the wall across from the couch where he had kissed her once. He had stared at that painting for a long time, then, while Claudia cried, her eyes closed, babbling about

Theodore. With only a few brushstrokes, Theodore had captured the way Claudia often stood, her weight on one hip, her hair in a ponytail just brushing her shoulder.

Theodore's paintings covered the walls of the apartment, and Adam could see Claudia somewhere in every one of the pieces. In some of them, she was off to the side or in the background. In others she was represented just by a splash of color, the particular blue of her eyes, like the blue of a flame. There she was on a dig; there, hiking in the woods; there, in the meadow in Central Park. Wherever she was, she held the viewer's eye.

Adam couldn't stand it anymore. He was through. "Enough bullshit, Claudia," he said. "I've known you too long. Don't tell me about all the favors you're doing for your department or how much you're helping me by stealing my work. It's always about you. You and your glory. It's like a drug for you, isn't it? The veneration? When Theodore died you lost your fix. And deep down, you know that no matter how successful you are, it's not going to be enough. You can tell yourself you want me in the department to buy my complicity in this farce, but that's not it. You're a star and you need an acolyte in orbit, right? You want me just close enough . . ." He felt his shoulders hunch and his chest tighten as his body folded in on itself at the thought. "No," he said. "No. Fuck you."

Adam could see the pulse throbbing in Claudia's jaw. The blood had drained from her face. "I'm telling you for the last time to get out," she said. She had inched toward the phone in the kitchen. That was fine with Adam.

"Go ahead, Claudia call the police. When they get here, I'll tell them what you've done. Maybe the press will want to hear about it. The tablet made one interesting story for them already."

She didn't reach for the phone. "Do you really think the tablet can save your career, Adam?" Claudia said. "I did want to help you, but not anymore. You're finished. You won't even be able to stay at Belmont when I'm through with you."

"What are you going to do? Call every reviewer and every publisher and tell them to blacklist me? Not everyone's your friend, Claudia." He walked toward her desk where her laptop lay open. He said, "I'm taking what's mine. Where's the tablet, Claudia? Give it to me."

"Do you think it's in my apartment?" She looked at him with incredulity, disgusted with his stupidity. "The artifacts are in Israel, you shit! You're never getting them. No one's getting them. The IAA will keep them tied up in red tape until I say to let them go."

Then it was just the photos after all. Adam felt his disappointment like a heavy weight. He could remember how the tablet felt in his hands when they had dug it up, the weight of it, its texture. He could almost feel the crevices in the clay as he ran his fingers over the letters in his mind. He took a step toward her. "The photos, Claudia. I want copies of the photos you took of the tablet—that's all. You can keep your notes. You can keep whatever you have on the other artifacts. I wasn't there for those. I'm not a thief. But I want those photos."

Adam had never seen Claudia so enraged, but Adam looked past her, to the computer sitting on her desk. He took his thumb drive out of his pocket. He thought for a moment she might move to intercept him, but he locked eyes with her and she stood fixed in place.

The chair at Claudia's desk had papers and books piled on top of it. Adam moved it aside. He dropped to his knees and slid the thumb drive into its slot in the computer. It took only a few seconds to find her recent images, copy them, and eject his drive. When he stood up, thumb drive in his hand, Claudia had her back to him. She was staring out the window, her shoulders tight.

Adam didn't say goodbye. He didn't say anything. He walked back through the apartment to the hallway. The elevator was still on Claudia's floor when he called for it. Adam could feel his heart pounding as he walked past the doorman and out into the street toward the subway station.

There were a few empty seats on the train, but Adam was too wound up to sit. He stood leaning against a pole, his thoughts chittering about his head like a swarm of bats, as the train rattled its way to the Bronx.

He told himself he'd lost nothing: a mentor who had been more than willing to sacrifice his career, a friend who betrayed him without a thought, a fantasy he had convinced himself was significant. But he felt sick.

He passed the biology building on the way to his office, and he called Steven on the phone as he walked by.

"Adam! What's up?"

"I took care of it," he said. "I got the photos."

Steven sounded surprised. "That's great! Good for you. Did she make a big scene?"

"I burned some bridges," Adam said. "It doesn't matter. It's over."

Steven asked, "Are you okay? Do you want to come by? I've got another hour or so in the lab before I can get out, but we could grab a drink or something afterwards."

"No, I'm all right," Adam said. "Just a rough afternoon. I don't feel like company right now. I'll call soon."

Big day, he thought to himself as he ascended the stairs to his office. Break into mentor's office: check. Show up at her apartment and refuse to leave: check. Sever relationship with the woman he had loved for a good chunk of his life: check.

He unlocked his office door, put down his bag, and sat down at his desk. He downloaded all the images, forcing himself not to look until they were all on his hard drive. He quickly skipped through them until he got to the lines he was most interested in reading, the ones just before and after the couplets he had been working on. He heard himself groan when he realized that the letters were too worn away for him to be able to say anything for certain about them. They were just lacunae sprinkled with the occasional letter or syllable. He rested his elbows on his desk and put his head in his hands. All for this for nothing . . . for nothing . . . He punched the table with his fist.

Adam sat for a long time without moving before he ejected his thumb drive. The only sounds were the hum of his computer and, lower, the flow of air through the ducts in his ceiling. When Adam finally put the drive back into his pocket, his hand brushed against the slip of paper that Detective Levy had given him: the one with her niece's web page and phone number. It seemed like weeks ago, he thought, but it had been just two days.

Adam stared at the paper. One more item to check off his list for the day. He typed the URL into his web browser: irenelevymusic.net. A faint, sepia photo of a Hebrew scroll made up the background of her home page. Adam stared at the writing for a few moments before he made out that the scroll was open to the final chapter of Song of Songs. Points for that, anyway. The center of the page said, "Irene Levy Music. Welcome." The menu at the top of the page offered, "About Irene," "Popular Music," "Liturgical Music," "Performances," and "Contact Irene."

Adam clicked on "About Irene." She didn't include much personal information. There was a brief, witty bio, but no photo. Adam smiled at Irene's description of her culture shock when she left New York to attend college in Michigan, where she studied composition. He read that she stayed there until moving to New York, about a year ago. She was a couple of years younger than Adam.

He clicked on "Liturgical Music" and a pull-down menu opened with a dozen songs to choose from. The first option was "Song for Sukkot (Jeremiah 2:2)." Adam knew the passage well: "I remember the devotion of your youth. You loved me like a bride and followed me in a land not sown." He clicked on the song, and a new window opened: a video. A woman, Irene presumably, was sitting at a piano in a green sundress. Adam expanded the video to full screen. The woman was shot in profile, and her light brown hair came almost to her collarbone, partially obscuring her face. Adam pressed play.

The piece began with a dense arrangement of unresolved chords that gradually grew sparser, more open. Adam shook his head, surprised, and he started the video again from the beginning. He hadn't been prepared for something so complex. And then the vocals began, warm and soulful, and for Adam, everything else disappeared. He realized only after the last of the song's Hebrew syllables had faded into silence that he had been holding his breath, his face very close to the screen.

He was about to play the song again when he decided instead to call her number. Her image still filled his computer screen.

She picked up on the fourth ring. "Hello?"

Adam cleared his throat. "Hello," he said. He hadn't planned what he was going to say. His mind went blank. "This is . . . my name is Adam Drascher. I was . . ." he cleared his throat. "Detective . . ." God, this sucked. Adam had almost forgotten how much this sucked. He told himself to start over. "I met your aunt a few days ago, Detective Levy—" A horrible thought struck him. "Wait, this is Irene, right?"

"Yes. This is Irene."

He let out a breath. That was something, anyway. "Your aunt gave me your number," he said. "Did she tell you I was going to call?"

"She thought you might," Irene said. "She didn't mention it would be this entertaining."

Adam winced. "I was hoping we could meet sometime. Maybe after the holiday, after Yom Kippur."

"I'm free Sunday," she said. "Does that work for you?"

"Sure. Sunday's good," Adam said, but he thought, Sunday was really soon. He said, "How about lunch? I could pick you up or meet you somewhere. I live in Westchester, but I have a car; I can drive. I mean, I can drive to you. Of course I can drive, or it would be pretty stupid to have a car, right?"

"It wouldn't be very practical," Irene said. At least she seems to have a sense of humor, he thought. Please let her have a sense of humor . . ."I can't do lunch," Irene said, "at least not early. We could meet in the afternoon somewhere, or we could meet for dinner if you want."

Why did that feel like a test? He said, "How about five o'clock?" and he berated himself immediately. Why did he say that? Was that supposed to be some kind of compromise between lunch and dinner? Who meets at five o'clock? Were they going to stare at each other for two hours and then go eat?

There was a pause on the phone. "All right," Irene said. Five it is." She told him the name of a bar she said was in Bayside. Adam had never heard of it.

"OK, great." Adam said. "See you then."

"Bye."

Adam pushed the off button twice to make sure he had ended the call and then he banged the phone against his forehead. He collected himself for a couple of minutes before texting Steven, "Crossed another item off my list. Date on Sunday. Talk later."

He had too much nervous energy to sit and work or even to make himself dinner. He scrubbed his sink, and toilet, and tub. He mopped his kitchen and bathroom. He even vacuumed, the chore he most disliked because he couldn't listen to music while he did it. Only then, finally, could Adam bring himself to return to the photos of the tablet.

As he organized the photos, Irene's songs playing in the background, Adam picked out several words and phrases from the tablet. Aside from the damaged lines he had focused on at first, the text was in remarkably good shape. There appeared to be a catalog of items dedicated to a temple. And he saw the word "king" appear several times. He didn't see another mention of the *Refaim*, but he did find a couple instances of *Elim*, "divine ones." Claudia was right. The tablet was rich. Now he just had to find some way to put his life back together.

Chapter 13

When the sun set, it would be The Day of Atonement, Yom Kippur. Adam showered and shaved as soon as he got home from work. He wouldn't be able to do either in the morning. He ate a simple dinner and drank several glasses of water to prepare for his fast, and then he brushed his teeth and headed out for his grandfather's temple.

When Adam entered the sanctuary, almost all the seats were filled. He scanned the room quickly and found Danny in his prayer shawl, sitting up near the front, but there were no empty seats nearby. That was all right with Adam. He would just as soon stand in the back near the door and be one of the first to leave after the service. But as he took a prayer book, an old woman with an empty seat next to her beckoned him to join her. He didn't feel he could politely refuse.

"*Shana tova*," the woman said quietly, as Adam sat down. She smiled at him. Adam nodded and smiled back. "*Shana tova*."

Standing next to Rabbi Mira at the center of the dais was Cantor Moser. He was no longer the barrel-chested giant Adam remembered. He looked stooped and frail. The cantor signaled the congregation to rise and he opened the ark, which was filled with Torah scrolls adorned with crowns and breastplates. He symbolically convened a traditional Jewish court by handing a Torah to Rabbi Mira and to a man Adam didn't know before he took one for himself. Then the cantor said, "By the authority of this court below and by the authority of the court above, it is permissible to pray with transgressors."

A hush fell over the congregation. The three figures on the dais stepped back and replaced the Torah scrolls in the ark. The rabbi flashed a smile and walked to the front of the dais as the congregation sat down. "Welcome, fellow transgressors," she said. Adam could feel some of the congregation's nervous energy dissipate as she let out a quick laugh.

She continued in a more formal tone: "For the sins between man and God, Yom Kippur atones, but for the sins between man and man, Yom Kippur does not atone unless the man appeases his fellow." Rabbi Mira paused for a moment, allowing the silence to register with the congregation before she added: "But repentance, prayer, and fasting avert the severity of the decree."

The rabbi stepped back and the cantor placed a chair next to the pulpit. A middle-aged woman in a billowy white dress ascended the steps to the dais carrying a cello and sat down. At the first stirrings of the bow against the strings, Adam closed his eyes. He had been waiting for this: Bruch's "*Kol Nidrei*." For as long as he could remember, Adam had associated Yom Kippur more strongly with the somber drones of the cello than with any other sensation, more than stillness, more than hunger, even more than regret. He leaned forward in his seat, covering his face with his hands, as the thrum of the strings pulled him out of himself and into the sacred time of Yom Kippur.

For much of the rest of the service Adam's thoughts floated disjointedly on the melodies and rhythms of the liturgy. But his focus returned when the congregation chanted their communal confessions: "We are guilty . . . For the sin which we have committed before You with knowledge

For the sin which we have committed before You in ignorance

For the sin which we have committed before You openly

For the sin which we have committed before You by deceit

For the sin which we have committed before You willfully

For the sin which we have committed before You under duress . . ."

They then sang "*Avinu Malkeinu*," "Our Father, Our King." When Adam was young, the cantor sang the song alone, but now, perhaps because his voice had lost so much of its resonance, the congregation sang with him at the prayer's refrain, adding their strength to his. As Adam left the service, the words still sang in his head, "Have mercy on us, pardon us . . ."

Adam got home late and fell asleep reading. The next morning, he arrived back at the temple in a crush of people and he grabbed the only empty seat in a pew a couple of rows from the back. He disappeared into the prayers until the reading from Isaiah deriding superficial fasts, empty of ethical content. Adam kept his book closed in front of him as he let the words pour over him: "Is not this the kind of fast I have chosen: to loose the chains of injustice . . . to set the oppressed free . . . to share your food with the hungry . . . to provide the poor wanderer with shelter . . . when you see the naked, to clothe them . . . and not to turn away from your own flesh and blood?"

Just before returning the Torah to the ark, the congregation recited the prayer for healing the sick. Then, the rabbi spoke. "In a couple of weeks" she said, "we will read in the Torah, 'It is not good for humans to be alone.' That may be the one statement in the Torah that I've never doubted. Loneliness and isolation are wounds, and everyone needs healing. That's part of what it means to be human. We spend our whole lives seeking connection through friendship, romance, work, prayer, study. I hope some of you have found connections here, in this place, as I have. I hope you feel connected today, as you look around this sanctuary."

The rabbi cleared her throat. "Some of you may have noticed that I'm expecting child number three." A number of people in the congregation laughed. Even in her white robe, she looked ready to burst. "You can imagine that when it came time to write a sermon for today, this is what I kept coming back to. A new human life! A new soul on the planet, experiencing everything for the first time, carrying our hopes for the future, accepting our love as a matter of course, as if it were his due, which, of course, it is; a baby full of flesh and trust and little else—a trust that we couldn't do other than love him. And yet, even that trust is a falling off from the state of absolute connectedness the fetus experienced in the womb, where no trust was necessary, where there was no such concept as 'trust' because we belonged to the same body.

"We all know that birth is a miracle. The days that my first two children were born were the most incredible of my life, so those aren't empty words to me. But birth is also a disconnection, a wound, an exile. When we are born, we are pushed from the womb and the umbilical cord is severed. We are in diaspora. We are cut off from the physical connection to our ancestors and the heritage that nourishes us, and there is no wound more profound than that.

"Maybe that's the reason the Bible describes a good death as one in which we are gathered to our ancestors. Perhaps that's an expression of the hope that, in death, even that first injury, that separation, can be healed. But I believe that healing is a life-long process and that we need to be gathered in every day. The bonds we share with each other and with God can be terribly damaged, but they can never be fully severed. We don't have to wait for another life in another world.

"Today, together, we confess our shortcomings as a community in covenant with God. These transgressors you're praying with? Don't worry, we're all praying with you, too. In community, we heal each other. Every moment calls out for us to be gathered in, in wholeness, with healing, with *refua shalema.*"

The crowd filed out slowly, families staying together but greeting other families on their way out. Adam looked for Danny. He had kept away from him for over a week, since Rosh Hashana, and he felt he needed to say something. Finally, he saw him come down the front steps and he called out to him. Danny turned his head and waved as he made his way to Adam through the mob of people. "How are you doing, Danny?" Adam asked. "Are you headed home?"

Danny took Adam's arm and pulled him in close so he could speak quietly as they crossed the street together. "It's good to see you Adam. Walk me back to the motel, okay? Fasting never agreed with me. In about an hour, I'm going to have a raging headache and I'll try to sleep it off." Adam nodded and he and Danny crossed the street so they could get away from the throng. "I thought you were avoiding me," Danny said.

"No. No," Adam said, avoiding Danny's eyes. "It's just been a crazy time." After a couple of paces, he added, "Detective Cheng paid me a visit."

Danny looked up. "What did he want?"

"To threaten me. He told me Calloway and Rose are going to come after me. They think I helped you attack Calloway, or at least that's what they're saying."

Danny looked horrified. "Shit, Adam, that's so unfair! If it weren't for you, Calloway would be in a lot worse shape than he's in now."

Adam bit the inside of his lip as he rejected the first several replies he wanted to make. "I need you to make this go away, Danny," he said, finally. "I don't have time for this. Cheng said he was going to drag me through the newspapers. I don't have the money for lawyers . . ."

"It won't cost you a dime!" Danny said. "Not a dime. I'll pay our lawyer if it comes to that. We just have to stick together."

Adam shook his head. "Make it go away, Danny. Don't ask me to testify to a lie."

"I'll do what I can, okay? But we need to keep a united front."

Adam knew that was as far as he was going to get that day. He asked how Henry was doing since Danny moved out.

Danny brightened at the mention of his son. "He's good. He's good. I've been seeing him every day. That's what keeps me sane." They were at Danny's motel now. "So, Adam," he said, "are you going to be at services for *Kaddish* later on?"

"Of course. Why?"

Danny looked relieved. "Well, for Hank, I mean. I might not feel well enough to make it, but if you're saying *Kaddish*, that's okay. It's covered."

"What do you mean, covered? What about the rest of the time? Have you been saying *Kaddish*?"

"Well, yeah. I wasn't sure you'd be doing it, and I thought someone should, so . . . why are you upset?"

Adam couldn't respond. He knew how it would sound if he said what he felt: that *kaddish* was his job and he was sick of Danny's always pushing his way in. So he said nothing. He felt ashamed. Finally, he said, "I don't know. I don't know. I don't even make sense to myself sometimes. I should go. We'll talk next week. I'll give you a call, okay?"

Danny looked concerned. "I'm sorry you're upset," he said.

"I'm sorry I'm upset, too."

Adam walked from Danny's motel out to Northern Boulevard and then west toward the city. He had never had much use for the first part of the Yom Kippur afternoon services. Many of the prayers were the same as in the morning, and the Torah reading was a text he had taught many times.

When Adam was almost at the Cross Island Parkway, the rich smell of mud and decay told him he was passing the Alley Pond Environmental Center. He lifted his head and saw the tops of the tall bearded reeds growing out of the bog, bent and swaying in the slight breeze like worshippers. Some of the reeds were broken and lay on their sides, half submerged in the mud of the wetlands.

Danny was insatiable, he thought. He was endlessly entitled. There was nothing he wouldn't demand of him, right or wrong: Babysit for me . . . save me from the police . . . deal with my wife . . . give me your grandfather . . . give me your father, who you barely had yourself . . . It was too much.

He entered the park without consciously deciding to, and he was instantly in another world, wild and eerie, hidden in plain sight in the middle of the city. Adam hadn't been there in many years, since high school biology, but he remembered it well. There were hiking trails filled with insects, and frogs, and birds. There were footbridges and acres of swamp grasses growing alongside and within brackish water.

The air was thick with putrefaction. Adam heard the soles of his shoes squelch when he lifted his feet, and when he looked down, he saw that they were soiled from his first steps, but he kept on, stepping as carefully as he could so as not to muddy his pants.

He thought of *Shahat*, the word from the tablet that meant decay, destruction, the Underworld. The ancient Canaanites were surrounded by deserts, but they pictured the underworld as a swamp. A desert is pristine, and for the Canaanites, death wasn't sterile; it was rot. It was mud. The underworld teemed with life that thrives on corruption. *UmiShahat mi yigaleni*, he thought, who will redeem me from this swamp?

Danny presumed on their relationship as if they were brothers, Adam thought, and he resented it even though he knew they might be, even though his resentment made him petty in his own eyes.

"Do not turn away from your flesh and blood," Isaiah said. Maybe Rose was right about him being a snob, he thought. He wouldn't have felt this way if it were Steven who might be his brother. He would have accepted those claims. He already felt them in any case, without any blood connection.

Adam knew what his grandfather would say. He would have said, "We don't choose family, and thank God. They're ours forever, regardless of anything. No matter what." His grandfather didn't even know Steven, but that had been his response when Adam told him about Steven getting kicked out of his house. They were in their junior year. They were roommates. Steven had come out to his friends at college that year one and two at a time, starting with Adam. They had been close since freshman year, or as close as Steven got to people before he came out. Adam was surprised at first, but in retrospect he thought he should have seen it. Steven's family was less understanding. They told him not to come home. Adam told him he would talk to his grandfather; he was sure Steven could stay with them for the summer. After all, Danny practically lived there half the time, and who the hell was Danny?

"His parents kicked him out?" his grandfather asked, over the phone. He sounded sickened, his voice thin, as if he could barely bring himself to speak the words.

"Yeah. They found out he was gay. They won't talk to him. Steven's okay. He says it's their loss."

"He's wrong," Adam's grandfather said. He spoke quietly, but Adam could hear his anger from the intensity of his speech, from the emphasis he put into every word. "It's everyone's loss," he said. "How do you disown a child? Your child?" Adam had rarely heard him like that. "Do they know how blessed they are to have a child? Do they understand what God gave them? To cut off your own child, out of self-righteousness . . ." Adam could picture his grandfather's fist clenched tightly around the phone, his knuckles white.

"Let me tell you something, Adam," he said, "I hope you already know it." His voice was the familiar growl now, like a lion's purr. "You're mine forever. There's nothing you could do that would change that. I don't care who you fuck. I don't care if you kill someone. You're mine even when we're both dead. That's it." He paused and Adam even remembered the pause, remembered hearing him cough and wondering if his grandfather's throat was as constricted as Adam's was.

"Everyone needs a home," his grandfather said. "Tell your friend if he needs a place, he can stay. Look at Danny. He needs a place sometimes, and whenever he does, he belongs here, too."

With the back of his hand, Adam brushed away the tears summoned by the memory of the call. He remembered the look on Steven's face when he invited him to stay that summer. Steven had been the only person Adam had ever told about what it was like living in that apartment where the sadness was so thick that Adam wondered sometimes if an outsider would be able to breathe there. In the end, Steven had won a paid internship in Berkeley for the summer and he hadn't needed to take Adam up on his offer. But to be welcomed and accepted made an enormous difference to him, he told Adam much later. It had helped him to accept himself when his parents chose not to.

His grandfather's words rang in Adam's memory, a rebuke: "Danny belongs here, too." He felt ashamed when he thought about his grandfather's openness, about his intuitive understanding of the need people have for belonging. Again, Adam's thoughts returned to the verses from the tablet that had been running in a loop in his mind for so long. "I am cut off . . ." To be cut off . . . Was that never to be gathered in, to have no home with the Healers? If it were up to his grandfather, Adam thought, no one would be cut off. They would all be linked together, the living and the dead.

Adam's grandfather knew how different he and Adam were, but it didn't matter to him. Adam was his, everything about him: his obscure passions, his friends, his moods. Adam remembered his grandfather's reaction at his thesis defense for his PhD. He sat there, enraptured. Afterwards, he took Adam aside, pride glowing in his eyes. "I didn't understand a word of it, Adam, not a word, but you're one of them! You taught them things they never thought of before, things that I guess no one ever thought of before!" He embraced him. "I hope someday you can feel what I'm feeling, Adam. It's indescribable." Even now, Adam could almost feel the strength in his grandfather's arms when they were wrapped around him.

Adam was on one of the footbridges now. He looked out along the clear stream that ran through the wetlands toward the sound. For most of his life, he could see now, he had thought of his grandfather as always in mourning. His view of his grandfather had gotten stuck, like a skeleton preserved in a tar pit. Living with his grandfather, watching him, grieving with him, somehow all Adam had been able to see was the old man's sorrow.

His grandfather had lost his son and his wife, Adam thought. He had Adam. And he had Danny. Danny had loved just to sit there in the apartment, telling stories, spending time, watching television. For Danny, the apartment had been a place where he was rooted and loved. For Adam, even though he loved his grandfather and knew he owed him everything, the apartment was suffocating. His grandfather's grief was suffocating. Adam could almost smell it every time his grandfather exhaled. But somehow Adam had managed to miss that his grandfather had wanted to go on living as much as Adam did, that he was trying to grope his way forward without letting go of his devotion to the family he had lost.

Adam saw now how badly his grandfather would have wanted him to share in his life. How, how could he not have listened when his grandfather mentioned Vivian? How could he never have asked about her? Worst of all, how had he never tried to understand what his grandfather saw in Danny?

Adam leaned against the handrail on the bridge and closed his eyes. He could feel the pressure of the bridge pushing up through his feet, his ankles, his knees.

It began as little more than a wish, a hope that they'd all be all right. It started with Henry, with thinking of Henry on his grandfather's lap, of their delight in each other, of Henry's smile, which was like the smile of no one else ever in Danny's family. And then, somehow, Adam was praying. He prayed for Henry, and Danny, and Rose. He prayed for Calloway. He prayed for Vivian, whom he had never met and whom he had not invited to his grandfather's funeral. He prayed for Maggie. He prayed for Steven and Todd and the mother who might give them a child. And he prayed for forgiveness: for his blindness, for his judgments, for his self-absorption, for the rage he had felt at Claudia.

When Adam opened his eyes, his mind felt empty. He watched the dragonflies darting over the marsh for a while before he felt ready to return to services. He made his way back to the park entrance where he used leaves and twigs to scrape the mud from his shoes as best he could before he headed out onto Northern Boulevard.

When he got back to the temple, Adam cleaned up more thoroughly in the bathroom before he took a seat. His muscles were warm and wooden, saturated with fatigue. When it was time to stand for the *Kaddish*, the words flowed from him like water from a full sponge.

At the end of the concluding service, the rabbi stood up one last time to address the congregation. On the walls, high above her, Adam saw the colors of the stained-glass windows faintly illuminated by the light of the setting sun. The rabbi's voice was hoarse and weary, and Adam wondered how much more difficult it was for her to fast when she was pregnant. "The day is almost over," she said. "Dusk approaches, and when it comes, Yom Kippur will be at an end. In a few moments, we will chant the *havdalah* prayer, and we will reenter everyday time. We've done difficult work together," she said, "but the real struggle begins then, when evening falls and we have to figure out how not to pick up our old selves and put them on again."

Chapter 14

It was a nightclub, it's neon color scheme aggressive and out of place in daylight. Irene was seated at the bar in a white V-necked blouse, her profile to the door. Her hands were clasped around a nearly empty glass. Though Irene's light brown hair was cut shorter than it had been in the video, Adam had no trouble recognizing her.

She looked nervous, Adam thought. Well, he was nervous too. He hadn't been on a date since the spring, and that experience had been typically horrible: small talk, miscommunications, and an early night. He took a breath and strode toward her. Irene's choice of meeting place didn't bode well, he thought. Mechanized beats and auto-tuned voices blurted from speakers that were mounted high on the walls. Across from the bar, Adam could see an unmanned DJ station under a circle of unlit spotlights. There wasn't much of a crowd, Adam thought, but then, the bar wasn't doing much to attract the day drinkers who might be interested in showing up early on a Sunday evening.

As he approached Irene, Adam had to swerve to avoid another patron who was backing up into his path. Before he could congratulate himself on his agility, he banged his right knee hard against a low table. He gritted his teeth and prayed she hadn't noticed, "You must be Irene," he shouted above the music. "I'm Adam."

Irene laughed and took his hand. "Very pleased to meet you," she said. She also shouted to be heard "Are you all right?" Even in the dim lighting, Adam could see she had the same penetrating gaze as her aunt.

Adam looked suspiciously at the bar before he leaned against it, as if it might roll out from under him. "Absolutely," he said. The volume of the music suddenly plummeted as the vocals and most of the instruments dropped out. Only synthesized trebly beeps remained to keep the pulse.

"I'm actually very graceful in my mind," he said. "Like Fred Astaire."

"But only in your mind?"

"So it would seem." The bass returned. He shouted, "What would you like to drink?"

A strand of her hair fell forward, and she absently brushed it back from her face. "I was just finishing my soda," she said, "and you've already almost fallen down. Should we just get a soda for you, too?"

"Sodas are fine with me," he said. "You don't drink?"

"Not much."

She must have seen his puzzled expression. "Why did I suggest a bar, then," she asked, "especially one this horrible?" She offered a quick smile and took his arm. "Come," she said. "I think it's a little quieter over there." She shepherded him toward the door. It was somewhat better. "I don't like to waste time," she said. "Some guys have trouble turning down a drink, or they can't stop after one or two. As for this place in particular, a friend recommended it. She's very hip. I'm not."

Canny and forthright were qualities Adam had always appreciated. "How about coffee instead, then?" Adam asked. "Or dinner if you're up for it. Would that be too much pressure for a first date?"

"I could eat," Irene said. "I know a place not far from here. Let's go."

Adam followed her out to the relative quiet of the street. Irene walked quickly and Adam had to angle his body as they passed through the crowd of pedestrians on the sidewalk in order to stay close to her.

As they turned a corner, Irene said, "I'm not really clear on how you and Aunt Sue met."

Adam didn't know what the detective had told her, but he had his answer ready. "She came to my office to ask me some questions related to a case she's working on," he said.

"She told me you're a professor. Did she want you for your expertise?"

Adam shook his head. "I'm an archaeologist; I'm not an expert in anything that's happened in the last twenty-five hundred years."

They stopped at the next corner to wait for the walk signal and Irene turned to look at him. "Well, you got her attention somehow," she said. "I hope you don't think I typically use the criminal justice system as my personal dating service. When Aunt Sue told me she met someone through work, I was pretty skeptical. I told her I'm not up for dating a cop. 'Don't worry,' she said. 'I know better than that. You don't have the temperament for that.' So, I said, 'What is he, then, a suspect? I was joking of course. Do you want to guess what she said?"

Adam definitely didn't want to guess.

"She said, you were a witness, mostly." Her tone was conversational, but she looked at him intently. "What does that mean? What's mostly?"

Adam didn't know what to say. The walk signal flashed and they crossed the street.

Irene stopped at the corner to face Adam. "I have to warn you," she said, "I got over my bad boy phase a long time ago. Are you in some kind of trouble? Because I'm not interested in any of that."

Adam shook his head. "I'm mild mannered. Really. An angel."

She gave him a skeptical look. "An angel, huh? What's the worst thing you've ever done?"

He hesitated as he pictured his grandfather, alone in his apartment, sick.

"Don't think about it," she said. "Just answer."

He tried to keep it light. "I've kept a secret I shouldn't have. Maybe two. I'm not sure."

She looked into his eyes. "That's the worst thing you've ever done? Keeping secrets?"

"It's the worst thing I've done this month," he said, "which covers anything your aunt might be interested in."

Irene nodded, her eyes still locked onto his. She gestured with her chin. "We're here," she said. "I hope you like Thai food."

"Who doesn't like Thai food?" He opened the door and followed her inside. It was a nice place, he thought, dimly lit, with dark, hardwood tables and waiters dressed in white shirts and black pants. The smell of ginger made him hungry despite the hour. A waitress came by with two menus and seated them at a table near the window.

While they scanned the menu, Irene asked, "So why did Sue give you my number? She couldn't have just suggested it out of the blue."

"She pretty much did," Adam said. "It surprised me. She said she had a feeling. She was very persuasive. She gave me your phone number and the URL of your website and she told me to call. She said you were very talented."

Irene held her face in her hands. "That's mortifying!"

"She was right, though," Adam said. "I listened to your music. You are really talented."

Irene looked at him, her head at an angle. She was weighing his sincerity, Adam thought. "Which song did you listen to?" she asked.

Adam was surprised at the question. "All of them."

"All of them?" She looked dubious.

"Do you want me to hum them?" He smiled.

The waitress came and took their orders: a salad and green curried tofu for Irene, spring rolls and chicken satay for Adam.

"Where did you get the idea for using the Jeremiah passage for a *Sukkot* song?" Adam asked. "That was my favorite."

She let out a short, quiet breath. "That felt really right. I wanted to do a song for the holiday, but I couldn't relate to all the agricultural stuff. What do I know about farming, right? I grew up not far from here. I couldn't exactly see myself writing about a fruit harvest. But the wilderness, the romance of it, that I thought I could understand."

"You know, the next line, which you didn't sing, does refer to the fruit harvest."

Irene laughed. "OK. You caught me. The song is a little bit about farming. But only if you know the parts I didn't sing." She spoke quickly. "The ending wasn't too much? I thought it might be melodramatic the way I held the last note. I had an idea for an alternate ending . . ."

"No, it was perfect. It was beautiful."

"You're flattering me," she said. "But I like it."

"I loved all of it. The pop songs, the liturgical stuff . . . even the background shot of the Song of Songs scroll was a great choice."

She smiled. "I didn't think anyone would pick that up. That's one for Aunt Sue. I'm glad she suggested this."

"Me too," Adam said. "I've always done very well with grandmothers and aunts."

"She was very insistent." Irene lowered her voice to a rasp that approximated Detective Levy's. "She said, 'Don't be a pill, Irene, I'm telling you he's your type. He listens to crazy music, he's read a lot of books, and he's written a few. I saw them on his shelf. He's polite, but he's got a sense of humor if you listen for it. And he goes to temple on the high holidays." She laughed.

Adam smiled. "Is that all?" he asked.

Irene blushed. She tried to lower her voice again, but her vocal cords were too taut now. "He's pretty cute, and he's tall enough; you could wear heels." Her voice broke as she snorted. She covered her mouth at the sound.

Adam laughed. He said, "I did mention to her at one point that I babysat. That seemed to go over well."

She winced. "I can see how it might have." After a pause, she asked, "Was archaeology something you always knew you wanted to do?"

"I probably got the idea when I saw the Indiana Jones movies as a kid. I'd bet a shocking percentage of archaeologists have a brown fedora up in their closet somewhere."

"There's probably not as much swashbuckling as you pictured at first, huh?"

"There's not much," Adam admitted, "but I wouldn't say there's none. And even when times are slow for swashbuckling, you get a certain amount of skullduggery. Academic politics can get pretty ugly." He thought of Claudia in her apartment, her back to Adam, her shoulders rigid as he downloaded his photos. For a moment, he lost his stomach for banter and he looked at his empty water glass.

The waitress brought all the food at once and they agreed to share with a gesture and a nod.

"Do you spend a lot of time in Israel?"

"I try to go most years, but I can't always manage it. More and more, I've been focused on the stuff I can do closer to home. Part of the thrill used to be not knowing what you'd find once you started digging, but as tenure gets closer, uncertainty is losing its appeal. I don't like the fishing expedition aspect of the work as much as I used to. What about you?" he asked. "Did you always want to write religious music?"

Irene shook her head. She answered him slowly, between bites. "I studied jazz and composition in college, and I've always played piano. I grew up listening to soul music and R&B and lots of 60s and 70s pop. Mom is a big Carole King fan. When I was in college, I majored in music, and I started listening to everything I could get my hands on, and I worked as a music counselor at a Jewish camp. That's when I started writing Jewish music."

She paused as she used her fork to mix her curry into her rice. "I initially had this fantasy that I'd put up the site and people would suddenly feel the need to commission new Jewish liturgical music. That didn't happen, so I diversified a bit. I'm teaching religious school and *b'nei mitzvah* classes. And I've gotten a couple of regular gigs playing in bars and a few small weddings, so that's helped to pay the bills. And I write when I can. I have a small piano in my apartment, and I try to write every day."

Irene's phone rang, and Adam saw her bite her lip as she looked at her purse. He nodded for her to go ahead and take the call. She looked at her phone and immediately silenced it and put it away. She looked upset. "I'm sorry," she said. "I would never usually have my phone on during a date, but I auditioned for a job singing at a restaurant once a month and they said they might call me back tonight. I think they liked me, and I need the work.

"Then I hope that wasn't them." Adam said. "You could have taken the call."

"No. That was Brian, my ex-husband." She fiddled with her fork. "Talking about your ex-husband is probably the classic ridiculous first date behavior, right?" Adam didn't answer. He felt like he could read Irene's emotions as they flew by: anxious, annoyed, self mocking, annoyed again. "OK," she said. "Real quick, only because it's such an absurd story. We almost never speak. We separated over a year ago. The divorce was finalized in June. He called out of the blue earlier today to tell me he's going through a 12-step program and he's supposed to ask forgiveness from the people he hurt. Apparently, I made the list."

"Congratulations?"

She offered a wry smile. "He never did get around to asking forgiveness. That plan got derailed when he shared his theory that if I were more supportive during our marriage then maybe he wouldn't have had to drink quite so much or cheat on me quite so often."

Adam winced. "It doesn't sound like twelve steps is going to cut it. Do they have thirteen or fourteen step programs?"

Irene flashed a rueful smile. "There's an upside, I guess. Think how easy it would be for you to look good by comparison. Besides, in a way, Brian helped get me here. I was getting cold feet before our date, but there was no way I was going to sit at home after that phone call." She finished off her water. "What were we talking about before I so rudely took out my phone?"

"We were talking about your music," Adam said. "I was about to ask if you ever thought about becoming a cantor."

She paused. She seemed uncertain of how much to say next. "Until this year, I could never have even considered it. Brian wasn't really respectable by temple standards. By any standards. I did take a couple of courses at Hebrew Union, and that was great, but what I l really love is composing. I'm not sure I'm cut out for working full-time in a congregation."

She looked at Adam thoughtfully. "So, speaking of congregations, where are you on the whole religion thing?" Adam hesitated for a moment, and Irene continued, "I know, I know. Religion isn't exactly a first date topic, but since I already ran off at the mouth about my ex, let's go with it. There couldn't be many spiritually inclined archaeologists, right?"

Adam took a bite of his chicken to buy time. She had to be the most direct person he'd ever met. "Well, there aren't a lot of literalists, if that's what you mean," he said. "Everything in the Bible before the monarchy is pretty dicey if you're looking for facts."

Irene smiled. "You're ducking the question," she said. "I asked if you're religious."

"How is your curry?" Adam asked.

Irene just looked at him.

"OK," he said. "I'll play, but you go first."

Irene absently pulled a cube of tofu through her sauce with her chopsticks. "Fair." She said. "All right." She dabbed at her mouth with her napkin. "Do you know that feeling when everything you see seems to be in focus and the air is so rich, when it fills your lungs, it's almost . . . nourishing? And you feel like everything fits, and you fit? I've only felt that really powerfully a few times, but when it happens, you feel really, profoundly grateful. At least, that's how I felt."

"I think you can appreciate a great feeling without necessarily believing in God," Adam said.

Irene nodded. "Of course you can. You can savor something without feeling grateful for it. But this was different. I felt like saying 'Thank you.'

But I don't think you can be grateful without being grateful to someone. So I guess I'm religious at least some of the time."

"What about the rest of the time?"

"Those are the times I think I'm at my best. I'd rather define myself by what I am at my best." She reached for her glass and sipped her water.

After waiting a moment for Adam to respond on his own, she said, "It's your turn. You can stroke your chin as long as you want, but you still haven't answered my question."

Adam felt his face turn red. He didn't feel ready to talk about this. "I'd probably give you a different answer if you asked me on a different day."

She peered at him intently.

"Maybe it was the fasting," he said, "or maybe I'm just especially susceptible to Yom Kippur music."

There was that head tilt again. "Don't worry," Adam said. I didn't have a vision or anything. I was walking. I usually walk on Yom Kippur. And I just felt like something that was stuck got loosened a bit. Like when you get over the flu and you realize you can take deep breaths again, or like when you're hiking and you take off your pack to look around. It's hard to explain. It already feels almost like it happened to someone else." He looked carefully at her expression. He thought she understood. He wasn't sure.

They chatted for a while about Queens and the neighborhoods where they had grown up. When Adam looked up, he saw that the restaurant was now full and people were waiting by the door. He looked for some signal from Irene, but she didn't offer any. "Do you want to go somewhere else for dessert?" he asked. "We could look for a café or something if you're up for it."

"Sure. That sounds good. There's a place I know not far from here."

Adam asked for the check. When the waitress returned with it, Irene picked up her purse, but Adam gestured that he had it. After he paid, he and Irene walked out. It was drizzling now, and growing dark, or at least the sun was down. Adam could still easily make his way by the red and orange lights of the shop windows and the white headlights from the oncoming cars. The light mist wasn't unpleasant, but it had thinned out the crowd somewhat, and Adam and Irene could walk comfortably side by side in the soft air.

They had been walking for a while when Irene slowed as they turned a corner.

Adam asked, "Where are we headed?"

She frowned and shrugged. "I'm not sure. I thought there was a pastry and coffee place on this street, but I don't see it." She looked across the street and back toward the direction they had started from. "I don't know. That's really too bad. I liked that place, but I guess they closed. Are you up for a walk? My apartment's not too far away. I have some ice cream in my freezer."

Adam smiled. Ice cream was on the short list of things Adam wanted very much. He gestured for Irene to lead the way.

When they got to Irene's corner, she took Adam's hand and peered down the alley adjacent to her building.

"Did you lose something?" He asked.

"No," she said. "My neighbor, Elizabeth, broke up with her boyfriend a few weeks ago. It was pretty ugly. Lots of shouting. I found out a few days later that he had hit her. She had been hiding it. I've caught him skulking out here at night twice this week. It's very creepy."

"Can't you just get your aunt to handle it?" Adam asked. "I would have thought having relatives on the police force would be very useful for something like that."

Irene shook her head. "I wanted to, but Elizabeth said no. He's always texting her to take him back. I'm afraid she might. She's only twenty-four, and this was her first serious relationship. I like Elizabeth a lot, but when it comes to Jonah, she can be a real idiot. Anyway, it doesn't matter. He's not here and I haven't seen him in a while. Maybe he found someone else to stalk."

They walked up the steps to her building and Irene pulled her keys out of her purse and unlocked the front door. They walked up four stories and came out onto a brightly lit hallway that opened into three apartments. "They're renovating that one," she said, pointing to the door without a welcome mat. It'll go fast. It has more than one room." Irene opened her apartment and Adam followed her inside. Her studio held a bed, an upright piano, a small, overstuffed easy chair, and a couple of bookshelves with no room to spare. Irene walked over to the refrigerator in the kitchen area, a nook that together with the small bathroom took up one wall of the apartment. She opened the freezer and pulled out three pints of ice cream. "Today we're featuring coffee, chocolate, and strawberry," She said. "Do you need time to think it over?"

"No need—I'd love some chocolate," Adam said.

Irene nodded. "Excellent choice, but then there are no wrong answers when it comes to ice cream." She pulled down two short glasses and a couple of spoons and scooped out a generous serving of chocolate for Adam and a small scoop of each flavor for herself. She gestured for Adam to sit in the chair and she turned the piano bench so that she could straddle it to sit facing him. "My next question, though, is terribly fraught. What kind of music do you most like to listen to?"

"That's kind of an intimidating question coming from a musician, isn't it?"

She shrugged.

"It's not like I can ask you about your favorite archaeological find, is it?" he asked.

She arched her eyebrows. "You're stalling again. You're a staller." She leaned forward and looked into Adam's eyes. It was very distracting.

"I'm a big Miles Davis fan," he said.

She looked skeptical.

"Don't look at me like that. I am. I love his fusion stuff. And the second quintet. Hancock . . . Shorter . . ." He paused. She was listening, anyway. "I guess Mingus might be my favorite," he said. "Even when he's leading a large group, you feel like you're hearing something from his soul."

She slid forward to the end of the piano bench and kissed Adam very lightly on the mouth, taking him by surprise. Adam moved forward and opened his eyes; he hadn't consciously closed them. But by then Irene had already stood up and moved her bench back to the piano.

"Come back," he said.

She smiled and sat down at the piano. "Soon. I think you might be interested in this." She played a simple, rhythmic bass figure with her left hand, insistent and repeating. It sounded very familiar to Adam, but he didn't place it right away out of context. Irene's right hand played a scattering of notes, slow at first, then faster, though the bass never changed tempo. After almost a minute, her right hand slipped into a counter melody that complemented the bass, and she began to sing. Her voice was soft and low, and in place of words, she scat-sang in the Hasidic style. Then, her voice trailed away, followed by the counter-melody, and finally the bass.

"You wrote that?"

"I did."

"It has such a specific mood. Is it a prayer?"

Irene bit her lip. "It is," she murmured. She looked down at her piano. "The abstract part with all those high notes was supposed to be reminiscent of raindrops. I'm still not sure about that bit."

"I liked it," Adam whispered.

"It's for an old, old prayer for rain," she said.

Adam nodded. Irene leaned in toward him. Her blouse opened slightly, but Adam saw only a shadow. "I'll tell you a secret," she said. She smelled like lavender with a hint of hot pepper, maybe from the Thai food. He had to restrain himself from reaching for her. "I cheated a little," she whispered. I stole the bass line from Cannonball Adderley's version of 'Autumn Leaves.' When you mentioned Miles Davis, I thought you might appreciate it."

"I do."

"Then you get another kiss."

Adam pulled her onto his lap and ran his fingers through her soft hair. He kissed her neck and she laughed. "Slow, slow . . ." he told himself. "You stole it?" he whispered the question.

She slipped off her shoes and pulled her legs up into the chair with Adam. She kissed his lips again, and he reached for her breast. She took a quick breath and held his wrists in front of her. Her fingers couldn't close around them. "I covered my tracks," she said, "I changed it a little, but the piece needed that driving . . ."

Adam kissed her. She slid her hands up to his palms and kissed the backs of his fingers. "You have to answer one more question," she said.

Adam brought his hands in close and kissed her fingers. He kissed her mouth again. "You've been testing me all night," he said. He kissed her on her neck, near her collarbone.

She kissed him back. "It's not working out too badly for you so far, is it?"

He put his arms around her waist, and she looked into his eyes from just a few inches away. When she whispered, he could feel her breath. "What was the secret you kept that you shouldn't have?" she asked. She brushed his lips with hers. She slowly unbuttoned her shirt. Adam could see the curves of her breasts through her lacy bra as she leaned forward.

He ran the tips of his fingers along her collarbone. He spoke almost in a whisper. "It doesn't matter," he said. "It's nothing." He leaned forward to kiss her, but she laughed and moved just out of reach.

She kissed his neck. Her hair covered her face, but he could hear the smile in her voice. "How about you let me be the judge of that?"

"I swear I'm not going to remember another thing as long as that shirt stays on," he said.

She laughed. "Have you got a condom?"

"No."

"Me either. But I think I know where I can get one. Hold on." She slid down from Adam's lap, buttoned up again and walked into the hallway. Adam got up and looked through the peephole and watched as Irene knocked on a neighbor's door. A tall blonde woman about twenty-five years old answered. They were speaking quietly, but Adam could hear the other woman saying "Good for you, Irene!" The woman went back into her apartment for a minute and handed something to Irene when she came back. Adam returned to the chair before Irene returned.

"You're in luck!" She held up the condom. "This is from Elizabeth, but she drove a hard bargain. It was her last one, and she insisted on a full report. Anyway, she could use a good story. We should try not to disappoint her."

Adam walked over to her and put his arms around her waist. She pressed her breasts against his chest. "Couldn't you exaggerate a bit if you needed to, just to help her out?"

"I don't think so. I'm a very honest person." Irene unbuttoned his shirt while he kissed her and then she removed her own. Adam grinned when she took off her bra

"What?" She covered her chest with her arms.

"A spiritual moment," Adam said. "I'm feeling very grateful."

She laughed and fell backward onto the bed, pulling Adam with her.

Chapter 15

"Adam? Adam?"

Adam woke slowly from a heavy sleep, his arm draped over Irene's thigh and his hand resting in the smooth space behind her knee. He remembered climbing back into bed with her after brushing his teeth with his finger, feeling the warm curves of her body against his, kissing her shoulders and the back of her neck as they drifted off to sleep. He smiled at the smell of her shampoo on his pillow, and he gently squeezed her leg as he drifted back to sleep.

"Adam! Wake up." She shook him.

"Is it morning?"

She was sitting up in bed, listening. It sounded to Adam like someone was pounding on a door out in the hallway. Not on Irene's door. He found his glasses and checked his watch. It was a little after two a.m.

Irene tiptoed across the room and looked out her peephole. "It's Jonah," she whispered. "We have to do something."

He was still a little groggy. Jonah . . . Jonah . . . That was the boyfriend. The stalker. Fantastic. "She locks her door, right?" Adam asked. He couldn't remember her neighbor's name.

Jonah was shouting now. His voice was hoarse. He sounded enraged. "I'd better not find you with anyone! Do you hear me, you fucking slut?"

A woman's voice answered, the neighbor, Adam assumed. Elizabeth. Her name was Elizabeth, he remembered. "Go away, Jonah!" she yelled. She sounded terrified. "Please, just leave my key and go away. I don't want to see you."

"You're gonna see me. Open the fucking door before I open it myself!"

Irene reached for her phone and dialed 911. "I'm calling the police."

Adam moved quickly. He felt no hint of drowsiness now. He slipped on his pants and shoes and pulled on his shirt, dimly aware of Irene giving her name and address to the person on the other end of her call, her voice deep in the background, almost drowned out by the pounding in his chest. He moved toward the door, his buttons still undone. Irene looked up at him. "You're not going out there?" she asked.

"How long before they get here? Five minutes? Ten? A lot can happen in that time." He unlatched the chain. "I'll just let Jonah know he's not alone up here and the police are coming. Maybe he'll go away."

Irene thought for half a second before she nodded to Adam and then turned her attention back to the phone. Adam went into the hallway and closed the door behind him.

Jonah stood in the hallway, unshaven and wild-eyed. He had at least thirty pounds on Adam and he was several inches taller. He looked to Adam as if he hadn't slept in a long time and wouldn't need to sleep for even longer. Steven would have known if Jonah was on drugs, Adam thought, and what kind. Steven would probably have told Adam to get the hell back in Irene's apartment, for that matter.

Jonah had unlocked Elizabeth's door and had left his key jammed in the lock. His foot was wedged in the narrow opening delimited by the chain on her door.

Adam approached slowly, as he would approach an animal. He rapped gently on the wall of the corridor to announce his presence before he spoke. "Jonah," he said, "the police are on their way. You should probably get out of here before they arrive."

Jonah turned and looked Adam up and down before he turned his focus back toward the door "Who the fuck are you?" he asked. "Irene's boyfriend? I'm not going anywhere without my stuff. I have books and clothes in there. I bought her a gold bracelet a couple of weeks ago. I want it all back." Jonah pushed his shoulder hard against the door.

The chain held, but Adam wasn't confident it could hold for long. "I'll make sure you get it," Adam said. "I'll deliver it myself in the morning if you want. Just go."

Jonah didn't respond to Adam. He shouted into the door, "You do not want to fuck with me tonight! Do you understand? You'd better pray I don't leave. If I leave now, I'm coming back with a gun." He gave the door another heave. Adam heard the doorframe creak. He could picture the chain loosening.

Jonah looked at Adam over his shoulder, "You can tell Irene she's already on my list," he said, sneering. "I know she convinced Elizabeth to break up with me."

Adam took a deep breath. Jonah couldn't have been much older than his students, he thought. "It's not worth it, Jonah," he said. "I can see how upset you are. I get it. But you don't want the police to catch you breaking in. Just go home. You can have your stuff in the morning and move on from there." Adam wasn't sure, but he thought Jonah might have leaned back a bit, easing the pressure he was putting on the chain.

Adam took a small step forward. "Jonah . . .

Jonah whirled, furious. He screamed, "Don't touch me!" as his fist connected with Adam's jaw, snapping Adam's head back. "You don't know me! You don't care what happens to me!"

Jonah swung again. Adam instinctively ducked under the blow and slipped between Jonah and Elizabeth's door. He had turned sideways, his hands up in a reasonable approximation of a fighter's stance as his grandfather had drilled into him over so many hours.

Adam tasted blood inside his mouth. He felt his heart pounding. Jonah was facing Adam full on. His eyes looked huge in the light of the hallway, and he was breathing hard.

Adam's jaw was already throbbing. He had no illusion that he could hold Jonah off for long, but he only needed to stall for a few more minutes, he hoped, just until the police arrived. Adam steeled himself for the pain that he knew was coming.

A siren rang out in the distance and grew closer. Jonah froze for a second and then grabbed for his keys and ran down the stairs. After a few seconds, Adam heard the chain on Elizabeth's door slide back and he stepped further into the hallway to let her out. Irene and Elizabeth both opened their doors and the sound of the siren grew much louder. Elizabeth ran across the hall to Irene's apartment and Adam followed her inside. Irene pushed a button on her keyboard and the siren stopped.

Adam looked at the computer and then at Irene. She was sitting on the edge of her bed next to Elizabeth. Elizabeth's head was buried in her shoulder and she was sobbing. Irene looked up at Adam. "Are you okay?"

Adam nodded slowly. He could feel each beat of his heart. His pulse was at least twice its normal rate. "I'll be all right," he said. He felt inside his mouth with his tongue. He had no loose teeth. He was still bleeding a little, but only on the inside of his lip.

"How did you do that with the siren?" Adam asked.

"Sue gave me a recording of a police siren when I moved in, and I made an mp3 of it in case I ever needed to convince an intruder to leave before the police arrived. It fooled Jonah, anyway."

"It fooled me, too," Adam said. He turned to Elizabeth, who was still huddled on the edge of the bed. "Are you okay, Elizabeth?"

She nodded and they made eye contact for a second. Her blonde hair was in a tangle around her face, and her eyes were red. She had been sleeping in a threadbare tee shirt that barely came down to her thighs. When she shifted her weight on the bed, Adam saw a flash of her light blue panties.

He looked away just a shade slower than he might have. "I'm glad you're all right," he said.

Irene must have noticed his brief glance. She shot him a look as if to say, "Really? Now?" She pulled a light blanket from her closet and draped it over Elizabeth's shoulders.

She turned to Adam. Her expression was grim. She said, "You're lucky he didn't have a gun."

"I didn't go out there expecting a fight. I really thought he might listen to me."

Elizabeth was huddled under the blanket, arms around her knees. "He really scares me when he gets like that," she said. "I knew I should have called him back. He gets so jealous when I don't call him back right away." She cleared her throat and looked up at Adam. "I don't know what would have happened if you didn't come out . . ."

Irene's expression was grim as she turned to look at Elizabeth. "You should have let me help you get a restraining order the first time he hit you," she said.

"He doesn't mean to hurt anyone," she said. "He just has a really bad temper." She turned toward Adam. "You don't know him from tonight. He can be really sweet and generous . . ."

There was barely room for the three of them in the tiny apartment. Adam moved toward the door. "I'm sorry," he said. "You two need to talk, and I'm in the way here. I should go. This is your aunt's precinct, right? I wouldn't look forward to explaining to her what I was doing in your apartment at two in the morning."

"No, please stay," Irene said. "It's not like leaving now would do you any good anyway. I called Sue right after I called 911 and she's coming over. Besides, you need to make a complaint to the police."

"It's just a sore jaw," Adam said. "I'd just as soon forget it."

"You saw what he was like," Irene said. Her teeth were clenched. She walked the few steps into the kitchen and motioned with her head for Adam to follow. "I'll get you some Tylenol," she said. When Adam came into the kitchen, she turned so that her back was toward Elizabeth and she whispered. "She isn't going to report him. If you press charges, we'll have an easier time getting a restraining order. Do you want him coming back here?"

Adam looked at Elizabeth and then back at Irene. He shook his head. It was going to be a long night. "No. No, of course not. okay." He took the pills and the water from her.

This time the police sirens came from outside. Adam buttoned his shirt and put his shoes on. He sat on the piano bench because it was as far from Irene's bed as he could get without standing in the kitchen.

Two officers in uniform came up the stairs. They knocked on Elizabeth's apartment first, but Irene opened her door. "It's all right. I'm the one who called. The man is gone. Elizabeth, the woman he was after, is here with me."

The older of the two cops pointed at Elizabeth. "That's your apartment across the hall?"

She nodded.

"I'm going to need some information," he said. He took out his pad and he looked around. "Do you want to step into the hallway?" Elizabeth led the officer to her apartment.

The other officer looked over at Adam. "Who's he?" he asked Irene. "Is this the guy?"

"I—" Adam started to say, but the officer cut him off.

"I'm asking her. Is this the guy?"

"No officer," Irene said, "he's a friend of mine. This is Adam. The man who was threatening Elizabeth is named Jonah Rudzik. He assaulted Adam and then he ran away."

The cop perked up. He glanced up from his notepad. "Assaulted?"

"Jonah hit him in the jaw," Irene said. "Adam didn't do a thing."

The officer turned to Irene. "I'm asking him. Don't answer for him." He turned to a fresh page in his notepad and peppered Adam with questions. "Did the assailant brandish a weapon? Did you know him? Did he threaten you or did you threaten him?"

Adam answered no to all the questions. "I was afraid that he was going to break into Elizabeth's apartment. I came into the hallway and politely told him that the police were on their way and he should leave. That's when he hit me in the jaw." Adam showed him his bruise. "He did threaten Elizabeth. And he threatened Irene, too. He said he had a gun and he'd be back. He blamed Irene for encouraging Elizabeth to break up with him. That's it. That's the whole story."

The police officer looked disappointed. "Are you going to make a complaint? Do you want to press charges?"

"Yeah."

Detective Levy arrived then. She was breathing heavily by the time she got to the top of the stairs. She looked at Adam for less than a second before she said, "You two didn't waste any time." She pointed at his chest. "You skipped a button."

Adam turned around to redo his shirt.

Sue gave Irene a hug and sat next to her on the bed. "Are you all right, sweetie?"

"I'm fine, Sue. Really. I probably shouldn't even have called you. The police got here pretty fast. And Jonah ran off when I played the siren recording anyway."

"They'd better have gotten here fast. They know if they get a call from this address, they run. Wait, Jonah was here? I thought you told me they broke up." Irene was about to answer when her aunt said, "Never mind. I'm not that old. They could have broken up and gotten back together three or four times since then."

She stepped back and gestured apologetically to the man who had been taking their statements. "Please continue, officer. I'm sure you've got a lot to do. I'll just wait here until you're done. Irene, tell him about the siren thing. It's pretty cute."

It took the police a long time to take their statements. Irene mentioned several times that Jonah had attacked Elizabeth in the past, but that it was never reported. Detective Levy let the police go about their business without saying another word. When they were done, one of the officers asked the detective if they should go to Jonah's apartment to pick him up. She considered for a moment and said, "No. Who knows if he even went home? I wouldn't, if I were running from a police siren. We can get him easier in the morning when his heart stops racing. He'll either be at home or at work then. Whoever is on duty can pick him up and Dr. Drascher can come down to the station then to identify him."

The police officers nodded and went on their way. When they were gone, Elizabeth came across the hall. "I just wanted to thank you both," she said. She looked embarrassed and exhausted. She turned to Adam. "You . . ." she couldn't find the words. "Hang on to this one, Irene. Not a lot of guys would have done that for someone they don't even know." Adam thought she might start to cry again.

Irene went over to her and gave her a hug. "It's going to be all right, Elizabeth. We'll get you a restraining order. He won't be able to come near you."

Elizabeth didn't answer.

"It's not your fault." Irene said. Her voice held a sharp edge.

Elizabeth gave no indication she heard what Irene said. "I have class in the morning, and I'm never going to fall asleep. I'd should go back to my apartment and take a sleeping pill." She hugged Irene and said goodnight to Adam and Irene's aunt before she left, closing the door behind her.

"I'm worried about her," Irene said.

"Maybe I'm being overcautious," Adam said, "but just to be on the safe side, maybe we shouldn't leave her alone with sleeping pills tonight. I had a student a couple of years ago who almost killed herself."

Irene nodded. "I'll make up some excuse to take the bottle and just leave her the one a pill. I'll be right back." She couldn't have been gone for more than a couple of minutes, Adam thought, but it felt much longer. The whole time she was out, Detective Levy just stared at the floor. She looked deep in thought. Irene closed the door gently when she returned and placed the pill bottle on her counter.

The detective turned to Adam and asked where he was parked. "It's late," she said. "You probably need to get back to your apartment."

Adam was about to respond when Irene said, "Adam and I have a lot to talk about, Sue. I think we'll be up for a while."

"OK," she said. "If you're up anyway, I've got some things to talk about too." The detective patted the mattress to signal Irene to sit back down and she slid over so she could look at Adam and Irene at the same time. "I don't like this," she said. "I'm very uncomfortable. I don't like violent men in my niece's apartment building in the middle of the night, screaming, hitting people, making threats. He could just be a punk, or he really could come back here with a gun next time." She looked down at the bed for a moment. "I wish I'd gotten a look at him."

"You think you could tell just by looking at him?" Adam asked.

The detective raised an eyebrow. "Don't doubt me. If I'd had a look at him, I'd know more than I do now, that's for sure. I've seen a lot. Too much. Tell me the whole thing again. All of it."

Adam and Irene repeated everything that happened from the moment they woke up and heard Jonah in the hall. The detective looked grave. "I don't like this," she repeated. "His language bothers me. I don't like the way you describe him, either. You said he's hit Elizabeth before?" When Irene nodded, her aunt continued, "What else do you know about this guy?"

There wasn't much. He worked for his family's carpet business and he was going to school at night, Irene said. He wanted to be a lawyer. He was studying for the LSAT, Elizabeth had told her.

Adam said, "Irene thinks you can get her and Elizabeth a restraining order if I press charges. I'll be happy to testify or sign any papers, or however it works. I can go down to the police station to identify him in the morning and take care of it."

The detective looked up at Adam and smiled, taking Adam by surprise. She turned toward her niece. "You see, Irene! Character. I told you he had character. One date and look how invested he is." She turned to Adam. "That's what I told Irene when I said she should go out with you. Yes, you've got some baggage, I told her, but who doesn't?" She looked to Irene for a second, as if for confirmation, and then turned back to Adam. "Sure, you could have been more cooperative. If I wanted to, I might make something of your being an accessory after the fact, but what would be the point? You didn't do any harm." She squeezed Irene's hand. "You can see it, can't you Irene? He really cares. He walks into a situation and he's in up to his neck before he knows what happened."

Adam looked from the detective to Irene. He wondered how much the detective had told her.

Irene was unreadable. She took a long look at her aunt, as if waiting for her to finish her thought before she said, "Aunt Sue . . ."

The detective shook her head briskly, as if to regain her focus. "Right," she said. "Never mind that for now. I was just distracted for a minute." She turned to Adam. "OK," she said, "so you're going to press charges, and we'll get a restraining order. That's fine. That's fine. We can do that. But a restraining order won't do Elizabeth any good if she invites him back or if she doesn't report him when he shows up, not to mention that people violate restraining orders all the time."

"But he did punch Adam for no reason," Irene said. "Look at his jaw. It's all swollen. Should we take a picture?"

"That's penny ante stuff," the detective said. "He took a swing at Adam in the heat of the moment when Adam interrupted a lovers' quarrel." She thought for a moment and shook her head in frustration. She rubbed her eyes. "I guess I'm feeling my age today. This middle of the night stuff used to be easier." She shook Adam's hand. "You did good tonight, Adam," she said. "Take care of business in the morning."

Irene stood up and Sue hugged her. "I love you, sweetie," she said. I'll talk to you soon."

Irene held her for a long time. "I love you, too, Aunt Sue," Irene said.

The detective smiled. "Of course you do, sweetie. I'm a momma bear. Who doesn't love a momma bear?" She gestured at Adam with her thumb. "You sure you want him to stay?"

Irene nodded.

The detective let herself out. Adam sat next to Irene on the bed. He took her hand and asked. "Are you okay? Do you want me to leave?"

"Accessory after the fact?" she asked. "What does that mean?"

Adam closed his eyes for a second. He couldn't do this. Not now. "It's a long story," he said.

"You said the worst thing you did was keep a couple of secrets." He was about to answer when Irene interrupted him. "Tomorrow," she said. "I can't tonight. It's too much. You'll tell me tomorrow. Let's just try to get some sleep."

Chapter 16

It was six-thirty when Adam awoke. His jaw was swollen and sore. He felt unsettled. He needed to move, get out, get some of his work done, but despite Adam's gentle nudge and tentative "good morning," Irene still slept. Adam knew there was no way he would be able to wait in her cramped apartment without waking her, so he left a brief note saying he would call from home.

Adam dressed, crept out, and called a car service. Now he regretted not having his car with him, but when he'd left home, he had been headed to a bar. The car wasn't cheap, but at least traffic wasn't too bad. By seven-thirty, Adam was in his own apartment. By eight, he had showered and dressed. He tried Irene on the phone, but he got no answer, so he texted her. He typed, "I'm thinking of you. I'll call after the police station." He sat at his desk and pulled up his files on the tablet so he could focus on the last line of the couplets he had been working on.

Adam recited the Hebrew text without looking. They were cut into his memory. *UmiShahat mi yigaleni*: "And from *Shahat*, who will redeem me?" Adam had spoken those words to himself many times over the past weeks. At first, it was half a joke, ironic, self-deflating. At some point, Adam admitted to himself, he had begun to identify with the speaker even though he didn't fully understand what the text meant. Redemption from what? What was *Shahat*?

Adam sat and thought for a long time. The couplet reminded him of something very strongly, but whenever he thought he was close to identifying it, it danced out of his grasp. He wondered if Irene were still sleeping, and he regretted leaving so early. He thought of the feel of her hip under his arm when she was nestled against him. Then he thought of the look she gave him after the detective had called him an accessory, and he almost picked up the phone. He shook his head. He'd call later, after he was done with the police. What would he say if he called now, that he missed her, that he was as good a man as he pretended to be? He had seen her an hour ago. He was what he had done.

Adam forced himself to get back to work. As he finished his cereal, he remembered what he had been thinking of: the phrase "*HaGoel miShahat*," the Redeemer from the Underworld. The wording was nearly perfect, and a quick search confirmed it was from Psalm 103.

Adam read and reread the psalm, but despite the similar phrasing, the context didn't fit. The speaker in the tablet was pleading for an inheritor to redeem him: "Who will succeed me?" The speaker wanted a son. But the redeemer in the psalm was God.

Adam paced around his apartment. He was sure he knew another text where "redeemer" was in parallel with "son." It wasn't in the Bible. He could feel it just beneath the surface of his mind, just out of reach. The rabbi had said something. "The son redeems the father," she had said, but she told him the phrase traced back to medieval Europe, three thousand miles and two thousand years from his text. Adam rinsed out his cereal bowl and left it in the sink. He went over to his computer. There was more. There was another reference he was thinking of. He could feel it.

He looked through his bookshelf. He stared at his maps. He thought he had something, a faint memory, the phrase, "Danel, the Healer's man." He pulled his book of myths from Canaan and Ugarit from his shelf and he opened it to the myth of Aqhat. There was a list there of the duties a son could perform for his father. One was to liberate the father's spirit from the underworld. The words were different, but concept was so close, he thought, much too close to be a coincidence.

Adam felt elated, almost giddy. He saw two possibilities. Either the idea of sons redeeming fathers is so fundamental to human experience that different cultures rediscovered it in different times and different places, or an ancient Canaanite tradition somehow persisted over thousands of years from Ugarit to Tel Arad, to modern Judaism. Either way, he was on to something significant, something that could make his career.

Unfortunately, he still had no idea what it meant. Sons redeem fathers, he thought: they liberate them from decay, somehow, from destruction. And they're expected to do it. It's their duty.

Language, he told himself: focus on the words. Hebrew has several words for "redeem." The one from the tablet was pretty common: *gaal*. Adam had translated it hundreds of times without really thinking about it. He thought it was time he did better.

Adam started a list of the uses of the word in the Torah. The most famous example was when God redeemed the Children of Israel from Egypt. That was certainly evocative, but it probably wasn't very helpful in this context. A man's son couldn't simply be expected to drag him out of the underworld by some miracle, or by brute force. Adam went through every instance of the word *gaal* in his concordance, line by line. It took him a while. None of the examples clarified the word's meaning.

He wasn't discouraged. He tried the noun form *goel*, "redeemer," and he found two examples so seemingly incongruous that he hoped they might prove illuminating. Boaz is called a *goel* because he marries Ruth, his kinsman's widow. And the blood avenger in the book of Numbers, a man who pursues the killer of his relative, is also called a *goel*. If Adam could figure out what the revenge and the marriage had in common with liberating the slaves from Egypt, he thought he might better understand the meaning of "redeem."

Adam looked up at his clock. It was almost ten. The police had probably brought Jonah in by now, and he should drive to Queens and identify him, but Adam could feel that he was getting close to something and he couldn't bear to lose momentum. Not yet. He looked up the police station telephone number on the computer and he called.

The officer on the line told him that they were processing Jonah just then. Adam asked if he could come in a couple of hours or if that would be too late. They put him on hold.

After a minute, Detective Cheng got on the line. His tone set Adam's teeth on edge. "Dr. Drascher, how nice to hear from you."

Adam suppressed a groan. Somehow, he hadn't considered that Cheng would be the detective working this case. "It's a treat for me, too, Detective," Adam said. "I just can't stay away."

"I hear you'd like to make an appointment. They said you're thinking noon-ish?" Cheng's voice dripped with sarcasm. "We don't usually take reservations, but I'm looking forward to it. See you then, Dr. Drascher."

Adam looked out his window. He felt claustrophobic. He grabbed his windbreaker and headed out, his quick strides taking him past the train station along Chatsworth Avenue.

Adam considered the blood avenger first. The whole concept had never made sense to him. That an accidental killing cried out for vengeance was mystifying. That the person who hunted down and murdered the killer was considered a redeemer was horrible. It was offensive. The barbarity of the text embarrassed him. He checked his watch; he had time. He wended his way along curving roads to the coast of the Long Island Sound. The wind was picking up. He noticed that the leaves on a few of the trees were just beginning to turn, the lush green giving way to buttery yellow.

His job was to understand the text, not to judge it, he reminded himself. He could see two possibilities. The *goel* redeemed his kinsman by avenging his kinsman's death, or he redeemed the life of his kinsman's killer the way you redeem a lottery ticket or your dry cleaning: by taking what belongs to you. Neither seemed to fit. He worried at the question for several blocks without a breakthrough, so he changed tack.

Unfortunately, Boaz presented just as big a puzzle. Boaz married Ruth and took possession of her land because he was related to her late husband, but whom did that redeem? It wasn't clear if he was Ruth's *goel*, or her dead husband's, or both. At one point, Boaz was even referred to as the *goel* of Naomi, the dead man's mother, Ruth's mother-in-law.

There was a park on the coast—just a green space with some pretty trails along the Sound. As he entered through the gate, Adam thought back to the context of the tablet. The speaker is cut off, Adam thought, with no one to succeed him. He cries out for a redeemer. He feels desperate. He wants something. What?

Adam was right at the coast now, on the crest of a short hill overlooking the water. Through low, dense clouds, he could just make out the high rises in Queens. His old neighborhood was further inland, well out of sight, but Adam thought of his grandfather and of Danny. He picked up a small stone and threw it out as far as he could and watched as it sank beneath the surface. My grandfather went down to *Shahat*, he thought, and all I got was a lousy brother. He didn't smile at his gloomy joke. But he had a flash of understanding.

It was about claim. The blood avenger was a *goel*, a redeemer, whether he caught the killer or not. What mattered was that he acknowledged that the person who died wasn't just some anonymous victim who belonged to no one but himself, to be discarded, forgotten. That would be decay; that was the loss that cried out for redemption.

The *goel* claimed the victim as his own. He claimed the injury as his own. He dedicated himself to redeeming that claim. It was the same for Boaz. When Boaz married Ruth, he obligated himself to live out his dead kinsman's commitments. He made his relationship to his kinsman and his kinsman's household central to his identity. To ask if Boaz redeemed his relative or if he redeemed Ruth or Naomi was to miss the point. He redeemed all of them. He made them all his. And in the end, Adam thought, maybe it wasn't the miracles in Egypt, the plagues and the splitting of the sea, that constituted redemption, but just God's assertion that the people belonged to him. "Fear not, for I have redeemed you," God said in Isaiah, "I called you by name; you are mine."

Adam looked across the Sound again and he thought of his grandfather's tape. His windbreaker flapped like a sail in the salty autumn breeze. Who will succeed me? he thought. And now he imagined his grandfather speaking. There were claims and commitments Adam needed to acknowledge.

When Adam got back to his apartment, he called Danny.

"Adam! What's going on?"

"What does your afternoon look like, Danny? I need to talk to you."

"I'm backed up for most of the day, but I have some time between one and three. Do you want to call back then?"

Adam grabbed his keys and threw what he'd need for the day into his bag. "I'm going to be in the neighborhood," Adam said. "I'll drop by somewhere in that window. I'll call again if there's a problem."

Adam arrived at the police station at ten after twelve and Cheng escorted him to a desk in a back corner of the room. The neighboring desks were unoccupied. Cheng stared at Adam in silence for a while, a self-satisfied smile on his lips. "So, you're sleeping with my partner's niece," he said. "That explains a lot."

Adam had no patience for this. He had spent enough time fencing with detectives. "Can we get down to business?" he asked. "I'm here to identify the man who hit me last night."

Cheng looked at him with mock sympathy. "We'll get there. Nasty bruise. But I'm more interested in your relationship with Detective Levy."

Adam locked eyes with Cheng. "I'm not here because of my goddamned jaw," he said. "Did you read the report? Do you not get that Jonah has hit Elizabeth already and that he threatened Irene?" He spoke slowly, deliberately, as if he were explaining something to a dim child. "I need you to take this seriously because if you don't, Jonah could come back with a gun. Do you understand?"

Cheng's sarcasm disappeared. His tone was stern. "I know how to do my job, Dr. Drascher. Don't doubt for a second that I take Mr. Rudzik very seriously. I know what he is." He held up a file folder that had been lying on his desk. "We picked Mr. Rudzik up this morning installing carpet out in Elmhurst. He wasn't happy to see us, but he's none the worse for wear. You can identify him after you review the paperwork."

Adam looked over his statement from the night before. "Is there anything you'd like to correct or add to this, Dr. Drascher?" Cheng asked.

"No. It's fine," Adam said. "The officers were very thorough."

"We aim to please. Follow me." Cheng showed him a lineup of Jonah and five other men about his age. None of the men made eye contact with him.

Adam picked out Jonah immediately. "That's him."

Most of the men from the lineup dispersed, and Jonah was escorted out, presumably back to his cell. Adam followed Cheng to his desk. He signed the papers Cheng gave him and he was about to leave when Cheng held up his hand.

"Keep your seat, Dr. Drascher," he said. "We're not done. I want to talk about my partner. Detective Levy has a lot of faults. A lot. But she's not lazy, and she's not stupid. So explain to me why she's been slow-walking the Calloway case. We could have had this wrapped up in a day, but she keeps coming up with busy-work to keep us occupied. What's going on? Has she been paid off, or is she letting Mr. Blumberg off easy because you're involved somehow, and she's protecting her niece's boyfriend?"

"I don't know anything about any of that," Adam said. "I've only had two conversations with Detective Levy, and you know about both of them."

"And her niece? How long has that been going on? Was that first meeting in your office just a charade for my benefit? Because I have to tell you, Dr. Drascher, I don't like getting jerked around."

Cheng's phone rang. He looked at it for a second as if he were deciding whether he could ignore it before he grabbed his notepad and signaled for Adam to wait. "Yeah?" He shot Adam a quizzical look. "And what am I going to see?" His smile was dangerous, Adam thought, predatory. "Really?" The sarcasm was back. "Fine. Tonight." Cheng hung up the phone and looked at Adam. "You continue to brighten my day, Dr. Drascher, even when I think you might be out of surprises for me. I'm going to go get a warrant, and then I'm going to check some things out. We'll continue our conversation another time."

Adam didn't like the sound of any of that, but he wouldn't give Cheng the satisfaction of seeing his concern. He turned so that the detective couldn't see his expression, and he walked out the door.

Adam texted Irene from his car before he pulled out of his parking space. "ID'd Jonah. No problem. Running errands here in Queens. Meet later?"

She texted back a few minutes later as Adam was driving to see Danny. He parked around the corner from the funeral home and checked his phone. It was a relieved emoji followed by, "Can't meet today. Tomorrow?" He texted back, "Great. Will call after work to arrange time and place."

Danny was waiting in the foyer, just inside the door, and he greeted Adam as soon as he walked in. He clasped Adam's hand in both of his. "How are you?" he asked in a hushed tone. "Thank you for coming." Adam wanted to laugh. He cocked his head and Danny smiled sheepishly. "Sorry, Adam," he said. "It's a thing you fall into. I guarantee if you worked here for a week, you'd sound like this too. Come to my office. We can talk there."

They walked down a short corridor to a dark, wood-paneled room. Danny's business must have been doing well, Adam thought. He was wearing a new suit, and the carpeting and the curtains also looked like they had recently been redone. They sat looking at each other across Danny's solid wood desk. Adam had a fine view of the somber floral arrangement that he imagined was intended to offer wordless, subliminal comfort to the distraught and susceptible. He felt as if he had walked into a life-sized condolence card.

"What did you want to see me about, Adam?" Danny leaned forward in his chair. His jacket bunched around his shoulders.

"A lot. You've got time, right?" Adam asked

Danny looked suspicious. "Yeah. I'm okay for a while."

Adam nodded. Now that he was here, he couldn't find a way to begin. "How are things with you and Rose? How's Henry?" He asked.

Danny moved his head back and forth, as if he were teetering between two possibilities. "There's something going on with Rose," he said. "She was crying the last two times I came to get Henry."

"Do you think it's about Calloway?"

Danny shrugged. "No clue. I don't think his injuries are that bad, if that's what you mean. He called me here. He wants to meet, if you can believe it. I have no idea what that's about, either."

"Don't go," Adam said. "That sounds like a terrible, terrible idea."

Danny nodded. "My lawyer said the same thing." There was an awkward silence and then, "Why'd you come by, Adam?"

Adam bit the inside of his lip. This was harder than he expected. "I have something I have to tell you," he said. He took the audiocassette from his bag. "I told you I found this when I cleaned out the apartment. It concerns you, too. I didn't know what to do about it for a while." He paused. "That's a lie. I knew what to do. I should have given it to you in the first place. Here." Adam slid the tape across the desk over to Danny.

"This is from Hank? He talks about me on there and you didn't tell me?"

Adam nodded slowly. "That's my only record of his voice. I need to make an mp3 of it and then I'll give you a copy to keep if you want. In the meantime, you can hang onto that for a while. You have a cassette player at home, don't you?"

"I've got one here," Danny said. "Lots of families bring in music on tape for memorial services. Can I play it now?"

"Now? Wouldn't you rather be by yourself?"

Danny looked surprised. "Why would I want to be by myself? It isn't secret or anything, right? You've already heard it." Danny slid his chair back and opened the cabinet behind him. A complete stereo system sat on the lowest shelf, with the capacity to play tapes, CDs, mp3s, even records. Danny flipped a switch off to the side before he started the tape. "That's so it comes in here instead of in the chapel," he said. "The speakers aren't as good, but I don't think either of us needs to hear Hank's voice coming from the ceiling."

The two men listened to the tape without interruption. Adam watched as Danny's expression moved from grief, to shock, to confusion. They were both silent for a while after the tape finished. Danny was staring at his hands. Then he looked into Adam's face. Was he searching for a resemblance, Adam wondered?

"It's a hell of thing," Danny said. He voice was humorless. "Hank was right about that."

Adam nodded. "If you want to get a genetic test and find out for sure, I'll do it."

Danny stood up and leaned against his desk. He looked down at his feet. "I don't know. I don't know what I want to know." He was pacing now. He spoke distantly, as if he were talking to himself. "I shouldn't have a record of it. If my father ever found out, he'd probably take the business from me and give it to my cousin. You know what he's like. He's told me enough times that I must have been switched at the hospital and he wishes he could switch me back."

"I had to tell you, right?" Adam asked. "I mean, you wouldn't have wanted me to keep this from you?"

Danny looked up at Adam and Adam felt the pain in his expression like a stab. "Don't bullshit me," Danny said. He was furious. "You've been keeping this from me since at least Rosh Hashana, anyway. That's when you asked me about Vivian."

Adam couldn't deny it. He said nothing.

"That was when you said I was as much Hank's grandson as you were. That really touched me, Adam." He walked around the desk toward Adam. His fists were clenched. Adam didn't know if he was holding back tears of sadness or rage, or both. He stood just a foot from Adam. "I thought you were being generous." He said. "Was that funny for you, telling me but not telling me?" Danny turned around and stared hard at Adam's face. "Was that your idea of a joke?"

Danny's eyes narrowed. "It wasn't, was it? You didn't think it was funny. You just couldn't bring yourself to let me know. You tragic son of a bitch! Did it kill you to think that Hank was mine as much as yours? That you aren't the only child? Well take a look: not only do you have a family, but it's me. I'm your little brother. That must eat at your guts, doesn't it?"

Adam couldn't answer. He wanted to deny it, but the words stuck in his throat.

Danny looked away. "I know what you think of me, Adam. 'His own family doesn't even like that jerk! He's loud. He's inappropriate. What does my grandfather see in him?' That's how you always talk about him, do you know that, Adam? Is that a conscious thing? I've known you more than half our lives and you still want to shut me out. You always say, 'my grandfather,' never 'Grandpa,' or 'Hank.' Like you're afraid I might take him from you. You want to make sure I think of him the way you do. As yours."

Adam swallowed back his first replies. Danny was right, he knew. Keeping the tape to himself wasn't an accident. He didn't owe Danny an apology for a mistake. He owed him an apology for who he was.

Adam took a deep breath. "I'm sorry, Danny," he said. "I am. I was resentful, I was scared, and I did a shitty, shitty thing." He tried to meet Danny's gaze, but he had to look away. Danny was staring at him like a wounded animal. "Look, Danny, this isn't easy for me, okay? But give me a little credit. He left it up to me what to do. It took me a little while, but I did tell you. Even before I heard the tape, I knew my . . . our grandfather chose you. I didn't need a genetic test for that. I asked for your help burying him and no one else because you belonged there. He wanted you there and I wanted you there."

"You asked Steven too."

"You said we needed more people. And you were right. It took all three of us working full steam. Look, Danny, I know I can never repay what I owe you for looking after him—"

Danny kicked over his chair. His face was red. "God damn it, Adam! You can't owe me for that. He was my grandfather, too! We both owe him the same . . ."

Adam winced. "I didn't mean it that way. I meant you did it all and I should have been there, too. You knew him better. You cared for him better." He tried again to meet Danny's eyes. "Look, Danny. Maybe I've been a crappy brother to you. But when you've needed help, when you're desperate, you've always been able to call on me, and I have always come through. Always. And that was before I ever heard this fucking tape. That's what he would have wanted. That's what family is, right? And now, with Calloway, I've stood by you while the police questioned me, while they've threatened me . . . Doesn't that mean anything?"

Adam saw Danny's hands clenching and unclenching at his sides. After what felt to Adam like a long time, Danny exhaled slowly and sat down, his hands lying on the armrests of his chair. He looked up at Adam. "So, what now?"

Adam let out a long, slow breath. "I need to make some repairs," Adam said. "It was wrong to bury him the way we did. "I thought that the loss was just yours and mine and it wasn't. I didn't know about his friends at the temple, or Rabbi Mira, or about Vivian . . ." He shook his head. He spoke in a whisper. "You could have told me."

"I tried. You wouldn't listen."

Adam suppressed his anger. He kept his voice level. "You should have tried harder. I hurt people he cared about, Danny. You could have told me!"

Danny folded his arms across his chest. Adam rested his forehead in his hands and counted slowly to five. "Look, Danny," he said, "I promised the landlord we would close out the apartment this week. I already took some things. Mostly books I grew up with. I want you to come with me to the apartment and help me pack it up and take what you want. It's yours, too."

Danny nodded silently, taking that statement in.

Adam continued. "I can't even imagine what Vivian is thinking. We need to try to make this right. Do you think she'd come to a memorial service? I can give her the box then, too."

"When?"

"Tomorrow's not enough time, is it?"

Danny shook his head. "No. I don't think so."

"The day after is *Sukkot*. We need to get this done. Sunday? Do you think we can do it Sunday?"

Danny considered, pursing his lips. "I think so. Vivian doesn't get out much. She has a book group and she plays canasta once a week, but I think she's free on Sunday afternoons. She's the most important one, right? The others will come if they can make it, and if not, that's okay."

"You've been in touch with her?" Adam asked.

"We spoke just a few days ago," Danny said. "I've been checking in. Do you want me to call her?"

Adam thought about what he could say if he were the one to invite her. How would he explain that he hadn't tried to meet her until now? Or that he hadn't invited her to the burial? "Yeah, if you could," he said. "I'll call everyone else. Please tell her I really want her to come. Say what you have to, but talk her into coming, okay?"

Danny nodded. "I want Henry to be there too. I'll get him and Vivian. We can be at the apartment by three."

"OK. I'll tell everyone else to show up at about four. I'll have everything organized before you come. You can figure out what you want before the others arrive."

Danny looked up at Adam again. He spoke very quietly. "You should have told me, Adam. You should have told me as soon as you heard the tape."

Adam took a long breath. "I know," he said. "I know. Look, I have to go. I'll see you tomorrow."

Chapter 17

Adam arrived at work the next morning with a feeling of hopeful expectation. He had come clean to Danny, which was a greater relief than he had anticipated. And as difficult as the memorial was likely to be, at least he had a plan. What most lifted his mood, though, was the thought that soon he would be seeing Irene.

But when Adam walked into his classroom, his heart sank. Gallo was seated at the back, filling in the top of an official looking form. Adam recognized it as a rubric for evaluating his class. He was only observed once a year, and he had always been given plenty of notice before.

Seventy-five minutes later, Adam thought it could have gone a lot worse. The students participated. The lesson plan was one he had used before, and it was effective. He didn't think there would be anything specific for Gallo to find fault with, anyway.

Adam hoped to avoid Gallo and to lock himself in his office and jot down notes for Friday's class, but Gallo took his arm and said, "I need to talk to you, Adam."

A conversation with Gallo was the last thing Adam wanted. He said, "I'm sorry, John. This week is crazy for me. Can we schedule for next week? Maybe Monday?"

"I don't think so, no." Gallo said. "I need to talk to you now. Come to my office."

Adam followed Gallo down the hallway. He looked questioningly at Teresa on the way into the office, but she just shrugged her shoulders. Gallo closed his door behind them and gestured for Adam to sit down. Gallo remained standing.

"What's this about, John?" It couldn't be the lecture, Adam thought. Even if Gallo thought it had gone badly, Adam had a long track record of good teaching reviews. One bad lecture wouldn't be enough for a meeting that couldn't wait.

"I received an email over the weekend that I thought you might be able to shed some light on." Gallo paused as if he thought Adam might already know what he wanted to discuss. Adam gestured at him to continue. "It has to do with your tenure. It's confidential, so I haven't printed it out for you."

Adam sat stone-faced. His mind raced back over the past few weeks as he tried to think of any grounds for a student complaint or any indication that someone in the department, or one of the deans, might be targeting him.

Gallo walked over to the window and stared out at the sky for a few seconds before he went on. "I'm in an awkward position here, Adam. I hope you appreciate that. I remember when I was up for tenure. The department would have meetings I wasn't supposed to know about, and no one would tell me what was said. Letters were solicited from everyone I had worked with, but I could never see them. It's barbaric, but that's the way the system works. This is different, though. I think a man has a right to know when he's being accused of something." Gallo tapped on his clipboard with his pen for about ten seconds as if he hadn't yet fully made up his mind how to proceed. Finally, he pulled out his phone, punched in his code, and handed it to Adam. "If anyone asks, I never showed this to you, Adam. We never had this conversation."

Adam took the phone. The email was from Claudia. There was no text in the body of the message, but the attachment read:

> Dear Dr. Gallo,
>
> It is with great sadness that I write this letter to you regarding Adam Drascher's candidacy for tenure. I have known Adam for the entirety of his graduate and professional career. I helped train him, and I have written letters to this committee and others on his behalf. I have revised my letter in support of his tenure (attached), and I request that you substitute this draft for the one currently in his file for your committee's review.
>
> Unofficially, to provide context, I feel that I have to let you know that I have recently observed disturbing behavior that makes me question whether Adam is competent to teach and carry out research in your department.

Adam blinked. He read that last sentence again and looked up for a moment to see Gallo's reaction. Gallo, though, had turned his back and was looking out his office window. Maybe he was too embarrassed to see Adam's face when he read the message, Adam thought, or maybe he wanted to be able to say he never saw him read it. Adam returned to the email.

In retrospect, the first clue that Adam was having psychological difficulties was his obsessive interest in a highly marginal and esoteric subtopic in our field, but at the time, I interpreted that as a lapse of professional judgment rather than the beginning of something more serious. Lately, he has demonstrated paranoia. He seems to believe that I am deliberately harming his career.

I'm sure you'll agree that my record of supporting Adam in the past shows that I have had nothing but good feelings toward him. Adam came to my office twice, looking for me, and just a few days ago, he came to my apartment and threatened me. I considered calling the police and I am still considering it, but I am reluctant to add legal troubles to what seem to be Adam's already considerable mental health problems. At the same time, however, I could not in good conscience leave you in the dark about this while you decide whether to grant Adam tenure.

Adam clicked on the attachment. The letter was vague, lukewarm, and possibly sufficient to torpedo his bid for tenure. She described him as "a competent scholar who had shown significant potential in graduate school that he might someday realize."

Adam handed the phone back to Gallo. He had been struck dumb. Maybe he should have seen that coming, but he hadn't. Claudia had made clear that she intended to hurt him. He had expected her to try to undermine his reputation in the community. It had occurred to him she might revise her letter, but never to such an extent. He hadn't dreamed she would attack his sanity to his tenure committee.

Adam looked up at Gallo. The betrayal wasn't important, he told himself. He had already grieved over that relationship. Gallo's opinion was what mattered. Adam studied Gallo's face to get a read on how close he was to losing his job, but Gallo's expression was neutral.

"Do you want to tell me what's going on, Adam?" Gallo asked.

"Do you believe her?" Adam asked. "Do you think I've lost my mind?" Gallo shook his head. Adam held his breath.

"I never believed her letters when they said you were one of the most brilliant and original scholars in the field, either," Gallo said. "I've found that Dr. Renaud's letters say more about Dr. Renaud than about anything else. Teresa hasn't noticed anything different about you, and neither have I. Your teaching is fine. And you know what I thought about the *Times* article. If you thought Renaud was trying to steal from you, that wasn't paranoia. She was trying to steal from you. But now there's this highly damaging letter in your file, not to mention this—" he threw up his hands, evidently at a loss for words "—email that I'm supposed to do I-don't-know-what with. I need to hear your version of what happened."

Adam exhaled. Maybe all wasn't lost. "That's very fair-minded of you, John. I appreciate that."

He took out his flash drive, handed it to Gallo, and directed him to the folder of images he took of the tablet. It only took a moment for Gallo to bring them up on his desktop.

"This is what we dug out of the site at Tel Arad this summer," Adam said. "Maggie and I, I mean. Claudia was there too, of course, digging nearby. We had agreed to collaborate on whatever we found. I had a family emergency and had to leave a couple of days early, with the understanding that Claudia and I would share all the data we collected, and we would leave the artifacts found at the site back in Israel. You saw the article in the *Times*. Claudia changed her mind without telling me. She decided to use what we had found as her exclusive property to draw a bunch of big names to her department. I think she made some kind of deal with the provost. She's going to be chair, apparently."

"You met with her, then. Did she tell you all this?"

"Pretty much. I saw her on campus before the article came out. Afterwards, she avoided my calls. I did go to her apartment. She didn't appreciate that. She was very unhappy when I reminded her that the artifacts from the dig didn't belong to her."

Gallo smiled. "I'll bet she was," he said. "Is that when she gave you that nasty bruise?"

Adam had forgotten about his jaw. It didn't hurt anymore except when he bit down. He wondered what his students had thought when they saw him. Adam shook his head. "It wasn't like that."

Gallo raised an eyebrow.

"I did question her ethics," Adam said. "And I explained that I needed the images of the tablet for my research and because I was coming up for tenure."

Gallo lowered his voice. "Did you threaten her?"

"No. She threatened to call the police, and I told her that would be fine with me. I said the journalists at the *Times* would probably enjoy the chance to do a follow-up story on how she was hoarding the tablet and trying to ruin my career."

Gallo chuckled. "I would have loved to be a fly on the wall for that," he said. "I hope it was worth it to you, though. I don't think she can retreat from this. You probably have an enemy for life."

Adam shrugged. That was nothing he didn't already know. "The tablet is going to be very big, John."

Gallo looked intrigued. "Show me what it says."

Adam gave him a brief summary of the lines he had analyzed and their significance. Gallo's field was twentieth century theology, about as far from Adam's work as it could possibly be, so Adam had to bring him up to speed quickly. As he talked, Gallo asked more and more questions, and Adam felt a rush. Gallo's excitement fed his own, energizing him.

"Is the rest of the tablet as rich as this part?" Gallo asked.

"I haven't had a chance to analyze it yet, but I've looked at it. There's a lot there," Adam said.

"This is a book," Gallo said. "Maybe a significant book, if you can beat her—if she doesn't scoop you."

Hearing that buoyed Adam's hopes. For the first time, he thought Gallo might support him. "I think I'm okay," he said. "Claudia doesn't ask the questions I ask. This isn't how she thinks."

Gallo nodded. "Tell me again about her plan for the artifacts. How is she going to keep them to herself?"

"She knows people in the Antiquities Authority in Israel. She made some kind of deal with them to prevent anyone from seeing the tablet and the rest of the objects from the site for a long time. It would be easy for them to do. Claudia intended to have the only photos."

Adam saw Gallo's eyes light up with avarice. "So Fletcher and Belmont are the only institutions in the world that can publish on this?"

Adam spoke slowly and deliberately. "Until I publish my first article, yes. That's standard. At that point, I'll share the photos with anyone who asks. That's also standard."

"Think about this," Gallo said. "This isn't a standard situation. You found something unique, something big. And Claudia is pretty much on record that she's going to cut off access to it. Maybe we can benefit from this and let her take the heat for it. If your first article is just on the lines you could read in your own photos, no one will have to know you have the whole text for quite a while, not until you've finished your book."

There was only one answer. He didn't hesitate. "No, John."

Gallo looked him in the eye. Adam could tell he was starting to get angry. "You're better than that? You know what the stakes are."

"You can call it what you like. I'm sharing the photos after the first article."

Gallo looked at the floor, deep in thought for several seconds before he looked at Adam again. He held Adam's gaze while he spoke. "This is what I need from you, Adam. This is the minimum. When the time comes, would you be willing to go on record that Claudia wanted you to keep the photos secret, but you were too goddamned noble? Can you give the department that much good publicity?"

Adam thought that would be his pleasure. "That I can do. You say when."

Gallo nodded. "I can work with that," he said. His tone turned businesslike. "You've put all this in your tenure application, right?"

"I haven't had time," Adam said. "I just wrote one sentence saying that we found a tablet on the dig that may be interesting."

"That's not enough," Gallo said. "Make sure these images are in there, along with as much of the translation as you have. Put in your plans for what you're going to do with the tablet as well, including what a book might look like, as detailed as you can."

"And Claudia's letter?" Adam asked.

Gallo stroked his beard. "You might be lucky, in a way, that you pissed her off as completely as you did. If it was just the revised letter, you might have an unsolvable problem. With that toxic email it's attached to, I think I can make the department see the whole context. She's clearly out to ruin you. You haven't lost your mind and you aren't delusional. No worse than half our department, anyway. Unless you start hallucinating or attacking people, I think the department will see that. Your supporting materials and the *Times* article will help fill in the blanks as well."

Gallo chuckled. "You must have made her so mad she can't think straight. If this email ever got out, she'd be a laughing stock in the field." He pursed his lips. "Of course, you might be ruined too. Someday I'm going to want that whole conversation you had, Adam, word by word—but that can wait until after your tenure decision. But I can't emphasize this enough: you never saw this email. And for God's sake, you can't go anywhere near her. No calls, no emails. Don't even go near the Fletcher campus."

Adam felt a flush of gratitude. "That won't be a problem," he said. "Believe me. I really appreciate this, John."

"Don't blow this opportunity, Adam." Gallo said as he returned Adam's flash drive. "I expect you to help our department. And the opportunity to see Claudia squirm is too much to pass up. I'm tempted to show you the letters she's written for you before, with her condescending asides about our department's limited resources, and our small size, and our lack of graduate students. I can still quote from the last letter she wrote for you: 'He more than meets any expectations your theology department might reasonably have.' I don't mind telling you that I voted against hiring you in the first place in part because I never wanted to see another letter with her signature on the bottom of it." He spoke now in a soft baritone. "I want you to take her down, Adam," he said. "I want you to kick her ass with a big boot that has 'Belmont Religious Studies Department' on its heel."

When Adam returned to his office, he pulled up Irene's website on his computer and he listened to her music while he worked. He badly wanted to see her. So much had happened in the last couple of days, and he was eager to tell her about it.

Chapter 18

They were meeting at a diner in Queens. Adam arrived early and jogged the two blocks from his parking space to the restaurant through the worsening rain. The waitress gestured for Adam to take a table facing the street. He dried his glasses on a napkin and called Rabbi Mira to ask her to come to his grandfather's memorial service. "I'll bring yarmulkes and prayer books and I'll tell the Brotherhood," she said. "I'm sure you'll get a good turnout. Everybody loved your grandfather." He called Steven and Todd next. "Of course we'll be there," Steven said, but he had to get off the phone. He and Todd were on their way to a movie.

Adam put his phone away and watched the storm through the window until Irene arrived, dripping wet under her inadequate blue umbrella. She went over to Adam and slipped off her poncho before sitting down. Her blouse was damp and strands of her hair were plastered across her cheeks and forehead.

"You look beautiful," he said. She did.

She looked down at herself and then back at Adam. "You have a generous eye." She wiped some of the water off her face and pushed back her hair.

They ordered coffees when the waitress came over to drop off their menus, and then they waited until she was out of sight before they spoke again.

"How is Elizabeth doing?" Adam asked.

"She's having a rough time. How did things go at the police station? Did you speak with him?"

"With Jonah?" Adam shook his head. "No. It was a lineup. I just pointed to him. The only one I spoke to was a detective."

She nodded. "Ronald Cheng. My aunt's partner. I spoke with him, too. What did you tell him?"

Adam said, "I told him I hoped he took Jonah's threats seriously, because I thought he was dangerous."

"And?"

Adam shrugged. "He made some snide comments about my being in your apartment."

"Nothing else?" Irene asked. Her expression when she peered at Adam's face unnerved him. Something in her eyes reminded him of her aunt.

"He didn't mention someone named Calloway?" Irene asked.

Adam didn't try to hide his shock. He couldn't.

"I can see you've heard of him," Irene said.

The waitress brought their coffees. Neither of them wanted to order food at that point. Before they could think to ask for waters, she was gone. "I don't know if Cheng was looking for me, but he found me," Irene said. "He was in my hallway. When I came upstairs, he was knocking on Elizabeth's door, but she was in class."

Adam felt his throat tighten. "What did he want?"

"He told me he had some questions for me, so I asked him in. He asked if I knew how Mr. Rudzik makes a living. I told him I knew Jonah worked for his family. Then he asked me if I knew anything about other work Jonah might be doing to supplement his income. I had no idea what he was talking about. He said, 'While I was speaking with Dr. Drascher at the station yesterday, I got an interesting tip. A concerned citizen said that Mr. Rudzik was selling amphetamines.'"

"I thought he was on something that night," Adam said.

Irene nodded. 'He was. Cheng said he tested positive. Elizabeth told me once he takes diet pills sometimes to help him stay awake so he can study after work."

"So, did they search Jonah's home? Did they find anything?"

Irene's face was taut. Her hands were shaking. "They did. They found diet pills. And some Adderall. They also found methamphetamine, enough to lock him up for a long time, and hundreds of empty pill bottles. Elizabeth says she never suspected for a second he was dealing drugs. She can't understand how he could do this to his family."

Adam didn't reply. He sensed there was more coming.

Irene swallowed. "Cheng told me he almost forgot the most interesting part of the whole thing. The anonymous tip, he told me, the concerned citizen . . . that was my aunt. He said she didn't even try to disguise her voice. 'Your aunt does not play games,' he said. 'Hats off to her. She wrapped Rudzik up for me with a pretty bow.'"

"What?" Adam asked. "I don't understand. What are you saying?"

Irene was biting down on her lower lip. She looked at Adam and then looked down and closed her eyes. Adam thought she might cry. "She was trying to keep me safe," she said. "And she was protecting you."

Adam was stunned. "How is she protecting me?"

Irene took a deep breath. "Cheng said, 'I met up with your aunt and we had a good, long talk. She knows that I want a transfer to narcotics in the 110th and she wants Rudzik off the street. Her price for giving me Rudzik was leaving your boyfriend alone. I'm supposed to drop the Calloway case. That's fine,' he said. 'I understand her reasons. Blumberg isn't a threat to anyone who isn't sleeping with his wife, and your boyfriend is just looking out for him.' He also said, 'Rudzik is a piece of shit.' That's a quote. He told me he looked him up and Elizabeth isn't the first girl he battered. Jonah put a girl in the hospital a couple of years ago in Connecticut, but she wouldn't testify." She swallowed. "Cheng showed me these terrible scars all over the inside of his arm, Adam. They looked like burn marks. He said, 'I became a detective to put people who abuse women and children in jail. We're going to lock Rudzik away, and as far as I'm concerned, Blumberg is clean. Your boyfriend is in the clear.'"

Adam could hardly speak. His stomach was in a knot. He felt sick. They were both silent for a long time before Adam asked, "What about the gun?"

Irene just looked at him.

"When they searched his apartment," Adam asked, "did they find a gun? He threatened you. He said he had a gun."

Irene shook her head. Her voice was small. "There was no gun."

Neither of them touched their coffees. When Irene finally spoke, it was with great effort. Her voice was so strained, it was almost a whisper. "Tell me everything you know about this," she said. "Everything."

Adam just looked at her. He didn't know where to begin.

"My aunt is involved in this, Adam! I'm involved in this. I think I deserve to know." The distress in her expression when he didn't respond was painful for Adam to see.

"I called Sue after Cheng left," she said. "She was at my apartment ten minutes later. She said not to worry—everything was working out. I asked her what she meant, 'working out.' Irene looked into Adam's eyes. "She said, 'Sweetie . . .'" Irene stopped and took a short breath. "'Sweetie, my job is to protect innocent people and sometimes that takes a little more than just figuring out who did what when.' She told me that sometimes in detective work you need to give things a little push. She said, 'Sometimes you have a criminal, and you have to nudge the crime a little to get everything to fit together. Or sometimes you have a crime, but the person who did it isn't really a criminal, and you have to squint a little to make it go away.'"

Adam felt sick. He muttered, "Holy shit."

Irene nodded. "That's right, 'holy shit.'"

"Are you saying she put the pills there for Cheng to find? Why would she do that?"

"She said when she read Jonah's file and saw what he'd done to his old girlfriends, she knew what she had to do. 'It all just came together,' she said, 'like the pieces of a puzzle. It's obscene how much easier it is to put someone in jail for selling drugs than for beating women, but that's the way it is. That's the world we have to work with.' When she saw I was upset, she told me, 'Talk to Adam. He's a good man. I like him. Tell him taking care of the Calloway thing him is my gift to him.' Then she left. So I'm talking to you, Adam, just like she said to. Are you going to tell me what's going on?"

Adam looked helplessly at Irene, searching for something to say.

She said, "You can start by telling me who these people are. Who is Calloway and who is Blumberg?"

Adam took a deep breath and let it out slowly. "Before my grandfather died, I would have told you Danny Blumberg was a guy from the neighborhood who somehow became really close to my grandfather. They looked out for each other. I found out why when I was cleaning out my grandfather's apartment." He swallowed. "Danny is my brother," he said. "No one knows that. Your aunt doesn't know that. I didn't know it until three weeks ago."

"You're joking," she said. "This is a joke."

Adam shook his head. "It's a long story," he said. "I promise I'll tell you, but let me get this out. Calloway is having an affair with Danny's wife, and Danny found out about it. I was watching Danny's son when Calloway came by. Danny arrived at the same time and attacked him. He put him in the hospital."

"That's barbaric," Irene said.

Adam nodded. "It is. It's a little more complicated than that, but it is."

"But what does that have to do with you?"

Adam wiped his forehead with his napkin. "When I heard the noise, I ran outside and I found them struggling. I bruised Danny's face while I was trying to break them up. When the police came, Danny tried to claim he was only defending himself—that it was Calloway who hit him and gave him the bruise. I never corrected him. Danny was afraid if they knew he was lying, he might lose custody of his son in the divorce, so I kept quiet. Your aunt figured it out right away."

"You helped him cover up an assault. You let him claim it was self-defense." It wasn't a question. She looked much more comfortable judging when it wasn't her aunt, Adam thought.

"The damage was already done. I wasn't happy about it, but keeping quiet didn't hurt Calloway. He's not being charged with anything."

Irene looked down. "That's what my aunt meant about becoming an accessory after the fact."

Irene's fingertips were pressed against her eyelids. "I can't believe this," she said. "I should never have . . ." A tear slid past her fingers and rolled down the side of her nose.

Adam opened his mouth to speak, but no words came. Irene wiped her eyes with the back of her hand. She took a deep breath and held it before letting it out. When she spoke again, her voice was hard. She said, "I asked Sue if you'd committed a crime, Adam. She asked me if I remembered her old partner, Bob, from when I was a little girl. I told her, sure I did; he was always very nice to me. When I visited the station, he used to give me dried apricots when she wasn't looking. Sue said she was always looking. She said, 'Do you think I'd take my eyes off you for a second in a police station?' She told me that when she'd just started as a detective, she walked in on Bob getting rough with a suspect. That was her term. My aunt is pretty tough, and Bob wasn't all sweetness and light; even as a little girl, I knew that, so I'm guessing it was pretty bad. She said to me, 'I saw something I shouldn't have seen, and I had two choices: I could follow the law and get a good cop thrown off the force or maybe even thrown in jail, or I could keep my mouth shut. And that's how a good person becomes an accessory after the fact.'"

"You're saying she didn't follow through with me in Calloway's case because she respected why I did what I did?" Adam asked.

"She did follow through!" Irene said, her voice rising. The waitress glanced up at them and Irene dropped her voice to a whisper. "She set us up on a date. Then she planted drugs in Jonah' apartment . . . She did follow through! God, I can't believe this. And she thinks she's helping me. She thinks she's doing me a favor."

"Maybe it won't work," Adam said. "If he never sold drugs, there won't be any witnesses or anything. Your aunt can't very well show up in court and say she was the anonymous call. Maybe it won't even go to trial."

Irene shook her head. "Jonah committed violent crimes before. He attacked you. He threatened Elizabeth and me."

"So, you think he'll go to prison if we just do nothing?" Adam asked.

Irene nodded. She looked pale. "I think so. I don't know, but I think so. I think his lawyer will tell him to plead guilty to a lesser charge." She looked accusingly at Adam.

"You said you wanted me to press charges," Adam said. "You thought he belonged in prison then."

"He does belong in prison!" It wasn't a shout, but it was loud enough to get the attention of the people at the neighboring tables. Adam thought for a second Irene might stand up, but she looked around and sank a few inches into her seat. She dropped her voice to a sharp whisper. "I know what he did, but he's a human being, okay? He deserves a fair trial. Do you not see that? He scares the shit out of me and he treated Elizabeth like a fucking savage, but he's still a human being no matter what Cheng says, or my aunt." Irene pushed her plate away. "Maybe he should go to prison, but not for this."

They were both silent for a while, not looking at each other. Adam's head was starting to throb. He drained his coffee, hoping to forestall the headache that he knew was coming. He noticed that Irene's cup was un-touched. "Look," he said, "can we get out of here? I can't sit here anymore."

"Into the rain?"

He looked out the window. "We won't melt."

The waitress came over. "Is everything all right?" she asked.

"Just not feeling well. Can you bring the check?"

Irene reached for her purse.

"I've got it," Adam said.

"You got last time," she said. "It's okay."

He shook his head. "Another time. I've got it." He pulled a ten out of his wallet and left it on the table. "We don't have to wait. Let's go."

Adam and Irene walked side by side in silence for several blocks. The streets were still mostly empty. Adam's thoughts were too confused for him even to speak. Irene spoke first. "You think we should let this happen, don't you?" she said.

Adam felt the cold rain slide down his shirt as he walked, and he pulled his jacket up higher over his neck. Beside him, an arm's length away, Irene pulled her poncho tight around her. After a minute, Adam said, "If your aunt had talked to me, I would have told her not to do it. I wouldn't have chosen this."

"But since she chose it, you're okay with it? We could still say the drugs weren't his. We could tell someone."

Adam shook his head. He could already feel the pain building behind his eye.

"Why not? None of this should be up to us. Calloway's not getting justice. Jonah isn't getting justice. This whole thing is corrupt. It's rotten."

"Do you think I don't know that?" Adam was shouting over the sound of a siren in the distance. He waited for it to die down before he continued. "Justice isn't up to us, Irene. We're in a shitty position. Some people got beaten and someone is going to jail. Maybe a few of us. That's what it is. It isn't going to come out all right for everyone."

"But you're going to make sure it comes out all right for Danny? Why? He sounds like an animal. Should he even be walking the streets?"

Before he could stop himself, Adam asked, "As long as we're asking, should your aunt be walking the streets? Who else is she planting evidence on?"

Irene stiffened and Adam stopped short. He reminded himself that pushing each other's buttons wasn't going to get them anywhere. "Danny's not an animal. He just wants to be close to his son and he did a stupid, stupid thing because he was afraid he was going to lose him if his wife ran away with Calloway. But Danny's not dangerous. He's so scared of his wife, he sent me in to get his underwear for him after she threw him out because he couldn't face her."

Irene looked skeptical. Adam said, "He's complicated, okay? We're all complicated. Danny loves his kid, and he loved my grandfather, and he also beat a man until he had to be taken to the hospital. That's all equally true. And I tried to do the best I could, and I helped cover up what he did."

Irene didn't answer. She trudged through the rain not looking at Adam, not speaking.

"Look Irene. Let's say they found out the evidence was planted. What do you think would happen to your aunt? I don't know what they do in prison to cops who plant evidence, but I'm guessing it's bad."

Irene stopped walking. Adam stopped too, and he turned to face her as the other people on the sidewalk stepped around them. Adam could see that her poncho had soaked through. "And you could go to prison maybe, too, right?" Irene asked. "An accessory after the fact?"

Adam said nothing.

"I should go," she said. The rain was pouring off her hair and down her cheeks. She spoke so quietly, it was hard to hear her over the sounds of the traffic. "I need to talk to Sue," she said. "I have to hear her out."

"My car is close by," Adam said. "Let me drive you home."

"No," Irene said. She looked miserable. "No. I need to think this through on my own." She turned, and Adam watched her walk away.

The pain in Adam's head was building. He could feel his pulse throbbing in his temple with each step. He imagined what his grandfather would say if he could talk to him. Probably he'd start by admonishing him. "How could you be so careless," he'd say, "letting that punk catch you on the jaw like that? You're lucky he didn't know what he was doing, or you could have been in real trouble." As if that were the problem. As if those were the lessons Adam had failed to learn. But he was in real trouble, Adam thought. He and Danny were both in trouble.

Adam got into his car and pulled out into the street. The pain in his head had moved behind his eye and was growing sharper. The migraine was coming. He could feel it. The nausea had already begun.

Adam wished he could tell himself at least part of the reason he felt so bad was because he was conflicted about what to do about Jonah, but he knew that wasn't true. He would stand by quietly while Jonah was framed for selling drugs. He wouldn't feel great about it, but he'd do it. And there could be no forgiveness for that, Adam thought. What could he say to Jonah if he met him again, years from now? That he regretted the necessity? That he did the best he could? That, bottom line, he agreed with Cheng and he thought Jonah was a piece of shit?

Adam was driving over the Whitestone Bridge now, headed toward the Bronx. He had to narrow his eyes into slits to cut the piercing intensity of the headlights of the oncoming traffic as the rain pounded on his windshield. It took all his concentration just to stay in his lane, but he kept thinking about Irene, about whether he would ever see her again even if she did decide that she might be able to keep the truth about Danny and Calloway to herself.

When he got to his apartment, Adam took four ibuprofen and drew the shades before he brushed his teeth and fell into bed. Despite his fatigue, he couldn't sleep. Snatches of a melody he couldn't place played on a loop inside his head. The night was half over before he identified it as part of Irene's song: the abstract bit from her prayer for rain.

Chapter 19

Adam spent the next three days in a fog. He was miserable. He struggled through his classes, but he managed almost nothing else. On Saturday, he called Steven, more out of instinct than from any explicit hope that Steven could help him.

Steven answered after one ring and he told Adam he was on speaker. Steven and Todd were in the car.

"We're having a baby!" Todd said. His voice exploded with joy. "It feels so good to say it. Everything is signed and ready to go. We just left our meeting with the mom."

Adam didn't want to bring them down. "That's great news," he said. "We can talk another time. I was just calling to say hi."

"Something's not right," Steven said. "What's going on?"

"It's nothing. I'm fine."

"You aren't."

"Are you home?' Todd asked. "We can come by. We could be there in an hour."

Adam shook his head, only half aware the gesture was useless over the phone. "We can talk tomorrow. I'll see you at the memorial."

"Oh, stop!" Todd said. "Talk to us. Tell us what happened."

Adam told them everything: the date, Jonah, the conversation with Irene.

"What do you think she'll do?" Steven asked.

Adam didn't know.

"You shouldn't feel bad about this, Adam. The bastard should be in jail."

Adam didn't answer. He knew Steven would always support him. After a moment, he asked, "What do you think, Todd?"

"I trust you, Adam. I trust your instincts. But I'm worried about you. Are you going to be okay?"

Adam shrugged. "It's been a tough time."

"I'd say so." Adam could hear Todd's gentle smile over the phone.

"I keep thinking about Irene," Adam said. "I miss her. I miss her a surprising amount."

"Call her, then."

"She said she needed time to think."

"So don't call her every five minutes," Todd said. "Call her once. Invite her to get together after the memorial service. Besides," this time Todd's smile sounded mischievous so that Adam smiled too, "we'll want to meet her."

So, Adam called Irene. "I know you've had enough of men who didn't know when to stay away," he said. "If you want me to hang up, I will, but I had to talk to you."

She sounded raw. "Why? You can't walk away from a disaster?"

He shook his head, frustrated at his inability to find the words he needed. Finally, he said, "I've been thinking about you. I'd like to see you."

"I can't talk now," Irene said, "Sue's here."

Adam didn't know what to say. Finally, Irene broke the silence. "I'll call you later, okay?"

His words spilled out all at once. "We're having a memorial service for my grandfather tomorrow," he said. He gave her the address. "It's at four, but I'm going to be packing up the apartment most of the day. Closing it up." He hated this. It felt like begging. But he didn't stop. "It would mean a lot to me if you'd come."

Irene hesitated for a long time before answering. "Will Danny be there?" she asked.

Adam let out a slow breath. "Yeah. He'll be there. There'll be a crowd: the rabbi, friends of mine, friends of my grandfather's. You don't have to talk to anyone you don't want to, okay?"

Irene was silent for several seconds. "I don't know," she said.

She wouldn't come, he thought. Irene would tell her aunt that match-making and detective work don't mix, and her aunt would say it had been worth a shot, but there were plenty of men out there and she would find the right guy before she knew it. And so Adam tried not to think about Irene. He tried all Sunday morning and half the afternoon while he worked in his grandfather's apartment, sorting through the treasure and detritus of three generations of Draschers. But when the buzzer sounded from the lobby, he knew it was too early to be Danny. And when he opened the door and saw Irene coming down the hallway, he could feel the constriction in his chest release.

"I know I'm early," she said. "My piano student canceled. I wanted a chance to talk." As she entered, she stepped around the boxes Adam had taped up and left in the foyer.

"I'm really glad you came," Adam said. "Sorry about the mess. I'm done excavating. It's just sorting now."

Irene looked around at the boxes and the off-colored rectangles on the wall that marked where framed pictures used to hang. "You grew up here?" she asked. "Sue told me you were raised by your grandfather."

Adam nodded. "I moved in when I was almost four, right after my parents died. I barely remember anything before." He cleared a path for her in front of a wall that still held its photographs, and pointed. "That's a picture of them there," he said. "All the ancestors are here." He had thought of this corner of the apartment as the wall of the dead for as long as he could remember. "That's me in this one, playing Boggle with Grandma." I must have been nine, or maybe ten."

"You have no more family?" Irene asked.

"Not living. Except for Danny." He took the pictures down from the wall and placed them carefully in an empty box. "And there's Steven and Todd. They're not technically family, but they'd tell you they try to look after me."

"Like brothers?"

Adam laughed. "More protective. Somewhere between a nanny and a German shepherd. Steven was my college roommate. Todd's his husband."

He beckoned for her to follow him. "This was my old bedroom," he said. He looked around at the bare walls and the empty bookcases. "It was my father's room before it was mine. I slept in his old bed, growing up."

Irene was quiet for a moment. "Are you okay?" she asked.

Adam shrugged again. "Being here always makes me a little crazy. It's been that way for a long time, since my grandmother died."

"How old were you?" She asked.

"Seventeen."

"My father died when I was twenty," she said.

"I'm sorry."

"It was my junior year. That's when I met Brian. We were both really lonely. He was the guitarist in my band, and we started seeing each other. Two messed up, stupid kids . . . we got married right after graduation."

"You were with him a long time."

"I'm a slow learner, but I get there." She tried to smile.

"Are you really done with him?" Adam asked.

"Oh, yes," she said. She was emphatic. "Very done."

She laughed at Adam's expression. "With everything that's going on, you're thinking about my ex? I guess I made a strong impression."

Adam shrugged. "It was a pretty great date until the police showed up."

Irene wrinkled her nose. "That's something I've heard Brian say more than a few times. 'It was a really great party until the police showed up.' 'It was a very nice Thanksgiving until . . .' you get the idea."

"Go out with me again," he said. "This time I promise not to get into any fights and your aunt can stay home, okay?"

"You haven't asked me about her, yet," Irene said. "Don't you want to know what she told me?"

Adam nodded. "Come to the living room," he said. "There's a couch. I'm going to want to sit."

She took a seat next to him. Adam rested his hands on his knees. "OK. What did your aunt say?"

Irene rocked in her seat for a moment before she began. "She said Jonah should be in prison and you and Danny shouldn't. As far as she's concerned, she shouldn't go to prison either, but she admits she may be biased. She told me I could take that with a grain of salt."

Adam didn't respond.

"It's bad, Adam."

He nodded. "I know."

"Jonah's family is devastated. Elizabeth told me. They dreamed of his being a lawyer. They were paying for his LSAT classes."

"Is Elizabeth okay?"

Irene nodded. "She is. And it's a good thing he can't get to her now. I know that."

Adam didn't say anything. He was ashamed of the sense of relief he felt.

"I think you were right," she said. "I don't think we have any choice."

"I'm sorry," Adam said. "I am."

They heard a key in the lock of the front door. Irene looked surprised. "It's still early, isn't it?" she said.

Adam sighed, "That must be Danny. I invited him to go through some of the stuff with me to see if he wanted anything."

"The assailant," Irene said. "The secret brother . . . I never told Sue about that, by the way. I didn't think she needed to know."

"You can tell her," Adam said. "I'm tired of secrets."

They got up to meet Danny at the door. "Danny might have my grandfather's girlfriend with him," Adam told her. "I've never met her. If it gets awkward, I might have to fake my own death. Don't be alarmed."

Irene nodded. "No worries. Just fall over on something soft. I'll tell them you've been under a lot of stress."

When they got to the front hallway Danny was already there, carrying Henry in his arms. Standing next to him was a short woman, slender but sturdy. She was wearing black pants and a black blouse, and she wore her straight, white hair cut to her chin.

"You must be Vivian," Adam said. Vivian's response was a turn of her head. She was silent, but Adam could see pain in her eyes. "I know how much you meant to my grandfather," he said, "I'm really glad you're here." Her mouth was set. It was like speaking to a stone. "Danny, Vivian," Adam said, "this is Irene. Irene, I've told you about Danny and Vivian."

Irene offered him her hand. "Adam told me that you two practically grew up together," she said.

Danny beamed as he shook her hand. "You didn't tell me you were seeing anyone, Adam!" he said.

"It must run in the family," Vivian muttered.

Adam smiled, surprised. It was a comment his grandmother might have made. He caught Vivian's eye, but she quickly looked away.

Irene ran her finger along Henry's cheek. "Who is this?" she asked. The boy smiled at her.

"That's Henry," Adam said. "He's a sweet boy."

"I can see that," she said.

"It's my night to have him," Danny said. "Rose says she needs to work. Of course, she lied to me for years when she was banging her coworkers, so who knows, right?"

"Henry is Danny's son," Adam said. "Rose is his wife."

"I'm keeping up," Irene said.

"They're getting divorced."

"Still keeping up," she said.

For a moment, Vivian's face came alive, Adam thought. He almost thought she would laugh. Irene turned to Danny. "Can I take him? He's adorable." Danny handed Henry to her and Irene made a face at him. Henry started playing with her hair.

Danny smiled at the two of them. "He likes you. He's already got an eye for the ladies," he said. "Do you have kids, Irene?" She shook her head. Danny sat in his old seat and turned to Adam. "Watch out, Adam. She looks pretty comfortable with a kid in her arms."

Adam flushed.

"Am I making you nervous, Adam?" Irene asked.

"No. Danny is making me nervous."

"You never know what I'm going to say, do you Adam? You don't need to worry. I'm not going to embarrass you in front of your girlfriend."

Adam thought that seemed overly optimistic on several counts. "Do you know when you're moving? Have you picked a place yet?"

"I'm looking at an apartment in Astoria, someplace drivable to Henry, but a little hipper, a little younger. I think being single is going to be a lot more fun this time," Danny said. "The way I figure it, I'm thirty years old, I've got a terrific kid, and I run my own business. That makes me sound like a pretty good catch, doesn't it, Irene?"

Before Irene answered, Adam said, "I was just giving Irene the tour, Danny."

Danny looked around and slowly made his way over to the couch in the living room. He turned to Irene and said, "This was always my particular spot, right here." He turned. "Remember, Adam? Hank would always be in his armchair." He gestured at the recliner in the center of the room. "We used to watch quiz shows together. This is where Miriam sat, Irene. Near me. She was Adam's grandmother. She usually got the answers before the contestants did. She's where Adam got his brains from. Hank always said that."

Adam looked over at Vivian. The mention of Adam's grandmother didn't seem to make her uncomfortable.

Danny gestured for Irene to hand Henry back. He held the boy tight, like he was holding a teddy bear, Adam thought, or a security blanket. Danny turned to Adam. "I've got a lump in my throat like a golf ball," he said. "There are a lot of ghosts in this apartment, a lot of memories here."

"It's always felt like that to me."

"Which was your spot, Adam?" Irene asked.

Adam was about to answer when Danny interrupted. "Adam would come and go. Usually he'd be reading or something in the other room, but he'd pop in for a few minutes and then go back to hiding."

Adam needed to change the subject. "You should take the chair and the couch for your new place, Danny. You can tell Hank and Miriam stories to Henry when you watch quiz shows together. Goodwill is coming Tuesday to take whatever is left. The clothes wouldn't fit either of us, so I packed them up. We could split his ties if you'd like. They're in the bedroom. Could you all come?" He turned to Vivian. "There's something for you there, too."

The bedroom closet was open. It was empty except for a rack of ties and a white box tied with a red bow. The box was labeled with Vivian's name in red magic marker.

"God," Danny said. He looked pale. "The empty closet is always the worst. All the mourners tell me that. It just gapes at you, doesn't it?"

Adam nodded. He handed the tie rack to Danny and said, "Take what you'd like. Check out the top drawer, too. I put something there for you."

Danny took just a couple of the ties before returning the rest to Adam, and then he opened the drawer. He pulled out a pair of heavy, black gloves and tried them on. Adam thought for a moment Danny might cry. Danny looked up at him and swallowed hard.

"He'd want you to have them," Adam said. He forced himself not to look away from Danny's tears.

Adam got the box down and offered it to Vivian.

She shook her head. "I'm not looking to accumulate more things at my age," she said. "I have a few photos of Hank in my apartment. That's all I want."

She gently placed the box on the bed and turned away, but Danny said, "You have to open it, Vivian. Hank left specific instructions. What's inside?"

Adam said, "I'm sure none of us want to pry, Vivian. Please, if you want to wait until you're alone before you open it, that's fine."

She shook her head. "I think there have been enough secrets already," she said. She slowly untied the ribbon and lifted off the cover. She pulled out a paper takeout menu from a Chinese restaurant. She looked at it for a moment, puzzled, before her face lit up. "This was where we got takeout on our first date," she said. "I ordered chicken with snap peas and Hank had orange beef. Look. He circled them. We watched a Cary Grant movie."

Next, Vivian pulled out a stack of eight or ten letters, all bound together with string. "I had no idea he saved these," she said quietly. "I saved his notes to me too . . ." She cleared her throat and pulled out the last item in the box. It was a photo. She showed it to Irene, who had moved next to her and was looking over Vivian's shoulder. Vivian started to explain the photo, but her voice caught in her throat. "It's just us," she said. She started to cry. Adam craned his neck to see. The photo was a close-up of their hands, pale and wrinkled, Vivian's palm resting on top of Hank's.

"There's something on the back," Irene said.

Vivian turned it over, but she couldn't get the words out. She handed it to Irene. Irene read softly and slowly. "Of all that I'm sorry to leave, Vivian, you were the hardest to say goodbye to. Please forgive me. Hank."

Vivian was sobbing now. Danny moved toward Vivian, but Irene had already sat down on the bed next to her and put her arm around her shoulder.

Adam said, "I'm sorry, Vivian. I miss him too." She didn't look at him. He knew he was intruding on her grief. Even Danny felt it. Adam could see it in his face.

The two men went back to the living room. "They really cared for each other," Adam said.

Danny nodded. "I know."

"I don't know what to say to her. I feel like shit."

"Yeah. I know," Danny said. "You're in a tough spot. I tried to put a word in for you. I tried to tell Vivian that it wasn't your fault you didn't talk to her before the funeral because Hank never told you about her." He gave Adam an apologetic look. "Looking back on it, that didn't make anybody look good."

Adam had no response. "Did you ever find out what Calloway wanted?" he asked.

Danny nodded. "I saw him. My lawyer almost had a heart attack when I told him I was going to meet with him. I guess he was afraid I'd hit Calloway again, but it was okay. It turns out he's moving. Rose has been pressuring him to marry her for months, and he can't take it. He's just an overgrown kid. He doesn't want to be a father. He doesn't want to be with Rose forever. He took a job at the company's office in St. Louis."

Adam was stunned. "Rose must be flipping out."

"It's not good," Danny said. "She's kind of a mess. But I'm not getting the brunt of it for a change. I'm doing fine. It cost me, but I'm going to get shared custody. I think at this point, Rose is just relieved to have someone to share the child care expenses and take half the weekends. I had to pay Calloway's lawyer, if you can believe it, and I had to give him a pile of cash, but it was worth it. I paid him for the damage to the car and to his face and some extra for him to disappear. He didn't even hesitate when I told him he had to sign over any paternity rights or there wouldn't be a deal. He's out. Full stop. It turns out since I was married to Rose the whole time they probably couldn't have taken Henry away from me anyway, but this way it's ironclad. When Henry gets older, I figure we can tell him we used a sperm donor. I got Calloway's medical history in case Henry ever needs it, and that's that."

"You're not going to tell him Calloway is his father? Not ever?" Adam was horrified. "When he's grown, he may need to find him, Danny. That's his right. You can't take that from him."

Danny scowled. "Don't look at me like that, Adam. It's not your business." He held Henry tighter. "I'm his father, not Calloway! That's all he needs to know."

"It's not my business? I'm his uncle, Danny. Have you forgotten?"

There was a buzz from downstairs, and Danny walked into the kitchen, muttering to himself, when Adam went to answer it. A few minutes later, Rabbi Mira came to the door flanked by a troop of five men who looked to be in their seventies and eighties.

"From the Brotherhood," Rabbi Mira explained, "Max, David, Norman, Allan, and Irving."

Danny emerged at the sound of the rabbi's voice, and Irene and Vivian appeared as well. Adam wouldn't have guessed that Vivian had been crying a few moments before. She looked composed and resolute as she stood beside Irene. Max seemed to be the Brotherhood spokesman. He offered their condolences to Adam. "Hank was a terrific, terrific guy," Max said. "He will truly be missed."

Adam introduced everyone as the throng closed in on itself. "You know Danny, I think," Adam said. "And this is Irene and Vivian." He felt like he was gasping for air as he pictured the flurry of handshakes and greetings that would follow. "Vivian meant an awful lot to my grandfather," he said quickly. "She and Danny probably knew him better than anybody." He looked toward the kitchen. "I'll be right back," he said. I'm just getting some snacks." He made a quick exit and Irene followed him.

"Did you just use Danny and Vivian as human shields?" she asked.

"Just being inclusive," Adam said. "They're mourners, too, right? And yes, the human shields thing. I'm not proud, but there it is."

She shook her head and smiled. "Let me give you a hand with this stuff."

Adam had stopped at the grocery store on his way in that morning. By the time he and Irene had arranged the cookies on a plate and poured the pretzels into a bowl, the buzzer sounded again. Adam and Irene brought the food and drinks into the living room and Adam got the door. It was Steven and Todd. Adam pulled them aside while Irene unstacked the cups.

"Thanks for coming," he whispered. "Listen, Irene's here, okay? I'll introduce you in a minute. Just be nice to her, all right?"

"What are you worried about?" Steven asked. "We're always nice."

"You can count on us, Adam," Todd said in his most reassuring voice. "We'll be tough, but fair."

Adam sighed. He tried to convince himself that they'd behave reasonably if he didn't rise to their bait. There was little he could do in any case. He brought them into the living room and introduced them to everyone.

To Adam's great relief, everyone chatted warmly. He kept himself busy at the periphery, refreshing drinks and refilling the cookie tray and nodding when it seemed appropriate.

After a short while, Rabbi Mira caught Adam's eye. Apparently, she had determined that all his guests had been adequately fortified. She cleared her throat. "Do we have a *minyan*?" she asked. Adam looked around the room. He nodded. The rabbi opened her bag and took out slim prayer packets to hand out. She also had yarmulkes for anyone who wanted one. Adam took one. So did Danny and the men from the Brotherhood. The rabbi was already wearing one. She led them in a brief service. Adam and Danny recited *Kaddish* together. When Adam saw that Vivian was hanging back, he whispered to her that he'd like her to read the concluding psalm.

Rabbi Mira stood up when Vivian finished. "Herschel was important to all of us," she said, "whether as a grandfather or as a beloved friend. I'm sure you can feel him in this room, as I do. We are all mourning today, but our love for him is still alive. Herschel's passing has made us a community of mourners, and I hope that we can support each other and help each other to heal in our time of grief. May his memory be for a blessing."

Adam went up to the rabbi to thank her. He was surprised when she took his arm and escorted him to the kitchen. "I've been thinking of you, Adam." She said. "Are you okay?"

Adam nodded. "I'm all right, Rabbi. I've had a lot on my mind."

"Danny told me about the tape," she said. "He spoke with me after services on Sukkot. He's really shaken, Adam. I imagine you must be, too."

"I'm fine," Adam said. "Danny was shaken by the tape?"

"You sound surprised! It's a big deal, don't you think? You'll keep an eye on him, won't you?" The rabbi must have sensed his discomfort. "What are you thinking, Adam?"

He hoped she could understand. "We're really different, Danny and I," he said. "He's . . ." Adam almost wanted to explain that keeping an eye on Danny could be costly, that he was afraid of being dragged into the mud of Danny's life. But he didn't have the words, and in the end, he knew it didn't matter. His grandfather loved them both, and love is thicker than mud. "I'll try," he said.

She smiled. "I know you will." She patted Adam's arm. Compassion flowed from her eyes. "You're a part of us, Adam. Don't forget that. Come see us at temple, sometimes."

They left the kitchen. The rabbi gathered up her prayer books and moved among the Brotherhood, collecting them together so that they could say their goodbyes and head out on their way. A few minutes later, Danny tapped Vivian gently on the back and they headed for the door as well. In the entryway, Danny shifted Henry's weight to his left arm and he shook Irene's hand with vigor. Then he rested his hand on Adam's shoulder. "Hank would have liked this," he said. "This was a nice thing." He looked from Adam to Irene and said, "Well, I've got to get Vivian home and then I need to get this little guy to bed or his mom is going to give me an earful."

Vivian held out her hand and Adam took it. "Thank you," she said. "I'm glad I came." She sounded at least a bit warmer than she had at the beginning.

"I'm really glad you did, too." He hesitated for a moment. "Look, Vivian, could I talk to you for a minute?"

Vivian hesitated. She looked quickly at Danny and then Irene. She nodded. Adam walked with her to the kitchen. "Vivian, I just wanted to tell you how sorry I am that I didn't get the chance to talk to you before today. I hope you can forgive me for not calling before the burial. I want you to know that I'm really glad you and my grandfather were together."

Vivian looked at him. "I just can't understand why Hank never told you about me."

Adam looked down. It was still painful to think about how poorly he and his grandfather had understood each other.

"He loved you tremendously, you know," she said.

Adam nodded again. "I loved him too. I would have wanted him to be happy. I just wish he knew that." He was silent for a moment. He meant to say goodbye, but surprised himself by his own words. "Maybe some time I could see you," he said. "I'd like to get to know you a little, if that's okay. I'd like to talk to you about him."

Vivian asked, "Would you be bringing Irene?"

Adam couldn't tell if she was teasing him. "She's very special," Vivian said. "I think Hank would have thought so, too."

"I'd like that," Adam said.

They walked back to the front entryway where Danny was telling Irene, Steven, and Todd one of his favorite stories. He was pantomiming Adam learning to parallel park, and making car noises. Adam caught Steven looking at the clock out of the corner of his eye.

When Danny saw Adam, he wrapped up his story and gave Adam a hug and tousled his hair. "All right, this time we're really going," he said. He inclined his head toward Irene. "She's out of your league," Danny said in a whisper they all could hear. He turned to Irene. "It was a pleasure meeting you, Irene. Anytime you want more embarrassing Adam stories, you know where to find me." He followed Vivian out, one arm at her elbow, one wrapped around Henry.

Chapter 20

Adam closed the door behind Danny and Vivian and he leaned against it. Steven smiled. "I know exactly how you feel," he said.

Irene laughed. She said, "Vivian was sweet, though."

Adam saw Todd give Steven a subtle nod. "We should go," Todd said. "You must be exhausted."

"I am, but stay for a few minutes. Tell Irene something nice about me. I can use the help. You can make it up if you have to." They went back to the living room and he passed the cookie tray to Steven and Todd as they sat down.

"Steven and Todd are adopting a baby girl," Adam told Irene. "They just signed the papers a couple of days ago."

"Congratulations!" Irene said. "How old is she? What's her name?"

"She's due around Thanksgiving," Todd said. "I just started making a list of names . . ."

Steven counted off on his fingers, "His mom's name, his sister's name, his aunt's name . . ."

Todd ignored that. "The mom is healthy. She's only seventeen, so her parents have been very involved."

"Better late than never," Steven said.

Todd winced. "Steven, don't judge. It's bad karma." He turned to Adam and Irene. "They seem like very nice people. Anyway, that's enough about us. Tell us about you, Irene. Start anywhere. We want to know everything."

"Irene's a terrific musician," Adam said. "She composes. She sings. I wish there was a piano here so you could hear her play. She's incredible."

"Let the woman talk, Adam," Steven said. "We can hear from you anytime."

"I agree, Adam. Hush," Todd said. He turned to Irene. "So, tell us what you think of Adam, Irene." he said. "Is it too early to tell if you see this going anywhere?"

Irene flushed, but she recovered quickly. "Adam warned me," she said. "I understand the two of you nominated yourselves for permanent guard duty."

Steven's smile belied the offended tone he put on. "Guard duty! I don't know when I've been so insulted!"

"Well, I'll wear that as a badge of honor," Todd said. "When I was about to meet Adam for the first time, I was already feeling nervous; Steven said, 'No pressure, but Adam has been my closest friend for my entire adult life, and if he doesn't think you're good for me, I'm going to have second thoughts.' I actually appreciated that. Steven isn't close to very many people, and I like knowing that he has people looking out for him besides me."

"Todd," Steven said, "I'll bet this is why Adam doesn't introduce us to the women he goes out with. You know, I don't think he's let us meet anyone since Beth."

"Oh," Irene asked innocently, "who is Beth?"

Adam groaned under his breath. "This might be when I fake my own death," he said quietly.

Todd turned to Irene. "Beth came to our Christmas party last year. She was very decorative, like an ornament. Do you remember how festive she looked standing next to our tree in that sparkly dress, Steven?"

"The tree had a better sense of humor," Steven said. "She really wasn't for Adam. You should be grateful that we helped you figure that out so quickly, Adam."

"You promised you'd be good tonight," Adam said. He remembered that dress. He had appreciated it on a level that he was pretty sure Steven and Todd couldn't.

Todd said, "Someone has to make sure you don't settle, right?"

"Look," Steven said, "seriously, I talked to her at the party for a while. She didn't get you at all. She was tired of being single, and she saw you as a stable guy with a decent job, but that's all. She said she liked that you were steady."

Todd said, "She actually used the word 'solid.' I didn't appreciate that."

Steven turned to Irene and said, in a stage whisper, "She wasn't talking about his physique." Irene laughed.

"Thanks for the clarification," Adam said. "You're a nightmare. Both of you."

Todd ignored him. He said, "You still haven't told us how you feel about Adam, Irene."

"Would you describe him as 'solid?'" Steven asked?

"We don't mean his physique either," Todd said.

Irene was bright red and laughing. "I think he has a certain appeal," she said. "Let's leave it at that for now, okay?"

Steven and Todd glanced at each other. "Good enough," Todd said. "That's enough mischief for one day. Now we really will go." They stood up and Adam and Irene walked them to the door.

Before the door had fully closed behind them, Adam and Irene could clearly hear Todd say, "I told you he should call her, Steven."

Adam looked helplessly at Irene.

"I like your friends," she said.

"I'm glad," he said. "They can be a lot to take."

"I'm glad I met Danny, too. I feel like I have a better sense of who he is."

"I hope that's a good thing," Adam said. He looked around. There were only a few boxes left for him to label and close up. He took up a black magic marker and a roll of tape that were sitting on top of the last box he had worked on.

Irene took a seat next to him among the boxes. "Let me help you with those," she said. Adam nodded his thanks. "Henry's really adorable," she continued. "Danny never wants to put him down, does he?"

"Nope. Not if he can help it. Henry is the center of his life."

Irene looked pensive. "He doesn't seem jealous of his wife. He's angry, but I don't think he wants her back. He seems over her."

"I think he is. They were always rocky. It's been bad between them for a long time."

They worked in silence for a while. As each box was filled, Adam would label it and he and Irene would tape it closed. Finally, her gaze still on her hands as she worked, Irene spoke. "It was never about his wife, was it?" she asked. "The assault, I mean. The man Danny attacked was coming between Danny and Henry, or Danny thought he was." She took her hands from the box she was working on. "Am I right?"

Adam said nothing. Danny's secrets weren't his to tell.

Irene looked hard at him. "I need to understand what happened, Adam. I was in a bad place for a long time because I didn't want to see what was in front of my face about my marriage, my career . . . everything. I promised myself when I moved to New York that I wouldn't make that mistake again. Do you understand? I need to know what kind of man you were protecting. I need to know why Danny did what he did."

Adam also stopped working. He thought for a few moments. He understood, he said. He told her about growing up with Danny and about Danny's marriage to Rose. He told her about the night of the attack and Danny's payoff to Calloway.

"And what about him?" she asked. "What about Calloway?"

Adam started working again. "What about him?"

"Is he okay? Has he recovered?"

"He's recovering," Adam said. "He broke up with Rose and he's moving to St. Louis. She wanted to get married and he didn't. He doesn't seem to be big on commitments."

"He doesn't want to be involved with Henry at all?"

They were nearly done packing up, now and Adam was surprised at how much ambivalence he felt to be finally leaving this place. "I was talking to Danny about it," Adam said. "I told him when Henry's older, he'll have the right to find Calloway if he wants to. My grandfather would have told him the same thing. I'll keep on it if I have to."

Irene shook her head. "If Danny just hadn't lied to the police . . ."

"I know," Adam said. "Danny has a way of making small disasters into larger ones."

"So do you," Irene said. "Sue was right. You do tend to get in up to your neck." Adam offered a wan smile. "Sue says you've never been married. Why is that? What's your story? You're a caring guy. You've got a good job. You're not bad looking. What am I not seeing?"

Adam knew what Steven and Todd would say: that he had been hung up on Claudia, that he kept himself too bottled up. "Maybe I should cultivate an air of mystery and tell you I'm damaged in some fascinating but not ultimately disqualifying way," he said. "Or maybe I just never met the right person. How about you go out with me again and we'll see which it is?"

The last box was overfilled. Irene taped the flaps together and reinforced the sides while Adam held it closed. Adam looked around. It didn't look like the home he had grown up in, now. They were done. There were just the boxes, the furniture they would give away, and the four walls. Even the air felt different, Adam thought, less heavy. This place where he had grown up wasn't his anymore. It was strange and unfamiliar.

Once he got home, Adam knew, when he didn't have tasks like the burial, the service, and the apartment to fill his thoughts, the slow mourning would begin. Gradually, insensibly, he would become more accustomed to living in the absence of his grandfather, another hole in his life that would never be filled, alongside all the others. Adam could feel his grief washing over and through him like water through a sand castle in a rising tide

Irene reached out to him and took his hand. "That box your grandfather left for Vivian was really romantic," she said.

Adam knew she was trying to distract him, to make him feel better. He closed his eyes and took a slow, silent breath. "He could have taught me a thing or two if I gave him the chance," he said.

"Did you save a menu from our date?" she asked.

"Maybe," he said. In spite of his sorrow, Adam couldn't help smiling a little.

"You do know that if you go back and get one now, it wouldn't count, right?"

"Maybe," Adam said again.

Irene got up from the floor and sat on the couch. "Come sit with me," she said. "Tell me what you're thinking."

Adam swallowed. He joined her on the couch and wiped his eyes. "Most of these boxes will fit in my car, and I can get the rest tomorrow," he said. He looked at her for a moment and then up at the empty walls. "It's going to be a rough night," he said. "I thought it would be easier saying goodbye to this place."

Irene nodded. She took his hand in both of hers.

Adam squeezed her hand. He said, "Danny was right. There are a lot of ghosts in this apartment." He looked at the wall of the dead, empty of its photos, now. He exhaled. He felt more in control. "We didn't used to think of them as ghosts," he said. "That's what I study. A long time ago, they were called *Refaim*, 'Healers.'"

She squeezed his hand. "What were they healing?"

"The breach between this world and the next, I think," Adam said. "A feeling of connection that death can't sever. I could use some of that, if it's on offer." He squeezed her hand back. "Can I show you something that almost no one else has seen?"

She raised an eyebrow. "Nice try, but I've seen it already."

Adam couldn't help smiling. "I'm being serious." He took out his cell phone and pulled up the picture he had taken just after he had found the tablet. "We dug this out of the ground this summer in Israel. It's thousands of years old. It mentions the Healers."

She nestled closer to look.

The writing was miniscule on his screen, but Adam recited from memory. "It says, '*Qirvu elai*,' 'Come to me.' '*Piqdu oti*,' 'Take notice of me. Watch over me. Keep loving me . . . Don't be gone.'" He looked down. "This was real to them. It's what we all want when we lose someone, right? To cry out, 'Come back! Come back!' and to have them there and feel their presence. The people who lived then, they had that, and when they died, they expected to find a home with the Healers. For them, that was real." He put away his phone.

"But we don't have that," he said quietly. "We're not children, right? At some point, we're supposed to stop asking. When someone dies, they're just gone." He still held her hand. "We're supposed to accept that if we want any kind of connection, it all has to come from us, from how we live, from how we choose to remember them, and that's not enough. There's nothing reaching back toward us from the other side. We're cut off."

Irene looked down silently for long enough that Adam wasn't sure she was going to answer. Finally, she said, "When my dad died, all these people came up to me trying to think of consoling things to say. Some of them were so clueless . . ."

She paused. Adam could imagine what she was remembering. He had heard his share.

Irene said, "A professor of mine sent me a very kind note. The last line was, 'Love is as strong as death.' I found that very comforting, somehow. Much later, I found the original verse. 'Set me as a seal upon your heart, like a seal on your arm; for love is as strong as death.'"

"That's from the last chapter of Song of Songs," Adam said, "That was the background of your webpage."

Irene nodded. She looked embarrassed. "I still miss my father all the time. I would do anything to see him, and you're right—I can't. No matter how much I loved him, I can't. But I believe love is stronger than death. And after going to all the trouble of creating us, I guess I can't believe God intends to be without our company forever. That's what I told Vivian before when she was crying. I told her I think she'll see your grandfather again."

Adam sat quietly next to her, his eyes almost closed. He so wanted to believe, to share her hope. Irene rested her head on his shoulder. They sat together for a long time.

"What are you thinking?" she asked, after a while.

"I could have been closer to him," Adam said. His throat was constricted. He could hardly get the words out. "I pushed him away. He loved me so much and I couldn't even see him for who he was. And he loved Danny, and I wanted to push him away, too. You asked me what was the worst thing I ever did . . ." He couldn't finish.

"Adam, don't." She looked into his eyes. "You're making things right with Danny. With Vivian, too."

Adam kissed her hand. He tried to force a smile. He stood up and looked around at the apartment again: here was the couch where his grandmother used to do crossword puzzles and listen to her jazz albums, and where he and his grandfather had settled Henry down to sleep; there was the table where his grandfather had made him so many egg salad sandwiches; there was the bathroom door that he and his grandfather had kicked in when they had feared for Danny's life. Adam tried to take all of it in, to seal it in his heart: the love and the pain and the day-to-day, so that he could have these memories along with the books and the photos and his grandfather's ties.

Irene stood up too, and she faced him. Her gaze was tender. "Let's get these boxes back to your place," she said. "I'll help you unpack."

www.ingramcontent.com/pod-product-compliance
Lightning Source LLC
Chambersburg PA
CBHW050401030726
47503CB00006B/1966